Lett

INCA RCER ATED

INGER IVERSEN

Incarcerated

Published by: Inger Iversen Books, LLC

Editing by: There for You Editing | Melissa Ringsted
Proofread: Crimson Tide Editorial | Victoria Schmitz
Cover Artwork by: Mae I Design Photography | Regina Wamba
Formatting: Inkstain Interior Book Designing | Nadège Richards

Inger Iversen
www.ingeriversen.com

TO REGINA WAMBA:

It is not just the words that bring readers to books. Those words are hidden at first. Hidden behind the beautiful covers you create. Your passion and courage to stand out in a crowd is inspiring more than you'll ever know, and if I have to, I'll PM you on Facebook every day to remind you!

TO VICTORIA SCHMITZ:

Yes, you rock. You force me to write without fear. You are one of the best editors/proofreaders I have ever worked with. Also, I added this AFTER you proofread the book, so if there may or may not be a mistake in here . . . Opps!

TO NADEGE RICHARDS:

You will change the world. I know it.
If you haven't already realized it, you will.
Thanks for being there when I needed it most.

P.S. PUBLISH 5 MILES.

Your readers love you and they'll love WHATEVER you write!

MOMMY, I LOVE YOU.
DADDY, I MISS YOU.

It's a terrible thing to be alone—yes it is—it is—but don't lower your mask until you have another mask prepared beneath—as terrible as you like—but a mask.

-KATHERINE MANSFIELD

JAN. 5TH

Kristen,

First off, I'd like to thank you for signing up for this program. Shit in here gets repetitive, and over time the routine gets old. I appreciate the time you take out of your day to write me. I'm sure you have better things to do with your time, but I hope you aren't writing me out of pity. No disrespect, ma'am, but I don't need it. All I ask of you is your time. Two letters a month is all I'm allowed so far, and I hope you fill that quota up 'cause I'll sure be filling my end of the bargain.

In your letter you said you weren't sure what we should talk about, but I've got a list in my head of things I want to ask you things I'd like to know about you if that's all right. First, I'll tell you about myself and answer the question I'm sure you want to know, but were too polite to ask.

I'm thirty-five years old, never married, and have no kids. Okay, I'll be honest. No kids that I know of. I was wild during my college years, and don't remember much from them. I went to Blue Grass Community and Technical College, and then transferred to the University of Kentucky and studied Business. Before I got locked up, I owned my own business and made good money. I've been in jail for eight years. I'm in here for robbery, conspiracy to commit a robbery, and assault with a deadly weapon. Before you throw the letter down and wonder to yourself what the hell you've gotten yourself into, let me just say this. I did it. I admitted to it, and I'm doing my time. When I get out of here I plan to get myself together and pick up where I left off after college. I don't make excuses for the things I've done. Even though I didn't know we were going to rob someone, when the time came for me to back out, I didn't and because of that I've lost eight years of my life.

Still, I'm not asking for pity, or even your forgiveness, I'm just asking for your time—two letters a month. If you could, in your next letter can you tell me about yourself? What you do for fun, what you look like, where you are from, and shit like that.

—Scott Logan

CHAPTER 1

KATIE

A FEW MONTHS AGO, Katie would have never believed she'd be having a conversation with a convicted felon. Of course, she hadn't actually spoken to him, but his letter had arrived at her PO Box just a day ago. Since then, she'd read it at least four times. Simple and straight to the point, Scott had explained why he was in prison and a bit about his life before the eight years he'd been serving. It was more than she'd told him about herself, but he didn't seem to mind. Actually, he'd asked her to tell him about herself, but didn't ask any of the questions Teal had warned her about. He didn't ask her to come and meet him, or what she liked to do when she was alone, and for that she was thankful.

Soothing jazz flowed from the iPod dock station while Katie sat at her desk in her study carefully plotting out her next letter. Pulling out her favorite bright yellow stationary, she picked up a pen and considered on what to tell Scott about herself. How personal did she want this to get? He'd been honest with her—as far as she could tell—and mentioned only wanting her time. Katie had a lot of that, and at twenty-five, she was looked at as an odd ball for being such a loner. She wouldn't dare tell Scott that, though. He thought her name was Kristen, but it was actually Kathryn, or Katie for short. This had been Teal's idea.

"Girl, you don't want those men to know your real name so they can come hunt you down for some lovin' when they get out of jail," Teal had warned. The problem was, Katie still worried about the Inmate Pen Pal Program. It had been her idea, and with her dad as the warden at Capshaw prison, it only took a few suggestions before Teal and a few other people were responsible for setting up the program. Of course, her dad told her that she wasn't eligible to join, but Teal, who'd worked an administration job at the prison, had gotten her in the program under the name Kristen. Teal raised a brow at what she called a "white sounding name", but Katie thought it normal. Yes, she was a black woman, and yes, people were surprised to see such a dark girl respond to the name Kathryn Rose Andreassen, but she never thought names had anything to do with a person's ethnicity. Her mother's skin shone black as night, as well as her biological father's, but he'd passed and her mother had remarried a European man. Katie refused to be defined by her name, but the world hadn't made it easy for her.

Name aside, Katie had also worried about her address making it on file with the prison, so she'd rented a PO Box. Teal had told her that she hadn't needed to; the letters coming to the prison were taken out of the original envelope and placed in a prison issued one, and then handed out at mail call. Katie, however, wasn't convinced, so she'd gone to the MailWerks across the street from her old job and rented a PO Box for thirty-five dollars a year.

The shrill tone of her cell's ringer pulled Katie from her desk, and into the living room. "Hello," she answered.

"Girl, I swear these people in here get on my last damned nerves!" Teal shrieked. Katie glanced at the clock, confirming that it was noon—Teal's break time.

Katie chuckled at her friends over exaggeration of her co-workers. "You always say that." She stood and headed to the kitchen to pull out the salad she'd prepared for lunch. "But anytime you need help with paperwork, or want to switch a shift, all of them are suddenly your best friends." She pulled the grilled chicken out of the fridge.

Teal sucked her teeth. "Whatever, but I'm telling you this . . . next time Stacie leaves her shit on my desk, I'm gonna cuss her out."

Katie could hear the radio blasting in the background. "Are you on your way over, or what?" she asked, ignoring Teal's whining. It was always one complaint after another and very few were founded.

"Yeah, and I don't want a damned salad, make me a cheeseburger or something." Teal let loose a loud moan. "I'm okay with being fat. Hell, haven't you heard? Big is beautiful!" Teal huffed.

Katie placed the chicken in the microwave and pressed the quick heat button. "Big may very well be beautiful, but high blood pressure isn't. Plus, you aren't fat." Teal was far from skinny, but Katie would never call her fat. She was one hundred and forty-five pounds, but she just barely made it to Katie's chin, who was five feet seven. "Plus, your doctor told you to watch your blood pressure, so you won't be eating any cheeseburgers over here." And Katie meant it. Her mother had had issues with her blood pressure, and it had gotten so bad that she had a stroke.

Suddenly, Katie heard Teal's Monte Carlo as she pulled into her driveway. The prison was only ten minutes away from Katie's house, which was one of the reasons she could afford the home on her own before she'd gotten an agent and then a book deal. Nobody wanted to live a few miles away from a maximum-security prison, so it had made her three bedroom home super affordable.

"I'm hanging up now. Come in through the back." Placing the phone on the counter, she headed to the sliding glass door and flipped the lock before running back to the microwave to pull out the chicken.

Teal walked into the kitchen, and was followed by a cold breeze. "Girl, why are you still in your damn pajamas?"

Katie looked down at what she was wearing; short sleeping shorts and a ratty T-shirt. She'd been up since six a.m. working on her novel, but she'd forgotten to change. When she glanced over at Teal—who was so damn well dressed and put together all the time—she cringed. She was taller and slimmer than Teal, but she never thought she looked as good in her outfits as Teal did. She'd tried, but there was just no contending with the fashion college dropout.

"You look a hot mess," she added with a raised brow.

Katie placed her hands on her hips as she watched Teal pull off her tweed pea coat. Underneath was a vibrant jade green silk blouse that hugged her chest, making her thick figure seem thinner. Her black pencil skirt elongated her short legs, and the pointy-toed, six inch black high heels scared the life out of Katie. She was strictly a kitten heel kind of girl, and didn't care what fashion guru Lauren Conrad said about them. She wasn't interested in breaking an ankle or her neck.

Katie sighed and turned her attention back to preparing the food. "I've been working all morning." It was an excuse she used often whether it was true or not. As an author, she made her own hours. However, that didn't mean she wouldn't put at least six to eight hours of time in . . . some days she even worked for twelve hours. The job was hard and sometimes very demanding, but often times people who didn't know she was a New York Times bestselling author often thought of her writing as a hobby.

Teal bumped her aside. "Go shower at least. Shit, you've been touching my food and you haven't even washed yet." Teal was grinning as she spoke, which was the only indication that she was joking.

Katie knew her friend. They'd grown up together, so she could tell when her friend was "kindly" insulting her. She held up her hands in mock surrender. "Okay, I'll be right back." She headed down the hall toward her bathroom. "And keep your mouth off that cheesecake in the fridge. I made it for my dad." She could hear Teal cussing from the kitchen, but ignored it and enjoyed a quick hot shower.

LUNCH WAS OVER FASTER than Katie had expected . . . mainly because of Teal's chatter about work and her love life or lack thereof. She'd all but forgotten the letter from Scott until Teal brought it up just as she was about to leave.

Teal shrugged on her pea coat and pulled her car keys from her pocket. "You haven't said anything about your pen pal." Teal frowned. "He didn't ask you some slimy shit, did he?"

Katie shook her head.

"Are you sure? What's his name? No wait, don't tell me. You're all quiet, but I know you didn't get a murderer or rapist or any shit like that." Teal patted down her sleek bob, as if what she said was common knowledge to Katie, but it wasn't.

Katie raised a brow. "I thought the Pen Pal Program was anonymous and random?" She shifted her weight and leaned on the table. "How do you know I didn't get someone in prison for murder?" She was confused. The way the program was supposed to be set up, was that forty inmates were preselected based on good behavior to be in the program.

To her knowledge, their crimes weren't a deciding factor in whether or not they could join the program. That was the point when Katie pitched the idea to her dad. She believed that some of them would benefit from a little compassion, and maybe even some written company.

Teal huffed. "Didn't your dad tell you?" She headed to the door. "Only twenty-five men were chosen based off of a few things: the crime they committed, the time they have left, good behavior, and some other shit your dad decided to throw in."

Katie took in a calming breath so she wouldn't curse, and bit her lip before she spoke. She could tell that Teal really thought she'd known. "That was not the point of this," she grumbled. "It was supposed to be for those who had no one, those who were stuck in that place for life. I think they . . . no, I *know* they need human interaction in some way. You keep them caged up in there like animals, and then society is surprised when they get out and act just like that—animals!" Katie was heated, but her tantrum didn't faze her friend.

Teal's eyes grew large. "Have you lost your fuckin' mind?" She threw her hands above her head and Katie watched as she visibly calmed. "Kay," it was Teal's nickname for Katie, "I know what you are going through . . ."

Here it was again. It always came to this, and although Katie was positive that Teal was about to drop some true knowledge on her, she didn't want to hear it.

"You're lonely and need someone to talk to, so you reached out and ended up not only getting played, but also hurt. Like always, you find some animal, or in this case twenty-five animals, to reach out to and help."

Katie looked away from her friend. She was tired of crying about the past, tired of explaining to people that all she ever wanted to do was be needed and useful. Teal placed a gentle hand on her cheek, and Katie couldn't help but gaze into her friend's concerned, soulful eyes.

"Let me just tell you this," Teal continued. "Those men are animals. You don't know the half of it, babe, and you never want to. Your father was right not to let certain people on that list. They are criminals, predators, and liars. That shit can get into a lonely woman's head and make her do things she'd normally never do."

Katie knew she was right. She'd let her own loneliness blind her to the facts. Sniffing, she wiped a tear from her eye as it tried to escape. "I know, I know. Now, get out of here before you're late to work."

Teal glanced at her phone and cringed at the time. "Yeah, I'll see you at Shea's Valentine's Day party, right?" Teal was heading out the door as she said this, and Katie followed behind. "I'm giving you a big ass heads up. You have weeks to get ready for this party, Katie. When I call, you better pick up the phone and tell me that you are ready to head out the door."

Katie hated parties and groups, but Teal was sick of her hermit behavior. "Okay." Katie didn't want to go, but she couldn't say no to another outing or Teal would come over and drag her ass out of the house.

Her friend pursed her lips and arched her brow. "You better be." She threw the comment over her shoulder, but stopped at the gate. She glanced pensively at Katie then asked, "You want to tell me the name of the inmate you got?"

Even though Katie knew it was against the rules, she was tempted to say the name. Teal could tell her everything Crashaw Penitentiary knew about Scott Logan. As soon as the word 'yes' formed on her tongue, it faded away. It didn't matter. She didn't need to know anything about him, just what he'd told her. They were pen pals and nothing more.

Katie shook her head, and Teal hesitantly nodded. "Okay." She still had a concerned look in her eyes, but Katie ignored it and went inside.

She was lonely, and nothing Teal said about Scott would stop her from picking up her pen and sending in a letter . . . nothing. Loneliness was a crazy thing; it cut so deep, Katie thought her wounds would never heal.

JAN. 14TH

Dear Scott,

I'm glad my letter got to you! Well, I was sure that it would, the prison is good at things like that. I'd like to say thank you for being so honest with me, but let me assure you, I am not writing you out of pity. That being said, it's my turn to be honest with you. I'm writing because I'm lonely. I have family and friends, but I still feel something is missing from my life, so I thought I'd reach out to someone else. Maybe this is to fill a void, or maybe I'm a bit selfish to place my loneliness on you, either way, I am glad you accepted me as your pen pal.

Let me answer a few of your questions. I'm twenty-five years old and from Virginia. I went to college for Nursing, but left and decided to pursue Journalism. I graduated from William and Mary two years ago, after receiving my Masters. You asked what I do for fun . . . that's a good question, and I'm not sure how to answer it. I'm a bit of a loner, so normally I'll read a book, see a movie, or go on a long ride up and down the mountain. Boring, right? I guess it is, but honestly I sort of like it. It's nice to sit down on a cold night and read a good mystery.

Do you read? If so, who is your favorite author? I am obsessed with crime writer, Karin Slaughter. My first novel from her was Triptych. I finished it in one night! Last night it was freezing, and the snow was falling fast and hard. I cuddled up by the fireplace and read two books.

Also, I've been thinking about something. We are never going to meet. I don't mean that to be rude or cruel, but in reference to your question about my looks, I think it's best if we both keep that to ourselves. Here is my reason for this: I enjoy this anonymity.

I'm not perfect, so if you tell me you have a million tattoos, body piercings, and all that jazz, it might make me feel different and maybe even a bit nervous about writing you. Please don't be offended. I've decided that you look like Colin Farrell and you have an Irish accent! Honestly, it doesn't matter what we look like. We'll never meet, but I will continue to send you letters and get to know you. Does that make sense? I hope it does.

Yours truly,
Kristen

CHAPTER 2

IN HIS CELL, LOGAN re-read the letter from his attorney. "Hell no!" He threw the letter on the bed and stood, pacing to cool his nerves. Unclenching his fists, he tried to remain calm, but blood raced through his veins a mile a minute, causing his heart to thunder in his chest. His fucking lawyer was a goddamned snake. Shit, he really couldn't be mad, that was why he'd hired him, but the bastard was asking for more money. More money for what? The letter wasn't clear. It'd just stated that fees were adding up and Logan was responsible for covering them.

"Who the hell else would be responsible for it other than me?" he asked aloud. He was alone in his cell as his cellmate was on kitchen duty. Both of them were close to release and had been moved to a different cellblock, which not only allowed them more yard time, but also the ability to sign up for miscellaneous jobs.

His anger deflated as he looked at the other envelope he'd picked up at mail call. He could see the yellow paper through the cheap white, reassigned envelope, and the sight of it excited him. Snatching it up, he ripped the envelope open and sat facing the door. If a guard or his cellmate came by, he didn't want them reading what his pen pal looked like; that shit was only for him. He'd asked her to tell him about herself and other things, but he really wanted to put a face to the woman he'd be writing for the next few months. Although he was positive that his idea of a tall, hot blonde with nice tits and a round firm ass wasn't the case, a man could only hope.

Logan opened the letter. He wasn't sure if Kristen had done it on purpose or not, but the scent of lavender and roses filled his nose. It'd been seven years since he'd smelled, touched, or tasted a woman, and the scent of Kristen's perfume or lotion drove him mad. Logan wasn't looking for a woman, not at all. It was because of a woman he got in the car with drugs and stolen money, and almost went across state lines with it.

As he read the letter, he was a bit stunned. She had all but admitted to using him as a link to the outside world, which seemed a bit off. Even though Logan was close to his parole date, he was still far from free or anywhere near the outside world. This woman had all of the freedoms he wanted, and she was alone? It was sad, but he expected that she was probably ugly, which was why she said she didn't want to tell him what she looked like.

In the program, inmates didn't know what state the letters where coming from unless the pen pal revealed it. He was sure Kristen would never tell him if he outright asked, so he took clues from her writing and he had a good mind to say she was in the same state as he. That was pushing it, though. It was snowing in Vermont and there were mountains here as well, but the same could be said for Northern Cali, Colorado, or Montana, just to name a few. His only other indication she was close was when she said, 'the prison is good at things like that.' Not prisons, but *the* prison. Did she know about prisons? She'd said that she went to school for journalism, so maybe her career had taken her on a path alongside criminals. Lord knows there were more than ten reporters who stuck a recorder in his face every time he went to court seven years ago.

Logan threw the paper down on top of the annoying letter from his shark-ass lawyer. He was used to disappointment. When he'd signed up for the program, he'd told Denise to make sure of two things. The first was that he got a white woman; he wanted someone he could relate to. Second, she needed to be hot. Denise was a steward in the kitchen in charge of handing out knives and such. She was a nice middle-aged woman whose husband, Graham, worked in administration. She'd said she made sure her husband paired him up with a white woman, and a name didn't get any whiter than Kristen Svensson. Logan knew a Scandinavian name when he read one. All he could see was a blonde-haired, blue-eyed, pale-skinned seductress, but Logan knew Kristen was far from that. What woman who looked like a snow bunny goddess sat in the house all day reading? He knew from experience that hot women spent more time making men chase them, than with their nose in a book.

Logan picked up the letter again and lay down on his bed . . . which was more like a cot. Nothing that thin and hard could ever be considered a bed. He read the letter again and chuckled at the tattoo bit. Hell yeah, he had tattoos. His chest, back, and arms were filled with them and he took pride in it. He'd spent at least twelve grand on his tats, and not once did he allow flash art or some snot-nosed kid on him.

Lifting his arm, he looked at his latest piece. A phoenix rose anew from the ashes of yesterday, and that piece alone had cost him eight hundred bucks. He'd flown to Miami to have the famed tat artist Ami James ink him. Looking back at the letter, he re-read the name of the man Kristen likened him to. "Who the fuck is Colin Farrell?"

The click of the door alerted him to his cellmate's arrival. "That mofuka's an actor that gots a lot more money than you'll eva see," the man snickered, but Logan ignored him. When Logan had first arrived, he'd had another cellmate who called himself an *AB* member. Logan had never considered himself a white supremacist, or a brother of the Aryan Nation, but with his last cellmate he'd learned that he shared a lot of the same views. Still, there were some major differences between his beliefs and the Nation's, and that's why when Aaron had asked him to join, he turned him down flat. Aaron let it be known that the invitation was always open, but he didn't have time for that shit.

Logan wouldn't mix with a race other than pure white, and he didn't have friends that weren't white; however, he would never hurt a person because of their race. It wasn't how he was raised, and being a criminal didn't make you racist.

On the other end of the spectrum, his current cellmate was a white boy who grew up in a ghetto where it paid to be black just like he had, but he had no respect for him. This douche had switched sides and there was no excuse for it. Iggy had been one of the few white boys on the block, and had decided to take on the verbiage and general attitude of a black man in the ghetto. It disgusted Logan. He'd never used the term "wigger" a day in his life, but suddenly he had the urge to spit it at the dumb fool every time he saw him. Logan sat up and folded his letters.

"You hear me, brotha?" Iggy asked, squatting down in front of him.

Logan gave him a hasty glance, then stood and pushed past him, almost knocking him down.

"Whoa, *shit*! All I did was answer yo question. You axed, and I answered." Iggy stood and wiped imaginary dust off his shoulder.

Logan had had his fair share of cellmates in the last year, but this one was trying every nerve he had. Coming up on parole, Logan had to play by the rules . . . no fighting being the one rule he was currently having trouble abiding by.

Clearing his throat, Logan shoved the letters in his manila folder on the only desk in the room. "What time is it?"

"Thirty minutes 'til chow time." Iggy jumped on the top bunk. "Wake me up when it's time to go."

Logan ignored the request and pulled out his legal pad and pencil. He sat down and started to write. He wasn't sure what he was going to talk to Kristen about, but he was damned sure it wasn't going to be about how lonely and empty he felt inside. That shit was reserved for no-damn-body. Especially not some stranger he'd never meet.

JAN. 20TH

Kris,

First, do you mind if I call you Kris? I like it even though it's a man's name. This is the last letter I'll be able to send you this month, so it will probably be long. Just bear with me. Let me ask you something. It may seem personal, but I need to know. You said that we don't need to know what the other looks like, but since you have that dude Colin for me, who can I choose for you? Who would you compare yourself to? I'll picture that person as I'm writing to you, like you do that Colin dude for me.

Anyway, please tell me why you are lonely. It doesn't make sense if you have family and friends. When I was out, the boys and me were always hanging at a bar or the lake. Go do some shit like that, and stop reading all the time. You're out of college now and too damned young to be stuck in the house with your nose in a book. Okay, so enough advice from the convict. (Ha-ha. But seriously, you are still young, so live your life.

I've been trying to figure out what to talk to you about, and I came up with an idea. My friend in the kitchen told me to try this with you. I'd like to get to know you better. This is how it works. You ask me two questions a letter and I'll do the same.

Most likely, that will spark a conversation each month. I'll go first.(You can be as personal as you want. I may or may not answer, though..)

1. *Have you ever committed a crime??*
2. *How much do you weigh??*

Yeah, I know it's rude to ask, but I want to know. It doesn't matter what your answer is. Even if you say three hundred pounds, I'll still keep writing to you. You already know the answer to number one for me. Number two is two hundred and fifteen. I worked out every day before prison, and have kept it up since I've been here. I take pride in my body. You only get one, and if you fuck it up that's it. I must admit that when I was younger I smoked—weed and cigarettes—but not anymore.. Have you ever smoked? I know that'd be three questions, but I want to know..

Don't take this the wrong way, but you seem real conservative. I like that you were honest about not liking tattoos. You're the first girl I've ever met to feel that way.. Tell me, what don't you like about them? Most people I know use them as a form of expression, or to tell their life story without even opening their mouth. Honestly, it's a beautiful form of illustration. One man in here has a big ass tat of the world on his shoulders. I thought that shit was amazing. His burdens went so deep that he tattooed that shit on his body. Even when his time comes, and it's all said and done, those burdens will still sit on his back.

Let me ask you this. What is so wrong with telling a story with ink? If you could tell a part of your story with ink, what would it look like. Let me guess. You'd have roses on your lower back heading down and onto your hips where they flare out. I only say roses because your last letter smelled like roses and lavender. Maybe you'd get a small rose on your shoulder. I can imagine you in bed at night, lying on your stomach with a white sheet around your waist. Your smooth skin and tattoos on display for me. Don't think I'm getting fresh, I'm just trying to paint a picture for you..

Kristen, tell me . . . if you could have any tattoo, what would it be, what would it represent, and what part of your life would you let it tell? I know we said that we'd never meet, and I think that's for the best, but give me your story in the form of art. Tell me who you are..

Scott Logan

CHAPTER 3

KATIE STARED IN THE mirror. It was six a.m. and she'd pulled another all-nighter. Her book wasn't going to write itself, and her agent was elated over the progress she'd made thus far. She'd have this book finished in record time. The last one had taken a year to write, but with this novel she was sure to be finished in six months tops. Pushing her curls out of her face, Katie picked up a wide tooth comb and started to detangle the mess on her head.

Her flat iron beeped, signaling it was ready for use. She sectioned off her hair and ran the hot ceramic over each parted section of hair, straightening the unruly tangle of curls. When straightened, her hair fell past her shoulders in jet-black waves. She loved her hair like this, but only did it for special occasions. Too much heat on her hair and she'd be managing a straw-like mess with split ends. It'd taken her years to decide to go natural. The perms—a.k.a. creamy crack—at one point had broken off her hair, but five years later she'd managed to get her hair healthy, long, and glowing again.

Katie ran her hands through her straightened hair and checked her makeup. Her weekly lunches with her father always went well. Her father stayed busy with work, and when Katie's writing finally took off, he was fine with her sleeping until noon and her hermit-like ways. Grabbing her keys, she locked up her house and headed to her car.

First, she had a stop to make at the MailWerks, to check for her letter from Scott. It'd been four days, and she felt a letter would be in her PO Box waiting for her. Katie hopped in her car and started it.

Looking for something to calm her nerves—because lately, leaving the house was a bit stressful—she opted for a CD instead of the radio. Katie pressed play and sat back, listening to the hauntingly smooth voice of alternative artist Charlene Soraia. Finally, she backed out of the driveway, singing along with the tune.

Pulling into MailWerks, the parking lot was empty, so it was a quick in and out. She checked her box and bought stamps. Back in her car, she was tempted to read the letter from Scott, but she needed to get to Mel's bistro. Being late would get her nothing but a lecture. Years as a prison warden had made him colder and a bit aloof, but Katie guessed her father needed to be that way. Dealing with murderers and rapists on a daily basis could change anyone.

Katie headed down Macon Street. Snow was coming down in sheets, but she considered herself a seasoned snow driver. Living in Vermont had taught her she didn't need sand bags in her trunk, seasoned snow drivers knew that to be a rookie mistake. She'd bought all-season tires and felt ready for anything. Katie didn't live in a big town, so it seemed like it took ten minutes to get anywhere.

Pulling up to Mel's, she searched for her dad's truck. Finding it, she parked her little Ford Focus next to his massive Ford F-250. Her father called her crazy for buying a little car—he worried about the snowstorms and blizzards—and had told her that the small car wasn't very practical. Regardless of his opinion, Katie had wanted the little red car as soon as she'd seen it shiny and new on the lot. He bugged her on a daily basis about checking her tires and gas gauge before she left the house.

He'd even gone as far as using his spare key to leave her his special concoction. A soda bottle filled with water, distilled white vinegar, and dish soap. He called it Jan-Erik's super ice melt. Being that her dad was from Sweden, where the snow fell on a regular basis, he was a snow expert . . . in his eyes. However, Katie had done her research; her front wheel drive and all-weather tires were perfectly fine for Vermont's snowy months. Also, that "super ice melt" was in her back seat . . . frozen.

Katie pulled on her gloves, grabbed her phone, and headed into the bistro to meet her dad. He sat with his back to the wall, watching the door. Her father had immigrated to the US back in the fifties. He'd joined the

Coast Guard, and after years of college, made a career switch to the Air Force. A proud yet stoic man, Jan-Erik had been Katie's rock when her momma died, and she often wondered if he'd had any time to mourn his wife's death. He'd been so wrapped up in picking up the pieces of Katie's shattered life that she was sure he'd never once had a moment to himself.

Jan-Erik stood and headed toward his daughter. "Sweetheart, it's a pleasure," he said, leaning in to kiss her cheek.

"Hey, Dad." Katie slipped out of her jacket with the help of her father and sat down. After placing the jacket on the back of the chair, he returned to his seat. "Are they bringing over some menus?" She asked, removing her gloves and laying them on the table.

He shook his head. "No, I've ordered the salmon and asparagus for both of us." Jan-Erik glanced at his Rolex. "I only have an hour before I have to get back to a meeting."

Katie never asked her dad what he made a year, but she was sure that it had to be up there. He was a Warden level five, which meant he was in charge of a correctional facility housing more than twenty-five hundred inmates, on all security levels. His job included planning and enforcing orders of executions mandated by the state. It was a job she often wondered how her father managed, but as of late his cold outer demeanor proved that a job like that could change any man.

Katie sighed and pushed back her chair. "You seem to have a lot of meetings lately." She looked up at him warily. "I even heard rumors about you stepping down, but I know that's not true."

Jan-Erik's ice blue eyes widened before he spoke, "Stepping down? Varför skulle jag göra det?" His surprise disappointed her. He'd asked her in his native tongue why she thought he'd quit.

Katie shrugged. "Oh, I don't know, maybe because you work twenty hours a day, you're never home, and you are close to . . ." she sat back and crossed her arms over her chest, before amending her words, "you are past retirement age." She eyed him, curious to see if her response had upset him. Jan-Erik was always a calm man, and it'd take much more than a comment about his age to set him off, but she wondered about how he felt being told it was time to settle down and think about retiring.

He didn't say a word, and Katie worried that maybe she'd hurt his feelings, but just as she was about to speak, the waitress ambled over to the table and noisily set their plates down in front of them.

"Here ya go, hun." The woman placed a plate of buttered asparagus and seasoned salmon in front of Katie. "Anything else I can get'cha?" She glanced between the two, but her dad kindly waved her off.

Katie felt sick to her stomach. She hadn't meant to hurt her dad's feelings; she'd only meant to tell him that it was his turn to settle down and relax like her mom had before the cancer took her.

Jan-Erik took a few bites of food before he sat his fork down on his plate. Katie could only nibble at the asparagus as she waited for him to speak. "The Inmate

Pen Pal Program is off to a great start." He took a sip of water. "So far, I have twenty-five inmates set up." Katie almost questioned her father on the number. When she'd proposed the program to her father, she'd asked for forty or more men, and at least ten of those men to be death-row inmates. Her father paused, and Katie was sure he was waiting for her to object.

Instead she said, "Good, I knew it'd go well. Who did you choose to head the project up?" She knew Teal was involved, but she'd never asked her much more than that.

Jan-Erik took another bite of his salmon, chewed, and swallowed before answering. "Martin Graham and Sarah Lawson are in charge of implementing the program, and Jason Batey and Teal will maintain it moving forward. There are a few things I need to tell you about the program.

"First, I only chose twenty-five men to start. It's a four person project, so I didn't want to overwhelm them. They have plenty of work to keep them busy, and this just adds to it. Second, death row inmates are off—" Katie started to protest, but Jan-Erik quickly nipped it in the bud. "Off the table." His eyes held no room for argument, and Katie's mouth snapped shut.

She picked up her water and sipped it in order not to say what she was thinking, or how disappointed she was at this revelation. Sure that her father sensed her emotions, she cleared her throat and said, "If you think that's for the best, I suppose it is." His response was a nod and smile. Katie guessed she should be happy that he'd even considered the Inmate Pen Pal Program to be implemented at the prison.

He continued. "I know it's for the best. No one on death row will be entered into the program. If they need to speak with anyone, they can speak to the priest or whoever is on their visitor list, but I refuse to give them an extra chance to send messages out to anyone." Her father's voice told her that on this subject, he would not give in. She only nodded and waited for him to continue. "Lastly, you are not allowed to join the program." He looked up at her. "I mean it. You want someone to talk to, you talk to me or your friend Teal."

Katie swallowed the lump of nervousness in her throat. She'd never been able to lie to her father, and the letter that sat in her car was a big fat lie. He'd told her that she wasn't going to be writing anybody from his prison when she suggested she be a part of the beta project. Submissively, she'd agreed, but cunningly made sure Teal was a part of the screening process so that Katie's alias Kristen made it through.

Katie sipped her water. "Yes, sir." She said nothing else, hoping not to incriminate herself.

He smiled. "Good girl." Katie hated when he did this, it made her feel like a little child or a puppy, but she smiled anyway.

After lunch, her father followed her to her car. Frantically, Katie peeked into her vehicle, hoping that she'd placed the letter from the correctional facility out of sight. Leaning in, her father kissed her goodbye before opening the car door. Katie instantly hopped inside, relieved that the letter wasn't visible. Her dad waved her off and Katie drove away, excited and nervous all at once, but ready to read her letter from Logan.

FEB. 1ST

Dear Scott,

I'm doing well, and I hope you are also. I don't mind you calling me Kris. My friend calls me Kay. I like your idea of the questions game. I think it will help us find plenty of things to talk about. So, let me answer them first..

1. Yes, I have committed a crime. When I was six, I stole a pack of gum from the grocery store. I felt so guilty about it that I told my mom, and she took me back to the store and made me apologize to the manager. He was nice about it, though, he even let me keep the gum for being so honest.

2. I weigh two hundred and ninety-nine pounds. Just joking. Honestly, I'm five foot seven and weigh one hundred and thirty-eight pounds. I've been trying to lose weight. I'd like to get to one thirty and stay there, but cheesecake seems to think I need to put on a few more pounds.

Also, Logan, I think I need to clarify something. I don't have anything against tattoos per se, I just don't want to picture you like some of the men I've seen in prison. I have a tattoo on my right shoulder of a bumble bee. I got it when I turned eighteen. Honestly, if I could have any tattoo. I'd get a little blue bird in a delicate, vintage cage. I imagine that even though the bird would feel trapped, she'd also feel safe from the outside world. I know you don't understand my loneliness and I guess you wouldn't. Maybe you feel the same way, but loneliness isn't just being alone. Yeah, I have friends and family, but I've lost friends and family too. It's hard to explain, so I won't even try.

I don't know about the tattoo your friend has since I haven't seen it, but I have to admit, I think it's a great way to tell a story.

About me saying that I'll picture Colin Farrell as I write you. Well . . . that was a joke, I won't picture anyone. Also, was that flirting I spied in the last letter? Lol! Okay, time for my questions:

1. What is your favorite tattoo?(I'm almost positive that you have them.?

2. What does it feel like to be high? (You said you'd smoked.?

Sincerely,
Kristen

P.S. Sorry for such a short letter. Work is piling up and I'm trying to finish so I can take a mini four-day vacation.!

CHAPTER 4

LOGAN SAT IN THE meeting room, waiting for his piece of shit lawyer. Jack was always late . . . always fucking late. Pressing his fingers into his temples, Logan hoped to ease some of the tension. His cellmate was itching to get his ass kicked, but Logan only had a few more months before he would be eligible for parole and he wasn't about to fuck that up. However, he was about to break a rule. He wanted to talk to Kristen on the phone. In the Inmate Pen Pal program, the inmates had strict orders not to ask for certain things or items, such as: money, addresses, pictures, or contraband. Yet, the people sending the letters were allowed to give their phone numbers to the inmates to call. Logan thought it was stupid that he couldn't ask, but Kristen could offer. He guessed it was to protect outsiders from the monsters caged within the prison walls, but Logan had a plan.

Letters leaving the facility were not screened. He knew this for a fact because he'd written and received letters from inmates in this very facility before he'd become a resident, and stamped on the top of the envelope was a message to the receiver stating outgoing mail was not screened. Logan either needed to convince Kristen to write to him out of the anonymity of the program, or convince her that talking over the phone was her idea.

The front door opened, and his tall, lumbering lawyer strolled into the room with a briefcase and big ass smile on his face. "Mornin' Logan," Jake said as he sat down and pulled some papers from his case.

Logan, silently brooding, took a deep breath before he spoke. "Why the fuck are you always late?" The smirk on Jake's face pissed him off even more. He'd gone to college with him, smoked weed with his ass, and scammed on women with the prick, and now he thought he was better?

Jake adjusted his tie. "Man, I had a long ass night. Got a new client that can't seem to keep his hands off his ex-wife." Jake's chuckle made Logan sick to his stomach.

"He hittin' on her?" Logan couldn't stand a man that hit a woman. He'd wanted to over the years plenty of times, but he'd be damned if he'd ever go that far.

Jake huffed. "The chick is taking him for over a grand a month and she got the kids. I swear, the law stands on a bitch's side no matter if they are crackhead whores who sell it on a street corner."

Logan shook his head in disgust. "Sounds to me like your new client should have worn a fuckin' condom and never said 'I do.'" It was the man's own fault for falling for the "okey-doke".

Jake leaned in close, as if he was about to reveal a secret, and he probably was. He was a no count lawyer with a nose candy problem and an ex-wife of his own he was still supporting. Attorney-Client privilege Logan's ass. "He got caught up with a nig—" Jake thought better of using the racial slur and continued, "black chick and her friend." Sitting back, he shook his head in revulsion. "Honestly, I think, it serves him right, but hell, with my bitch ass ex-wife on my ass I've got to make this money."

Logan listened quietly, hoping the disinterest was clear on his face. If Jake's new client didn't know that black chicks were a bad way to go that was his own problem. He cleared his throat and leaned forward, wanting to make sure Jake saw how serious he was when he threatened him. "Listen here, motherfucker."

Jake's head snapped up and his eyes bulged in surprise. He started to speak, but Logan held a hand up, stopping the words in his throat.

"If I find out you are out there spreading my fucking business around, I will kick your ass, are we clear?" Logan sat back, sure his point had been made. "Now, how fuckin' soon can I get out of here?"

GOOD BEHAVIOR AND OVERPOPULATION. The words replayed in Logan's head. He had wondered why he'd been moved to the East Block so soon, but he didn't ask any questions when the guard came and told him to pack his shit up. At first, he thought he was in trouble, but there was no better inmate than Logan Whyte. He'd entered the system with a plan: keep his head down and get out as soon as possible.

Make no mistake, Logan was no punk, but he knew he had better things to do than rot in prison with murders and rapists. He planned on getting out and making a life for himself, even if it meant moving back to the ghetto and working in his uncle's shop until he could get his shit together and open up another shop of his own.

Logan's life had never been easy, even before prison, but he'd survived. He'd lied to Kristen when he'd told her he went to the state college. Logan made it as far as community college, but when he was arrested for possession of an illegal substance, all of his financial aid had dried up, so he was forced to pack up and move closer to his uncle. His whole life, Logan had been surrounded by lower class citizens, at least that was what he was always called. But moving to the ghetto to live with his Uncle Nate taught him that there was a new low. He'd moved into a neighborhood where he was the minority, and he was reminded of the fact every day.

At twenty, Logan was no scrawny kid. He'd always been taller than most kids growing up, and after a few incidents, he took advantage of that by going to his neighbors and lifting weights. Yet, the problem wasn't that the black kids thought he was a punk . . . it was that they knew he wasn't, which resulted in being jumped by several black kids—sometimes on a daily basis.

This was the way, until he met a man by the name of Trent. His friendship with Trent was the spawn of his hatred for black kids. Initially, his hatred had nothing to do with the color of the skin on the kids kicking his ass, at least not until Trent started to point it out. "*Only the niggers came over and kicked your ass. The spics just watched and laughed, but me? I'm willing to stop them, willing to stand up for you. Why? 'Cause us whites gotta stick together.*"

After that moment Logan realized what the black kids already knew—there was power in numbers. Logan got a membership to a gym the next town over and worked out daily; he made sure when he walked home alone that he kept Trent's gun tucked safely in his pants. He even went to a few of Trent's secret meetings.

Back then, he didn't even know what the KKK was. Sure, he'd learned in school that they hated everyone other than whites, but what he hadn't learned was that the group was also a family. Whenever he needed something, he could depend on Trent and the gang to make it happen for him. When his uncle was too drunk to open up the shop, Trent and a few of his buddies did it for him.

Logan had learned a few things back then, but it was only when he arrived in prison that he learned how clueless he really was about the KKK also known as the AB Brothers. In prison, lives were lost over the color of one's skin, while out on the street with Trent, he'd never seen any of the boys kill and rape a person based on skin color. Yeah, racial slurs were thrown around and he'd even done it a time or two, but back home on the streets it was just for protection. There was a code: You don't fuck with us and we don't fuck with you. Here, behind these bars, was a whole other story. Behind these walls spun a new world full of hate and anger, a world Logan wanted no part in.

Sitting at his desk, pencil poised over the legal pad, Logan was ready to respond to Kristen's letter. He wondered how much about himself he should truly reveal. So far their letters were just a bunch of meaningless words and avoidances, and something in Logan wanted more. He wanted to tell her more, but he also wanted to know more about her. Maybe it was the excitement about his last few months being reduced, or maybe it was because he assumed Kristen actually lived in the same state where he was living out his sentence.

As much as he told himself he didn't want to meet her, there was that little voice inside of him that couldn't lie. Logan was the type of man that liked solving problems—he liked being in control—and there was nothing better than soothing this woman's isolation because Logan knew all about loneliness.

FEB. 7TH

Kris,

I was thinking. I know we are never going to meet, and getting to know one another on a deeper level may seem stupid, but listen to this idea I have. Tell me your deepest, darkest secret. No one will ever find out. Plus, it won't matter that I know because I won't ever meet you. I figure, by telling me this you can get it off your chest and work on that shit. I'm only asking you to do this because of the tattoo you'd get to explain your life. This is why I love tattoos. If you take the time to think of what you want, you can tell a true story about yourself. Sometimes you don't even realize who you are until someone forces you to sit down and think about that shit. Ponder that. Also, some things are hard to convey in a letter, so if I misconstrue anything you say, sorry. Talking is easier than writing.

So, what I'm taking from your letters is that you think this program is a cure for your loneliness, but here's what you need to do. You have to open up. Just writing a bunch of meaningless words on a piece of paper won't help. This is going to sound far from manly, but I'll be honest, to defeat loneliness you need to form a personal connection with another person. I read that in a book. Think about that for a bit..

Scott Logan

P.S. You seem like a good girl. You don't need to know what it feels like to get high. Stay away from that shit.

CHAPTER 5

BEFORE KATIE HAD EVEN read Scott's letter, she was thinking of ways to give him her number without seeming foolishly indecisive about how far their communication should go. She'd told him she would never meet him, but she still wondered what he looked like, or what his voice sounded like. He was from Kentucky, so he most likely had an accent. Katie had been born and raised in Virginia, which was considered the South's New York, but he might think she had an accent as well. Whenever she'd visited her family in Atlanta, they always told her how 'Northern' or 'proper' she sounded. Her uncles weren't so nice about it. They'd teased her, saying she sounded like a snobby white woman.

He asked her to reveal a deep, dark secret, something she'd never told anyone before, but Katie couldn't think of anything worth telling him. She had a degree, a successful career, and a loving father. On the outside, everything seemed boring or normal; yet, deep inside, there was always a silent storm brewing. Her life was far from perfect. She'd watched her mother die, her ex-boyfriend Ramon had left her shortly after, and Katie had suffered a miscarriage that she'd told no one about. *There it was!*

"Damn," she whispered to the dark, empty bedroom. It was two a.m. and she'd been awakened by a storm outside. Scott was right. It had been more than a year, and Katie had all but erased that day from her memory. He'd forced the memory from her with a simple question. What was she supposed to tell him? The truth she guessed.

Why did she want to open up to this stranger? Could it be that he was a man she'd never have to face? Katie reasoned it'd be easier to tell a person whose opinion of her really didn't matter, and how could Scott's opinion matter? He was an admitted criminal.

Katie sat up in her bed. It'd been several days and Katie hadn't written Scott back yet. Every time she'd started her reply, trepidation and uncertainty kept her fingers still as they lingered over her bright yellow stationary. She didn't want to write her secrets on a piece of paper because that would just be too damned much. There'd be proof out there somewhere if she did that, and although she thought she was ready to move on, she feared her words would give her fears new life. She just couldn't deal with it again.

Her decision was made.

Katie jumped out of bed and power walked to her desk. Fear be damned, what she was about to do was completely against the rules of the Inmate Pen Pal Program, but not only had her curiosity gotten the better of her, but she desperately needed someone to talk to. Grabbing a yellow sheet of paper, she scribbled the digits she'd promised Teal to never give out.

COLD AIR SLAPPED KATIE in the face as she strode toward Teal's SUV. She smoothed down the flyaways from her sleek ponytail and slid into the vehicle.

Teal gave Katie a once over and rolled her eyes. "You could have a least dressed up," she muttered as she started the SUV and backed out of the driveway.

Katie looked down at the pink cashmere sweater and tight, black skinny jeans with pink stitching. "What? This is nice," she said, then looked to see Teal's attire.

Her best friend had her hair hanging in loose black waves. She wore gold hoop earrings to match her gold leggings. Her sweater was so sheer, Katie could see the gold bra beneath.

Teal headed down the road to their friend Shea's house at what Katie thought was too damned fast for the way the snow was coming down. "Katie, you look like you are going to a grade school party. I told you to dress *sexy*. I knew I should have come in and picked something out for you to wear."

As Teal reached over and turned the radio on, Katie looked at her outfit again and could not find anything wrong. Yeah, she wasn't diva'd up like Teal, but she hadn't meant to be. "Whatever, just drive safe. I'd like to make it to the party in one piece." Katie huffed, ignoring the ache in her chest. She stared out the window, already regretting the choice she'd made to come out tonight.

That afternoon she'd sent the first draft of her novel off to her editor, and normally as a reward to herself, Katie would pour herself two glasses of wine, pull out her sixty dollar box Godiva chocolates, and soak in a steaming hot bath. Yet, here she was, on her way to a party she didn't want to attend, being scolded about how she was dressed.

Teal let out a sigh, and then pointed to the glove box. "Look in there. I think there are some earrings that will match that pink, and since you straightened your hair and put it in that cute ass lil' ponytail, they'll look real good on you."

Katie assumed this was Teal's way of saying sorry, but she still wished she declined the invitation. Teal thought she needed to get out more and maybe even start dating again, but Katie wasn't ready for all of that. Plus, most men weren't willing to stick around and deal with her baggage.

Opening the glove box, she searched for the earrings. "Who is showing up tonight?" Katie hoped it'd be a small gathering, but with an event coordinator like Shea, there was sure to be at the very least fifty people showing up.

Teal gave Katie a sideways glance. "Now, you know good and well half the world is going to show up 'cause of that damn blabber mouth, Shea." The car slowed, and Katie glanced up. "See?" Teal shouted. "Look at all those damned cars."

Katie's chest tightened and she sat back, abandoning the search for earrings. "What the heck?" She looked at her friend, whose eyes softened.

Teal placed a hand on her shoulder and gave a light squeeze. "I know you've been having issues with large crowds, but I'm here with you. You'll be fine." The SUV slowly started to move again, as she navigated the vehicle into a parking spot.

Katie was still staring at the amount of cars lining the street. Shea and her husband, Cuddy, lived in a nice neighborhood with a sprawling front and back yard. Though covered with snow, the lawn was packed with partygoers and smokers. Katie's stomach dropped even lower when she saw Joe's BMW parked out front.

She turned to Teal, and in that moment she wished looks could kill. "You said it'd be a small gathering of friends." Katie jabbed her finger in the direction of the cars. "Does that look like a small gathering to you?" She knew her voice got louder and squeakier when she was angry, and the smile on Teal's face only made her angrier. "Seriously, even Joe is here."

Teal leaned forward, glancing around. "Where? I don't see his pickup truck."

Dryly, Katie responded, "He bought a BMW."

Her smile resembled the Cheshire cat. "Dude bought a beamer?" Teal's eyes located the car and Katie couldn't do anything but curse under her breath. Pulling on her coat, she checked her hair in the rearview mirror. "Honey, that man is nothing but chocolaty goodness wrapped in a successful wrapper. You better not be a fool and let him get away." Teal stopped primping in the mirror. "You do know that man wants you, right?"

Tired of this conversation—which had gone on for the past year—Katie grabbed the door handle and opened the door. "Yeah, I know, he's said it before. And like I've said again and again, I'm not ready." She hopped out the SUV, careful not to slip on the ice. In her mind, there was nothing worse than a man who thought the phrase "not interested" meant "please keep trying."

They quickly made it past the small crowd of smokers and into the warmth of the house. Katie looked around for a corner or chair to escape to, but as soon as she moved in the direction of a chair, Teal hooked her arm into hers and pulled her into the middle of the fray. Everyone from Dadesville had shown up, and even a few from Capstone, which was the county over.

Katie struggled not to shoulder bump people as Teal dragged her toward the kitchen. There, she spied Joe leaning against a wall, talking to another female who was dressed more like she probably should have dressed. Her tight outfit hugged her generous hips and made her waist seem nonexistent. Katie would never have been caught in a dress like that. She considered herself flat chested, but Teal always pointed out that at least she wasn't an A cup, like some women.

Once Teal had dragged Katie into the kitchen, she stopped to pat her on the back. "See, that wasn't so bad, was it?"

Katie gave her a withering glare and pointed to the array of alcoholic beverages there were to choose from. "If you take one sip, I'm driving us home and you know I can't drive that big ass SUV." Teal raised her lip in mock disgust and opened her mouth to speak, but was cut off by the warm yet husky voice of Joe.

"Ladies," he said, yet kept his eyes glued solely on Katie.

"Hey, Joe." Teal smiled and went in for a hug.

Katie waited for them to separate before she said, "Nice to see you, Joe." She smiled warmly in greeting.

"Katie, baby." She hated when he called her that. Terms of endearment were only for those in her life that she held close to her heart, and Joe was not one of them.

He cocked a brow at her. "Now, honey, I know I can at least get a hug. It's been—what?" Joe glanced at Teal, but she shrugged and shook her head; he placed his hand over his heart as if he'd been wounded. "It's been at least three months." He moved in and wrapped his big arms around her.

Katie returned the embrace and placed her head on his chest. Joe always smelled good, and tonight he smelled like smoky vanilla with a hint of light sandalwood. She pulled away and placed her arms at her side. No matter how familiar Joe smelled, there was always something that held her back. He didn't give her that warm feeling in her stomach. In fact, she felt nothing for him at all.

Teal cleared her throat. "I'm going to get a drink." Katie threw her a sharp glance. Holding her hands up in mock surrender, Teal added, "Of water. You two want anything?"

Joe lifted his glass, of what Katie assumed was bourbon—his signature drink—and shook his head. "This is all I need for the night." He regarded Katie. "You want anything, sweetheart?"

With a shake of her head, Katie declined the offer. Once Teal left, Joe hooked his arm with Katie's and led her out of the kitchen. "It really is nice to see you again, Kay." He led her down a hallway, easily maneuvering her past guests as they chatted in hushed murmurs.

"You, too, Joe." Her heart thundered in her chest. Where was he taking her? It wasn't like she was afraid of Joe; she just didn't want to be alone with him. He'd ask her what he always did, and it was a question she'd been able to avoid for the past three months. She figured she'd preemptively apologize. "Sorry I haven't called. I've been busy with my book and stuff." Whether it was true or not, it was her go-to excuse. In this case, it was the honest truth.

Joe stopped in front of French doors, which led to what looked like an enclosed patio. He opened the door, and a gust of warm air rushed over them. The patio was heated, and Katie made a mental note to see about adding one to her home. After leading her inside, he shut the doors behind him.

Guiding her to a loveseat, they sat down. "How is that little book of yours doing?"

Katie tsked and sat back in the seat. "That little book is doing just fine." She was tempted to tell him that her "little book" was still on the New York Times bestseller's list, or that the same little book was being translated into four different languages at the behest of fans all over the world. Not to mention, that little book had bought and fully paid for her house and a car, meaning she walked away with both, purchased outright.

Joe blatantly checked her out, and she tracked his eyes as they landed on her chest. "That's what's up. I'm doing good too. Not that you asked." Joe pouted, causing her to laugh.

Okay, so she wasn't interested in him, but that didn't mean she needed to be rude. She loosened up a bit. "Okay, Joe. How are you doing, and what have you been up to for the last three months?" She didn't even have to feign interest because she was actually interested to hear his answer.

Joe leaned in closer as he explained, "Well, as you know, I was offered a job as a Compliance Specialist with G.W. Savings and Trust. It's good money and offers a bright future." He grinned and added, "Now, I'm just looking for a proper woman to go along with everything else in my life." He took her hand in his.

For the life of her, Katie couldn't figure out why she didn't scoop Joe up and let him take her out. It wasn't just her past stopping her, but something more. He was handsome, but—as Teal would say—his game was off.

Joe's grin widened and his white teeth shone bright. The pearly chips were a perfect contrast to his dark chocolate skin and his angular face was more than a pleasant sight to behold, but that was it. Katie just wasn't interested.

He tried too damned hard and his go-to was always his finances. Katie supported herself and didn't need someone throwing their financial stability in her face all of the time. He was sure to make some other woman very happy, but she had better things to focus on than Joe and his need for a future wife.

Pulling her hand from Joe's, she ignored the frown on his face. "Joe, we've talked about this, and I've told you—"

He pulled away abruptly and stood, straightening his pants. "I know, I know." He looked at her, and his soft brown eyes burned with anger . . . no, annoyance. "You know, Katie, when your damned dad begged me to ask you out, I had to admit, I almost laughed."

She shook her head, and her stomach filled with dread. Katie had no idea what Joe was talking about. "What?"

He paced to the window, and perched on the edge. "Yeah, you can imagine how surprised I was when he came into my office, begging me to take out his baby girl." Joe's voice had taken on a cruel edge. "You know what I was thinking as he sat there explaining why I should take you out?" His eyes were dark, and even though Katie knew that he wanted his words to cut her, she was powerless to get up and leave. All she could do was sit there and listen to Joe explain to her how her father had tried to play matchmaker. "I was thinking that I wasn't the right shade . . . if you get my drift."

Katie let out a humorless laugh. "Excuse me? What the hell makes you say that?" She'd heard it before, but never from Joe. Men always assumed she only dated white men. It was hurtful and confusing, but she still wanted to know why he felt that way.

He sneered. "You have got to be fucking kidding me. You always walk around here like your shit don't stank. Like you're better than the rest of us niggas 'cause of that white man who saved you and your momma from the ghetto."

Katie's eyes widened with shock, and she finally stood. "I've never acted that way!" What the hell was he talking about?

Joe laughed. "The fuck you haven't!" He strode to her. "You dress, act, and speak like a damn white woman, and everyone knows your black ass wishes you were white." Katie threw her hands in the air and screamed. She was so sick of hearing this shit, but before she could open her mouth to tell Joe how she felt—before she could curse his ass out—the French doors were flung open. Teal stood in the doorway looking ready for war.

She glanced between Katie and Joe. She must have seen the hurt on Katie's face because she turned to Joe and snarled, "What the fuck did you do?" She marched into the room on her six inch heels and got into his face, but he softly pushed her away.

He placed his hands in his pockets. "You and Jan-Erik got a lot on your hands with this one." Katie's eyes narrowed at the comment. Had Teal and her dad tried to set her up? "Too much for this brotha' to handle." Joe left the room, cursing under his breath as he went.

Teal eased over to Katie and wrapped an arm around her shoulder. "Let's go." When Katie didn't budge, Teal nervously asked, "What?"

At first Katie thought she was going to cry, but then she wanted to hit something. First, she needed to ask the question she truly feared the answer to. Before she even opened her mouth, she could see the guilt in Teal's eyes, changing her question to an accusation. "You and my dad set this up from the start."

FEB. 14TH

Scott,

802-654-5555

Let's form a connection.

-Kris :)

CHAPTER 6

EVEN THOUGH KITCHEN DUTY sucked, Logan was damn glad to be on that detail. Still, getting patted down and strip-searched every Wednesday and Friday—before and after he entered the kitchen—felt degrading. His job for the day was to cut the potatoes for the massive pot of mashed potatoes he was preparing. Logan pushed aside what he'd just finished cutting.

"Danko, you got some more peeled and ready?" he asked the Russian inmate whose job it was to peel. Just that . . . peel. He peeled any and everything that needed to be peeled, and he was also the only inmate in the kitchen who wore a hot pink jumper. Logan's white pants and white shirt were a sign that he was well behaved, so the stewards knew they didn't have to worry about Logan sticking his dick in the homemade peanut butter or showing it to any of the female stewards. Danko, on the other hand, was a damn freak.

He enjoyed whipping his shit out for laughs, which only ended up with him on restriction or in the tombs.

Danko passed Logan the big bowl of peeled potatoes under the ever-present eyes of Steward Jones. Danko had yet to show her his dick, and that might have been because Steward Jones promised him that she'd, *"take that lil Vienna sausage, put it on a bun, eat it, and shit it out a day later."* That'd been three weeks ago, and Danko hadn't so much as readjusted his junk in front of her.

"Da, I like with skin on," he muttered as he walked away. So did Logan, but when it'd gone up for voting, the prisoners had decided they wanted them peeled.

Logan picked up his knife. The number six engraved into the steel as well as the plastic handle reminded Logan of the cage in which he resided. He couldn't wait for the day when he could go into a kitchen and make a sandwich, without having to sign out a knife or ask a person to unlock the pantry. He felt like a toddler, constantly being watched and scolded, but it was still better than maximum-security lock up. Logan looked up at the white washed walls and the steel cabinets; cold and impersonal. Logan was no sissy, but hell if he didn't wanna see color in a kitchen; some photos on a wall, or something.

"What are you staring at, Whyte?" Steward Jones asked. Logan glanced up at her and noticed that her eyes were still on Danko.

Logan continued cutting. "Nothing," he answered. Even if he thought Jones was nice to him, he still wasn't about to open up and tell her how he missed the smell of biscuits in the oven, or the pictures that lined the grimy wall in his old apartment back in Kentucky.

"You sure? You got that look in your eye." She leaned in a bit. "The one that says you got someone at home you can't wait to get home to. You comin' up for parole, ain't you?" Logan knew she knew the answer to that, so he didn't respond. "I know you can't wait to get the hell out of here. Shit, I know I can't wait to clock out every day."

He only grunted in reply, but Jones was right. He was ready to leave, and the words "overpopulation" had never sounded so good.

LOGAN HELD THE LETTER in his hand. He could see that there was very little writing on the page, and he wasn't sure it that was a good or bad thing. Maybe she'd caught on to the fact he wanted her to call him and it pissed her off. She did say at least twice that she wanted anonymity, but Logan knew that she could still have that even if she called him.

Placing the letter on the bed, he sat down. He'd been on his feet for a good part of the day and his back was sore from his work out, but Logan found familiarity in it. He enjoyed the pains of a job well done.

Logan heard Iggy shuffle in the cell.

"Every time I come in here, you got yo ass laid out on the bed with fuckin' letters spread around you." His cell mate chuckled and hopped up on his bunk.

Lights out was in thirty minutes, and Logan had gone the whole day without kicking Iggy's ass, but as the man lay above him rapping some dumbass rap song, Logan had had enough.

"I don't know how you've survived so long in this place." Sitting up, Logan scrubbed his face with his palms. He was tired and needed take a piss, so he went to the little toilet—if you could call if that—in the corner.

Iggy was quiet for a moment, and Logan was more than grateful.

"Whatchu' mean, man?"

Logan finished using the toilet and turned to the sink. "You know what I mean. It seems to me like you are confused." After washing his hands, Logan dried them and leaned against the sink as Iggy sat up in the bed, now giving him his full attention.

"Oh, I see what this be about," Iggy shook his head.

Logan smirked. "Do you now? You know what I'm talking about?" Iggy didn't respond. "You're a white boy. Your ass better realize that shit, and you better get back over on this fuckin' side . . . and do it real quick." Logan was used to using his height and weight as intimidation. He'd only been in one fight since he'd been in jail, and he assumed it was his icy demeanor that kept other inmates at bay. Iggy was a skinny white kid who needed to be reminded of his ancestry.

Seemingly unfazed by Logan's intimidating stare, Iggy burst out laughing. He actually held his stomach and lost his breath to the laughter. Once he calmed, he wiped the tears from his face and straightened. "My man, that is not the first time I've heard shit like that in a place like this."

Logan was sure that was the truth, but he didn't find it funny. "Then you might want to heed that shit." He shoved away from the sink and yanked his shirt over his head in anger.

Iggy cracked his knuckles just as the first warning for lights out sounded overhead. "Fuck dat shit. You don't know me, man."

Logan could tell that Iggy was serious, but now it was his turn to laugh. He thought back to his time in the ghetto when he'd gotten his ass handed to him by the black kids more times than he could count. Those black kids would just as soon beat the shit out of Iggy before they accepted him into their hateful ass group.

He grunted. "Yeah, I know your ass. You're one of them little boys who wants to be all gansta, but you aren't dark enough to be."

Logan wasn't interested in arguing with the man; he'd seen his kind over the past seven years, and they were all the same. They all wanted to be the next Eminem, and thought pretending to be black and date black chicks was the way to get there. He laughed. They were fucking douche bags. As far as Logan knew, Eminem may have acted black, but his ass married and knocked up a white woman.

CHAPTER 7

KATIE HAD SAT BY the phone waiting for it to ring for the last two days. She felt ridiculous, but at this point she didn't care. Held up in her house since Valentine's Day night, she had way too much time on her hands. The editor would most probably have her manuscript for another week or two, and Katie had already cleaned her house from top to bottom . . . twice.

Teal had called a couple times to schedule a breakfast, lunch, or dinner with her, but she pretended to be too busy. Although Katie was mad—no, she was *livid* that they had once again tried to control another aspect of her life—she tried not to let Teal see the pain it caused her. And she sure as hell wasn't going to confront her dad about it. She already knew how that would turn out. Her father had a way of making Katie feel like a needy child, and she supposed she only had herself to blame for that. Growing up, Katie didn't fit in, so she leaned on her parents for companionship.

When her mother married Jan-Erik, she had only been eight. Jan-Erik moved his new family to Northern Virginia in an affluent suburb and placed Katie in a private school. She'd notice the differences between her and her classmates almost immediately, and if she hadn't, they had no problems reminding her.

As if the obvious outward differences weren't enough, Katie had to deal with going back to her old hometown to visit family for the summer three years later. Her friends had all gone to public schools and seemed so different than her, or at least that's what they'd told her when they'd called her names like: bougie, stuck up, and Bougetto. For the life of her she couldn't figure out what any of those names meant in reference to her, but one in particular stuck with her from childhood until now, and that was Oreo.

Of all the names she was called as a kid, Oreo had to be the most confusing. She was not mixed and she didn't think she "acted white". She would always ask, *"How do you act white?"* It made no sense that speaking properly and not using slang was looked at as "acting white". Especially since Katie thought she was just speaking the English she was taught in school.

When Katie realized that her friends from the past, as well as the new students of St. Augustine's Preparatory School for Girls, weren't interested in her friendship, she turned to the only two people who accepted her—her parents.

Katie wasn't sure how long the phone had been ringing, but as soon as her inner thoughts released her from the past she grabbed the receiver and squeaked out a greeting. "Um . . . yes, hello?"

Anxiety heightened, she listened as the automated voice explained, "You are receiving a collect call from Crashaw Correctional, Inmate #92510." The recording stopped, and the voice she'd been waiting to hear came on the line as he said his name to the recording that would play for her. She didn't have time to think much about the gruff, rumbling voice on the other end of the line.

Since the automated operator cared nothing about Katie needing to calm her nerves, it continued, "If you'd like to accept these charges, please press one. If not, please hang up the phone."

Before Katie could think, or even second-guess herself, she pressed one and covered her mouth, hoping to trap the nervous squeal bubbling in her chest. The line was silent for a moment before Scott's southern accent filled the line.

"Hello?"

Katie hadn't been sure what to expect from Scott's voice since she'd never set foot in his hometown. She heard as he cleared his voice and tried again.

"Hello, Kristen?"

The fake name she'd given him surprised her, and she almost wished Kristen were her name. She found her voice just in time to sound like a fool. "Um . . . yes, this is her—I mean, I . . . I'm Kristen." She slapped her forehead, but his warm chuckle stopped her embarrassment and heat blossomed in her chest.

"Sounds like someone is nervous," Scott teased.

Katie laughed and swallowed her nerves. It was just a phone call, why was she acting so ridiculous? "Just a little," she admitted.

"Well now, what's there to be nervous about?"

Katie could hear indistinct noises in the background, and she assumed that Scott wasn't alone in the room. After all, he was in prison and she'd seen the phone pods before. There were eight if she remembered correctly, and since he was in the minimum-security ward, they were free to come and go as they pleased.

"Honestly, I don't know." And that was the truth. Katie had lingered by the phone like a crazy person waiting for this call, and now that he'd phoned she was lip-locked.

Scott's voiced lowered. "Well, can I start this conversation out by saying you have a beautiful voice?"

At that, Katie let out a short burst of snorting laughter, which she was sure would change his mind about her "beautiful voice."

He laughed as well. "No, seriously. It's soft and sweet, the way a woman should sound."

Blushing profusely, Katie smiled. "Thank you, Scott. I like your voice, too. I wasn't sure how you'd sound, but I like the light Southern accent."

"Shit, honey, you should hear me when I'm angry. I can make every word one syllable and a paragraph turns into four words."

She laughed. "Oh yeah?"

"Yeah. I honestly thought you'd sound more Southern, 'cause you said you were from Virginia."

"Yes, I am, but I'm from Alexandria. It's far up north, close to DC, so I don't really think I have an accent. If you go further down around Suffolk, Virginia Beach, or even to the west, like Clarksville, you'll hear a bit of the South." Katie relaxed a bit as she talked to Scott about her hometown.

Though while growing up, the place was stressful, it was still familiar and helped erase a bit of the stress in her life. "Now, if you go north all the way up to New York, they'll call you a Southerner, but if you head down to South Carolina, they'll call you a Yankee!"

She and Scott laughed, and Katie couldn't help but enjoy the timbre of his voice. Heavy and deep, the sound traveled through the phone and settled in her ear, pleasing the part of her that missed a man's voice.

"You don't sound the least bit Southern to me."

Katie scooted back in her chair and got comfortable. The muscles in her neck loosened, and she took a deep breath. "Of course not, Mr. Kentucky, you are west of Virginia."

Logan chuckled. "True."

There was a moment of silence, and Katie almost panicked, but instead she thought back to the letter he'd sent her. "Hey, why did you really want me to tell you a deep, dark secret? Planning to use it against me later?" She chuckled nervously. If Scott ever found out that Katie was the warden's daughter, would he use her words against her?

"Yeah, about that . . . Kristen, I just thought you might need to talk to me about something. I say this because, when a woman reaches out to a stranger, a convicted felon no less, there might be something behind it. You told me you had friends, so I'm wondering what's going on in your life that has you reaching out to a stranger instead of your friends."

Good question. "Hmmm . . ." She didn't really have to think about it, but she needed to stall for time. She wasn't sure what she was going to say to him. However, Scott was smarter than she gave him credit for and called her out.

"What's this, 'Hmmm'? You know what it is, and I think you want to tell me." Scott's voice lowered, and if possible got even sexier, but Katie ignored the warmth in her belly and focused on his words. At her silence, he added, "You want me to go first?"

Her mouth moved before she even knew it was happening, and she whispered, "Please."

He wasn't silent long, but she still felt his hesitance. "Shit, honey, I'm not even sure if these calls are recorded or not."

"Yes, they are." Katie knew this for a fact.

"Okay . . . but I'm still gonna do it. I'll still tell you because I can't expect it from you and not do the same in return, right?"

"Right." Katie was nervous for her turn, but curiosity about Scott and his maybe dark deeds excited her to the core. He was in prison, and Katie could think of a million things he could confess to her. "Don't tell me anything illegal, Scott," she pleaded. She wouldn't tell a soul, but she also wouldn't be able to talk to him anymore.

Gruff laughter emerged from the phone. "Honey, I wouldn't sully your ears with more of my crimes if I had any. You aren't a priest, and I ain't asking for your forgiveness. Just your time and your honesty."

Katie didn't speak. Actually, she was relieved he was so frank with her.

Scott coughed, and lowered his voice to a whisper. "Okay, a deep, dark secret. After this call, I'm going to go back to my cell, lay in my bed, and think of what it would be like to make love to you."

Bumbling idiot that she was, Katie dropped the phone . . . and in her several attempts to pick it up again, she pressed about twenty buttons. Once the phone was back to her ear and she'd settled down, she expected to hear Scott laughing, but was greeted with silence.

"Shit, I hung up on him," she whispered dejectedly.

"No you didn't, sweetheart. I'm still here."

Katie wasn't sure if she should be relieved or hang up. "Oh, okay."

Still, there was no chuckle on the other end. "I didn't mean to embarrass you. I was just being honest."

Katie took a deep breath and placed her head down on the desk. "I appreciate that, Scott, but my secret isn't that I want you in my bed, it's darker and more painful than lust." And with that, Katie hung up the phone.

"Shit." She slammed the receiver down again. Of course all he wanted to do was talk about sex. He was a freaking criminal who'd been hard up for several years.

He didn't give a damn about Katie, and she was a damned fool for ever believing that he did.

CHAPTER 8

YEP, HE DESERVED THAT, but her anger didn't stop Logan from redialing Kristen's number twice until she finally picked up the phone again. Only this time, she wasn't the shy, demure girl who was so nervous that she rambled on and on about his accent.

"Scott, I'm not sure what you think this is, but it's not that. No, not at all," were the first words out of her mouth when she accepted the collect call.

He thought to apologize, but from experience he'd learned that saying 'I'm sorry' could oftentimes make the situation worse, so he just listened and waited.

"You told me you wanted to form a connection, and I assumed you meant in the way of a friendship . . . at least that's what I had hoped you meant. But if you think that I'm going to be on this phone with you talking— speaking to you like that—you are seriously mistaken." Her tone was sharp, and Logan considered himself duly chastised.

He waited for her to catch her breath before he spoke. He owed her a truth after fucking up so badly. "When I was eighteen, I moved to a small town in Kentucky from Lexington because I'd gotten arrested for possession. Before my mother kicked me out and sent me to live with her drunk of a brother, she asked me what made me try weed since, as she knew it, I'd never tried it before. I was so pissed at her for siding with my stepdad to get rid of me, that I told her I'd been smoking weed and I'd tried meth twice." He heard her breath catch.

"Jesus, Scott."

"Yeah but, Kristen, my secret is that I'd never done any of that shit." He'd always thought the day he told his mother that lie was the day it sealed his fate.

"Then, why? Why would you tell her that if it wasn't true?" Her voice was so soft and comforting that Scott actually told her the truth.

"Because I wanted to hurt her the way she was hurting me. I wanted her to feel like a shitty parent, because at that point, that's what she was to me. There was no worse person in my life."

"But—" Katie abruptly stopped, as if thinking about what to say next. "Scott, being a parent can't be easy. What if she was just trying to help by sending you away from what she thought was a bad situation?"

The curiosity in her voice kept Logan from getting upset. Most people had pity for his mother. They'd say, "Well, she probably did what she thought was right."

Scott knew the truth, but over time his anger had subsided and he'd put the past behind him. It'd taken years, but he'd done it.

"No, my mother remarried. From the start, he and I didn't get along, and it wasn't for my lack of trying. The man was a hard-ass. He was in the military and I wasn't used to that shit, but I still tried. Nothing was ever good enough, so over time I stopped trying—period."

"Was it that you just couldn't live up to his standards?" she asked, but Logan could hear the understanding in her voice. Maybe she'd gone through some of the same shit, but he wasn't about to ask her. Any personal information she gave him would have to be voluntary.

"Something like that."

"What about the drugs? Why did you have them?"

Logan laughed. "Now, I've done told you that I take responsibility for my own actions, right?"

"Yes, you did."

"I was holding for a friend when I got pulled over. I'm no damned snitch, so I just told the cop it was mine. Now, by this time I'd been living with my asshole stepdad for a few months, and when the cop said he wanted to call my father to pick me up, I let my anger get in the way and told the cop to take my ass to jail."

"Geez, that was stupid!"

"Well, I was eighteen and dumb. What I didn't realize was that the cop was trying to do me a favor that night. Instead, I ended up with a drug charge. So, that's my secret. I'd never done drugs, yet by telling my mother that, I all but made sure her ass sent me away."

Unsure of what to make of Kristen's silence, Scott didn't say anything.

"I was dating a guy named Roman for two years, and I thought he'd pop the question eventually, so I never bothered him about it, but then my mother was diagnosed with cancer. I guess after hearing that— I mean, I don't know, I just fell to pieces. Roman was there for me and all, but something wasn't right with him."

Logan didn't want to interrupt, but he needed to know. "What do you mean, 'something wasn't right?'"

"He was distant and aloof. I foolishly thought I could solve it with sex, because at that point we knew that my mother wasn't going to make it, and I couldn't stand losing Roman and my mother at the same time."

The word 'sex' hadn't gone unnoticed by Logan. "Death is hard, but a part of life." He hoped he didn't sound insensitive. "I mean, what about your father? Didn't you have him still?"

"Yeah, but he handled it differently. He's from Sweden, and he would always say Europeans mourned differently. I think it's silly, but I wanted to keep everyone in my life. One night, I came home to Roman packing. I freaked and tried everything I could to convince him to stay. I thought keeping him with me would numb the pain. However, it was too late, and he wouldn't stay. Even when I found out I was pregnant, he told me to figure it out."

Logan wasn't sure what her secret was, but he was starting to get a clue. "What happened next?"

Kristen sighed and continued on a shuddering breath. "Fast forward two months later, my mother is going into the hospital for the hundredth time, I was reeling from keeping my pregnancy a secret, my friend Teal was juggling college and work, my father wasn't accepting the fact that my mother had signed a DNR, and I was so stressed that I'd lost ten pounds and hadn't slept in days. One night, I woke up and was bleeding. I panicked, but there was no one I could call. No one knew about the baby, and I couldn't call an ambulance for fear my neighbors would call my dad. So, I drove myself to Mercy General."

Mercy General? Scott had wondered if Kristen lived in Vermont because of how fast he'd gotten her letters. He knew there was a Mercy General in Vermont. "You had to drive yourself to the hospital?"

Logan could hear the sadness in her voice. "Yeah, I had a miscarriage that night."

"And you had to handle it alone?" he asked.

"Yeah."

After a beat of silence, he said, "Thank you, Kristen."

On a sigh, she asked, "For what?"

"For forming a connection with me. For telling me your secret. Thanks." Logan really had wanted to form a relationship with her; however, his earlier comment about thinking of sleeping with her had been true as well. However, after listening to Kristen's sincerity and honesty, Scott wasn't thinking with his dick as much; he was actually content with just getting to know her.

CHAPTER 9

KATIE POURED ANOTHER GLASS of ice water and handed it to her father. She knew the day would come when he found out what had happened between her and Joe, and she was ready for it. Not ready for an argument, or anything like that. She was actually ready to apologize.

Jan-Erik sat at the dining room table, and his coat jacket hung off the back of the chair. He took of his suit coat and stood.

"I got it, Dad." Katie took his coat and hung it up in the hallway closet. "I hope it stops snowing soon," she called over her shoulder as she hung it up.

"There's a storm coming in the next few days." Katie walked back into the dining room and sat in the chair across from him. "Maybe you should pack a bag and stay over at the house with me."

Her father's statement may have seemed innocent enough, a father looking out for his daughter, but to

Katie, it felt like he was trying to keep her under his thumb. She had lived on her own since college, and had already lived through quite a few snowstorms. But it never failed, her dad always wanted to keep her close during a storm, which was understandable, yet Katie knew she could take care of herself.

"I'll be fine here." She wrapped her shawl around her shoulders and watched as he sipped his water.

After placing the cup down, he pushed it away. "And if you lose power?" He raised a brow as if to say, 'what then?'

"Dad, I've got plenty of fire wood and a cell phone if the power goes out. I'll be fine."

Not one to give up, he added, "Maybe you can call Teal over. Then you can have a sleepover, or whatever it is that you girls do." He rubbed his eyes and Katie could see he was tired.

He'd stopped over before work, which was early as hell since he was always in the office by seven thirty. Katie listened as he spoke. There was never a day she thought her father wanted anything more than the absolute best for her, but his methods had grown tiresome.

"We don't have sleepovers, we go out to dinner, have lunch, or get coffee." Katie wiped imaginary crumbs off the table, waiting for the real reason he'd come over.

He pulled his Blackberry from his pocket and placed his thumb on the reader. "Just make sure you call her," he said as he read what she assumed was an email.

Jan-Erik didn't do text messages; he'd ignore the texts or respond to it in email form. It used to annoy her, but over time, she realized her father had a reason for everything he did. That didn't change the fact that oftentimes, it made absolutely no sense to her.

Katie smiled, of course her father would want someone with her during the storm, but the only person Katie could think about was Scott. They'd spoken every day since his first call, and she'd come to look forward to the icy, compassionless automated voice that introduced her to her daily escape.

She looked up at her father, who was tapping out an email. She thought of her confession to Scott and the words burned her lips, willing—maybe even begging—her for their escape. Her heart hung heavy in her chest as she imagined the disappointment from her father if she told him her secret. But, damn how good it'd felt to tell someone, even if he was a convict serving time for armed robbery. She'd be damned if she'd judge him anymore than she already had. She hadn't expected such honesty from him, but he'd given it freely and she'd given him the same in return. It was because of that honesty, Katie had decided that when he called this afternoon, she'd tell him her real name. He at least deserved to know that.

Thick fingers appeared in front of her face and snapped, once and then twice. "Where'd you go, little girl?" Jan-Erik's look of concern pulled her from her thoughts.

She rubbed her eyes and shook her head. "Nowhere, it's early and I'm still a bit tired." Her father stood and took his glass to the sink.

"Who was on the phone?"

Silently, Jan-Erik rinsed the glass out and placed it on the drain board. Something like indecision or confusion spread across his face before he asked, "You want to tell me something?" He turned to her, and Katie's heart jumped into her throat.

Swallowing hard, she forced words out of her mouth. "Umm . . . no, not that I can think of." If he knew she'd been talking to Scott he'd put an end to it real quick, but looking at her father she wasn't sure if he was talking about Joe or Scott.

He nodded, but Katie could tell there was something important on his mind. "I forget sometimes that you are twenty-five." His comment threw her off.

"Okay?" Her brow furrowed and she narrowed her eyes.

He crossed the room and placed a gentle hand on her shoulder. Katie reached up, grabbing his warm hand. His smile was sad and had her a bit worried. Maybe it was something completely different, she thought. Maybe he had bad news of some sort. However, before she could ask him, he spoke.

"Your father can't be the one to find you a man, can he?"

Katie expelled a breath and squeezed his hand again. "No, Dad, you can't."

Jan-Erik moved away and reached for his coat. "Make sure you call Teal," he reminded her as he put on his suit jacket and walked into the foyer. "And I'll have David bring over some batteries, candles, and more fire wood."

Sighing, Katie rolled her eyes. "Dad, I have all of that stuff right out in the shed." She reached for his coat, removing it from his hand. "I don't need anymore. There's like a hundred dollars' worth of batteries out there now." She helped him into his coat, and then stood on her tiptoes to give him a kiss. "I sure as heck hope batteries don't go bad."

He wrapped his arms around her and pulled her close. "That's the first problem, all of the things you need are outside when they should be close, and you know better. Now, make sure you check the box for an expiration date."

Katie ignored the admonishment and hugged her father closer. She loved him with all of her heart, which was one of the main reasons she wouldn't tell him about the miscarriage. She couldn't take a grandkid from him even if it'd only been two months old and the size of a jellybean. Her stomach fluttered, and the absence of her child brought tears to her eyes. The fact that her father had tried so hard to find her a good man, in hopes she'd someday marry and have kids with him, burdened her. She'd let him down, and she didn't have the courage to tell him.

CHAPTER 10

"**I FEEL LIKE I'M** in high school again," Katie admitted with a smile. She was of course talking about the good days in high school when she wasn't being teased or ignored.

Scott chortled in what sounded like disbelief. "What? How so?"

She didn't want to sound like a moonstruck fool, but waiting by the phone for a guy to call brought back good and bad memories. She cuddled up under her blanket, moving the phone to her other ear so she could get comfortable. "Well, I guess you wouldn't know what I'm talking about since you were never the one sitting by the phone waiting for a guy you liked to call you."

He groaned, and Katie smiled at the affect she had over him at times. "So you do like me? And here I thought you only tolerated me because you had nothing else to do but wait for your novel to come back from the editor." Katie could hear the laughter in his voice.

"Maybe it started that way, but things change." She wondered if things were different, if they'd spontaneously met, if he would be interested in her. She didn't know what he looked like, but his damned voice made her stomach drop and her heart thunder.

Scott's voice grew serious. "What changed, Kristen?" At the sound of her fake name, Katie realized how silly it was to think that the two of them could ever be anything more than pen pals. What was even more ridiculous was the fact that she had told him about the night she'd lost her child, but she couldn't tell him her real name. She wanted his time and honesty, but she hadn't given him a hundred percent of what she demanded of him.

"Kathryn Andreassen," she blurted.

"Who?"

The confusion in his voice almost made her laugh, but fear that he'd be pissed she lied kept the laughter at bay. "Scott, when I first signed up for this program, I . . . I didn't give my real name."

"Oh yeah?"

There was an edge to his voice that she'd not heard before. It didn't sound like disappointment or even anger. "I was nervous about what I was doing and I—"

"You wanted anonymity," he finished. "I get that."

Yeah, well, at least she had wanted it at that time. "So you aren't mad?" She sat up, comforted by how well he'd taken it.

"Not at all."

Confused, Katie asked, "Why?"

A beat of silence passed before Scott spoke. "Because I did the same. My name isn't Scott, its Logan. Logan Whyte. I lied for a different reason, though."

The relief she'd just felt plummeted, and goose bumps settled over her skin.

"I didn't want you to look me up and see what I'd done before I had a chance to tell you myself. By the time we'd gotten to the point where we could be straightforward with each other, I honestly forgot to tell you my real name."

Katie was about to speak when the one-minute warning sounded, alerting them that the collect call was about to disconnect.

"Kris— I mean Kathryn—"

"Call me Katie, everyone does."

"Okay. I'll call you right back, I need to talk to you about something." Logan hung up before Katie had a chance to reply.

She pressed the end button, got out of bed, and went to glance out the window. The snow was coming down in sheets, but in Vermont that wasn't a big issue. It was the low visibility that worried Katie. The phone sounded and she placed it to her ear, listening as the automated voice droned on. Once she pressed one, Logan's deep voice came on the line.

"Sweetheart, I want to talk to you about your phone bill."

Katie groaned and sat down in her desk chair; she was scared as hell to look at her bill.

"Yeah, I know, but I enjoy talking to you. Your voice is the highlight of my day. I have an idea though."

Katie perked up. "I'm listening."

"Good, that's my girl." Whenever Logan called her things like his girl, honey, or sweetheart, her heart fluttered. "I'm going to get my lawyer to add money to my canteen. That way, I can call you and they'll charge it to me. How's that sound?"

Katie bit her lip. They hadn't talked about financials, and she wasn't sure what money Logan had . . . if any at all. "Are you sure? I mean, I haven't gotten my bill yet, so it might not be too high."

Logan grunted, and Katie had heard that sound enough to know that he didn't agree. "No, it's going to be sky high, and if you have a hard time paying it you let me know." He sounded so sincere that Katie's stomach fluttered.

"I'll be fine," she whispered.

"Don't be shy. If you can't pay it, you let me know." He repeated.

"I will." She knew she could afford it, but she wasn't excited about seeing it. "So your lawyer is going to give you the money?" Seemed like a nice thing to do, but Logan had expressed to her many times that he didn't like the man.

"No, my friend, Trent, sends me my money. I sold my truck and put him in charge of my finances. I trust him with my life," he said earnestly.

"Sounds like a good guy." Katie felt the same way about Teal, even though the woman seemed to want to take her dead mother's place.

"He saved my ass from the black kids that constantly thought they saw a target on my ass. I swear, I was eighteen, white, and a bit chunky, and that's all it took for those thugs to want to kick my ass." He let loose a hollow laugh. Pain radiated from it, and Katie heard it loud and clear.

She wasn't sure what to say, but if she hadn't known before she knew now that Logan was white. That discovery aside, Katie had also had her share of times when black kids picked on her, but it wasn't just black kids. It was black and white kids. Both races had their assholes.

"I know the feeling. When I was younger, I was never sure what made kids think I was such an easy target, but they did and I suffered."

Logan's voice grew gentle. "Baby, it's because they are jealous of you. I know that's a parental thing to say, but it's true. They want what we have, and when they can't have it, they steal it. Mexicans, too. They just stood and watched as I got the shit kicked out of me."

Katie couldn't help but feel sorry for Logan. "At least you had Trent. I'm glad you didn't have to go at it alone." And that was the honest truth. She had friends, but never ones who would stick around long enough, or even through the entire year. Logan's situation would have been a lot worse if not for Trent, Katie was sure of it. She at least had her mom and dad and later on, Teal, but Logan only had his drunken uncle, Luke. "Things could have been real bad if he hadn't helped, huh?"

"I probably would have gotten killed, so yeah, things would've been real bad if he hadn't come along. Trent was into some real crazy stuff, and those thugs went running scared." He laughed. "After that, I shaved my head, worked out every day, got a few custom tattoos, bought a gun, and dared those assholes to come near me." Katie imagined a tall, well-built man, covered with tattoos, and a gun in his waistband. Besides the gun, the rest made a very sexy picture, even if she couldn't imagine his face.

She lowered her voice, hoping to change the subject. "The picture you just painted doesn't sound very intimidating to me."

"Oh yeah?" She could hear him lick his lips. "What kind of picture are you imagining over there?" The timbre of his voice changed, leaving behind the anger and bringing forth something sexier, decadent even. After he'd hit on her during their first phone call—forcing her to hang up on him—she noticed he'd been choosing his words very carefully. However, little by little he'd been breaking down her walls, and on top of that, her loneliness was starting to get the better of her.

"Well," she adjusted herself comfortably on her bed, "I can't see your face of course, but you've said you are six foot two, you've worked out for the past fifteen years, and you eat right, taking pride in your body." Katie sighed, and then let loose a little moan of appreciation. "You see what I'm getting at here?"

"Shit," Logan whispered. "Yeah, I think I can see where your mind is going. You want to tell me more about that?"

Katie exhaled. "What the heck am I doing?" She sat up, her face hot with more than just nervousness. "I'm sorry."

"Goddamn, girl. Don't be sorry, be honest and tell me what you were thinking." His voice was gruff, but not with anger.

Katie covered her mouth to keep her delighted laughter in.

At her silence, he whispered not unkindly, "Tease."

"You know I don't mean to be," she said honestly. Katie was horny and so was Logan; she guessed eventually they'd joke and flirt about it, but that was it.

He cleared his throat, but she caught laughter in it. "I'm not sure. Babe, I'm gonna let you go. I need to call Trent and set up the money transfer to my canteen."

Katie placed as much pout in her voice as she could. "Fine." She could keep him on the phone longer if she wanted to, but she really did want him to set up a calling plan for them.

He groaned again, and Katie wasn't too sure he was actually going to be making a phone call when he hung up, but maybe handling some personal business. Shame hit hard. She wasn't a tease, and she didn't want Logan rubbing one out on his own because of her. She sweetened her voice and said, "I have some preparing to do for this storm anyway, so I'll talk to you tomorrow."

"Okay, I'll have the calling plan set up by then. Talk to you later." At that, he hung up.

Standing, Katie stretched her legs. The warmth in her belly hadn't subsided, and she realized she wasn't the only one who needed some sort of release. She couldn't keep teasing Logan, because in the end, she ended up suffering the same—if not more. Okay, maybe not. After all, Katie had the privacy of her own home to "double click her mouse" but if Logan wanted to enjoy the "five knuckle shuffle" he'd have to do it with some unwanted company.

Katie giggled as she headed down the hall to dress for the storm starting outside. Her dad was right, she should have gotten the firewood earlier, but the weatherman claimed that she still had some time to prepare for the upcoming blizzard. However, once outside, Katie thought differently. Snow fell from the sky with a vengeance, the wind howled loud and long as she headed to the shed with the key in her hand. She was on a mission: batteries, her cordless phone to talk to Logan, and more firewood.

Snow fell in heavy sheets all around her, and after living in Vermont for the last few years, Katie had learned the difference between heavy snowfall and a damned oncoming blizzard. Weatherman and his week be damned, a very bad storm was coming and Katie prayed she was right when she told her dad she was ready for it.

CHAPTER 11

LOGAN ENDED THE CALL before he could say some sappy shit like, "miss you." He dialed his buddy Trent's number and placed the phone to his ear. Katie's last name sounded familiar, but more so it sounded European. She'd told him that her father hailed from Sweden. Still, the name bounced around in his head, tugging at his memory.

After Logan recorded his name and waited for his call to be accepted, Trent's gravelly voice filled the line. "What's goin' on, man?"

Logan enjoyed his familiar voice; it reminded him of home and all of the days before prison. "Nothing, just waiting 'til my time is up," Logan answered. "How is Shayla doing?" Shayla was his on-again, off-again crazy ass girlfriend. Logan always thought she was more trouble and drama than she was worth, but Trent never listened.

He sighed into the phone. "Bein' a terror as usual. She packed up and left, took my fuckin' truck, too."

Logan had had his fair share of women who'd added more stress to his life than necessary, but he wasn't like Trent . . . no amount of sex could make him deal with the heap of shit Trent was dealing with. "I told you, man, she was going to take that truck. She was always asking to drive it. Anyway, I need you to fill my canteen so I can make a calling plan." Logan could hear Trent moving around in his place, most likely to get his ledger out of his desk.

"All right, how much you need in there?" Trent asked.

From what Logan understood, collect calls from prison were expensive, he just didn't know the cost per minute. "How much is it when I call you?"

"'Bout twenty-five cents a minute, so a fifteen minute call is 'bout three dollars and seventy-five cents. Debit and prepaid calls are twenty-one cents a minute. So, what do you need? Like thirty or forty bucks?"

Logan called Katie at least four or five times a day. The call center was open from eight a.m. to ten p.m., and whenever he missed her voice, he'd call her. "More like two hundred," Logan corrected.

"Damn, man, who you callin'?" Trent exclaimed. Logan could hear him scribbling in the ledger; Trent was in control of Logan's finances until he got out.

He wasn't sure how to explain Katie to Trent, so he didn't. He'd wait and see if it went any further than letters and phone calls, because if it didn't, then it wasn't worth mentioning. Regardless, there was something else he wanted to talk to Trent about. "Oh, yeah, I forgot to tell you. Jake came by to see me not too long ago." Logan moved the receiver to his other ear. He'd been on the phone with Katie for a while, and the right side of his face was starting to hurt.

Trent snorted. "What'd that asshole lawyer of yours want? You know he's still pissed at you 'bout that Dawn situation years back." Trent snickered. "Can you believe that shit? Years later, he's still mad cause you fucked some chick he liked."

Logan groaned. He couldn't really stand Jake either, and it'd taken bribing him to get him to represent him in court. Although Logan barely remembered his college days, he did remember the night he'd spent with Dawn. He hadn't been a virgin, but she'd taught him a few things that'd made him real popular with the ladies later in life.

"Pshhh . . . man, I know. But he's good at what he does, and my funds were severely limited at the time." It was true. When he was arraigned, he couldn't even afford to make bail. Logan had to sell his truck and a few other things just to keep his account from going in the red.

"Well, partner. You're lookin' good over here. I got you back up to eight grand, so when you get out you ain't gonna be livin' in the streets, and you know you have a place here with me."

Logan knew he could depend on Trent. "Good, brother." He was starting to feel better about his release. If anything, he was nervous about getting back out in the world after so many years. He needed to get his business up and running, and all sorts of other shit.

"As a matter of fact," Trent's voice held Logan's attention, "that sugar-nosed freak owes you 'bout three hundred. I overpaid him on the last installment. I thought you owed him eight hundred and sixty to pay him off, but it was five hundred and thirty. You want me to call him and tell that crook to add it to your books?"

He remembered the letter his lawyer had sent asking for the money. "No, I'll call him now." Logan didn't want to because his ear was aching and he had to piss badly, but he would get it done.

"All right, brother."

Trent hung up, and Logan dialed Jake's number, recorded his name, and waited.

"Jake McCallister." The formal greeting grated Logan's nerves.

"Put that extra money on my canteen for a calling plan," Logan demanded.

"What extra—"

"Don't fuck with me, Jake." Logan wasn't in the mood. In fact, in Jake's case he was never in the mood.

"All right, but who the fuck are you calling that you need that much money? Aren't you doing that Pen Pal Program?"

Logan failed to see how that was any of Jake's damn business, but how the hell had he known?

At his silence, Jake explained, "I signed you up for consideration. They said you were eligible, and my buddy Graham made sure you got in. You know

Graham. He told me when he talked to you about it that you asked for a hot white woman!" Jake let out a wicked laugh. "Oh wait, I see. Is that who you are talking to?"

Logan hung the phone up. He was pissed at his meddling ass lawyer, but he couldn't be too pissed . . . Jake's actions had introduced him to Katie.

CHAPTER 12

KATIE DECIDED SHE WANTED to change her career again. In her mind, she felt a weather woman was where she needed to be. As she stoked the fire she'd started the second the power was lost, she calculated the cost of returning to college.

In preparation for the long night ahead, she'd already hooked up the cordless phone, put all of her faucets on a slow drip, moved her food to the freezer, and started the fire.

After calling her father four times, she knew the prison's power was still up. He had told her they were sending home all nonessential personnel, which meant she could call Teal to come over. However, she hadn't because she was actually excited for the snowstorm. She was looking forward to Logan's call. It'd be like spending the night, or at least a few moments with him on a cold, snowy night. Katie hadn't been held in a man's arms in years and she longed for that. If she couldn't have it, she'd settle for Logan's warm voice and conversation.

Katie stood and went to her room. Grabbing an afghan and pillow, she brought them into the living room with her. In front of the fire, she'd arranged a cozy setting for two, but sadly enough it'd just be her. A bottle of white wine and chocolates were set away from the fire to keep them chilled, a bit less romantic were the bag of chips and dip. Katie shook her head and placed the afghan and pillow in front of the fireplace. She sat down and poured a glass of wine just as the phone rang.

The automated voice greeted her with its familiar words. Katie accepted the call and went right into her thoughts. "Logan, I'm switching careers."

"What, why?" His voice sounded sleepy, but she'd expected it to. It was Friday, and he'd worked all day; in the kitchen and then cleaning bathrooms.

She lay back and propped her feet on the coffee table. "Because Atmospheric Scientists, including Meteorologists, have a median annual wage of eighty-nine thousand dollars. And the best part? You don't even have to be accurate!" She giggled. Yeah, she made well more than that a year, but writing was hard ass work.

Logan's grunt sounded as if he agreed. "Yeah, I bet. When I was back home, the weatherman was always saying there'd be rain in the summer, but it'd sprinkle and then be hot as hell. So other than deciding to spend your life's savings on college again, how was your day, baby?"

Katie struggled to hold in the sigh wanting to escape her lips. Normally, she hated being called anything other than her name, but with Logan she enjoyed it. It was the rough timbre to his voice and the way he lowered it for only her to hear.

"Umm, nothing much. Got the manuscript back from the editor, but I'm lazing off that. I lost power a few hours ago and I set up a fire."

"Good, keep my baby safe and warm."

Katie loved the fact that he hadn't treated her like an invalid, asking if she was prepared, had a check list, or whatever. No, he just wanted his baby safe and warm. "Am I your baby? Is that what I am to you?" She kept her voice low.

He hesitated, and that worried her just a little. "What do you want?"

"You paused."

Logan laughed. "I'd hate to have you hang up on me again," he joked.

She was sure he knew she would not hang up on him again. Their flirting had so far been harmless, but lately he'd been calling her baby and sweetheart. He'd also ask her how she was feeling, and she knew he'd been insinuating if she needed him in ways a phone call couldn't satisfy. Still, Katie had to think of reality. How could anything come from what they had? Her father would flip, and Katie and Logan were still practically strangers.

"Logan," she paused. Even though she was nervous about the answer she might receive, Katie still needed to know Trent's thoughts on a "what if" situation. "If you weren't in prison and you met me and felt the way about me that you feel now, what would happen?" She wanted honesty, she wanted him to want her, but she also wanted her fantasy to match reality.

There was no hesitation, no reluctance in his tone. "Katie, if I wasn't such a fuck up and I was out there, I'd ask you out. Forgive me for being blunt, but as beautiful as I know you are, I'd take you out. Then, we'd go home and I'd make love to you all night long. In the morning, I'd want you to stay."

Katie swallowed hard. Logan had told her that he was coming up for parole, so there was a true chance that she would get to meet him. "Logan."

"Yes, baby?"

His voice was so deep and gravelly, Katie closed her eyes. "I want you. I want to meet you, but I know I can't."

He heaved a sigh. "Maybe one day, baby. I know you are here in Vermont, and I wouldn't ask you to come to this hell hole and see me, but if you wait just a little bit longer, we can meet. I'm not asking for much more than a chance to see the face of the woman who keeps me sane and grounded in here." Logan went silent for a moment, and then spoke again. "Katie, can I ask you for something—something I don't deserve?"

Her heart thundered in her chest at the possibilities. "Yes."

"Be mine. Keep talking to me, and if things go good when I get out, we'll meet and you can decide how far this will go." Katie listened to his words, and while they were everything she wanted to hear, she'd feared hearing them as well. Her fantasy and reality seemed so damned far apart.

He cleared his throat. "Don't be silent, baby, if you don't want this—"

"I do," she blurted. "I want to try, but I don't know, Logan. We are still strangers." And they were. "Not only that, but my life is complicated. My family, too." She hadn't told him that her father was the warden, but if she were to expect something more from what they were doing, she'd have to be honest. "Like my dad—" She could hear him shuffle the phone to the other ear.

"He isn't going to like it, and I understand that. However, you're a grown woman, and only you can decide who you date."

"Yeah, okay, but first . . ." Sitting up, she braced herself for an onslaught of curses. "We said nothing but the truth from here on out, and if we are planning—" She stopped, not quite sure what they were planning.

Logan filled in the blank. "To be together and see where shit goes when I get out. And for you to be my woman until then."

The biggest smile spread across her face. "Yeah, that. Well, I have to tell you something about my dad." When he didn't speak, she continued, "Do you know the name Jan-Erik?" She waited as he thought.

"Nope, why?"

"That's my dad, and he's the warden at the prison you're in," she said in a rush. Better to get it out than to keep it in. "I mean, I should have told you, but I didn't think it mattered since we weren't trying this thing we are trying—"

"Not trying, Katie. As of now, I'm your man and you're my woman." His voice was soft, as if trying to calm her worries about her father.

She let loose a sigh of relief. "Okay, I thought you'd be pissed."

"No, I get how this started. I knew your last name sounded familiar. I'm more familiar with assistant warden Jamieson. I should have known the second you told me, but my mind was elsewhere at the moment."

Katie grabbed the glass of wine and took a long sip. "Okay, so I'm dating an inmate?" She giggled and sipped more wine. "I'm sitting in my living room, drinking wine and talking to my boyfriend in prison on the phone." It all seemed surreal and a bit crazy.

"Baby, I am no boy. I am *all* man." Logan's deep voice echoed his words.

With another gulp of wine, Katie responded, "Yes, yes you are. Just— I can't tell my dad, you know? One, I wasn't supposed to enter the Pen Pal Program; and two, I'm sure he'll flip his lid."

"I know if I was a father and I was in his situation, I'd kick my ass. So yeah, to make sure the rest of my stay here isn't hell, let's tell him later."

Katie agreed, and with another sip of wine she finished the glass . . . and poured another.

CHAPTER 13

LOGAN HADN'T MEANT TO get a woman while he was in jail. If anything, he thought he'd end up with some inmate chaser; one of those women who loved to latch on to a man she thought she could change while he was in prison. Yet, as he listened to a buzzed Katie talk about the things she wanted to do with Logan when he was released—unfortunately nothing naughty was said—he started looking forward to meeting her.

A small hiccup escaped her lips, and Logan thought about telling her to slow down, but instead he just listened to her. "I think we should go to dinner first, you know?"

He didn't, but he let her continue.

"I mean, like a first date. When you get out."

Now he got it. He agreed, but in all honesty, he wasn't much of a dinner and movie type of man. "Oh yeah?" Logan didn't have high hopes for what would happen between Katie and himself after he found out who her father was, but he wasn't giving up just because of Jan-Erik. He liked her, understood her, and actually enjoyed conversations with her.

"Yes, I mean—"

The one minute warning sounded.

"Baby, I'll call you back in an hour. I need to take a shower and use the bathroom." He looked around as the room filled up. With the storm coming, he knew that other inmates would want to call friends and family in Vermont.

"But you just called," she whined.

"Yeah, baby," he said hurriedly so the phone wouldn't hang up on them. "I know, but I'll call right back. Don't fall asleep! I'll—" The phone disconnected and Logan cursed.

"My turn, yeah?" another inmate, who was standing a little too close to Logan, asked.

The underlying threat was there, and although he wanted to sit there longer to teach the motherfucker to wait his turn instead of walking up and invading his space, Logan stood and walked away from the phone, returning to his cell.

After his shower, Logan picked up an envelope and searched the manila folder holding the meager belongings he was allowed to keep with him. He rifled through the few photos he had of himself, looking for something decent to send to Katie.

There was one of him and Trent—he was in his prison garb—the first year Logan was locked up, and another of him and his uncle. There was also the one his uncle's wife had sent him from when he was just a teen. He couldn't send a picture of him when he was only nineteen years old, but he understood why Aunt Elma had sent it. Flipping it over, he read the back.

Do your time and come home.

Miss you,

Aunt Elma.

His aunt had taken a bus up to Vermont and stayed throughout his trial. The moment the verdict was read, he heard her weep. The day he was sentenced, he'd heard her weep. And the day Trent had called two years ago to tell him his Aunt Elma had passed away, Logan feared that the whole world could hear him weeping.

Pushing the picture back into the envelope, Logan removed the one of Trent and him, turned it over, and scribbled his name on the back. Flipping it back over, he realized that she had no clue which one he was, and he be damned if he'd let her fantasize over Trent. He circled his face and pushed it into the new envelope. After he scribbled a short letter, he pushed it in as well.

On the way to the mail slot, he wondered if Katie would send him a picture as well. In the cells of other inmates, he'd seen pictures of pretty and not so pretty women hanging from their beds or lying on their desks. The thought of having his woman's face on his pillow did a few things to him. The first was the stir of lust in his pants, but not only that . . . Logan could imagine holding Katie in his arms, her blonde, red, or dark hair splayed over his pillow.

When he reached the mail slot and pushed the envelope in, he headed to the phone room. Logan didn't have a preference when it came to hair color, as long as the carpet matched the drapes and it was long enough that in the heat of the moment Logan could pull it without complaint.

As far as body type, Logan had spent the last fifteen years of his life working out and eating right, so he wanted a woman just as fit and healthy as him. Like every man, a nice ass and perky tits were desired, but not required. When it came to Katie, Logan had fallen for her personality first; he didn't really have a choice since he couldn't see her first.

He had been pleasantly surprised when he'd talked to her . . . her voice was amazing. She spoke so prim and proper, which he attributed to her father, who was probably stern and demanding. He noticed that Katie still worried about her father, which to Logan was odd. She was twenty-five, not five. Then again, maybe she was a daddy's girl. Logan rounded the corner, and saw that all of the phones were in use, so he sat down to wait. If these men were anything like him on the phone with their women, he'd be waiting a while.

KATIE SNUGGLED DEEPER INTO the covers, pushing her head under the pillow to stop the annoying ringing in her ears. The loud bray continued, and suddenly she remembered that she was waiting for a call from Logan.

She reached for the phone. "Hello?" It sounded more like a croak, but luckily the automated voice kicked in with its usual statement. Katie sat up and cleared her throat, groaning when her head started to spin. She placed her hand over her head. Pressing one to accept the call, a dizzy and drunk Katie lay back down and waited for Logan's warm voice to invade her ears.

"You fell asleep, didn't you?"

"Mmhmm." Yawning, she lifted her head to look at the clock. "You said an hour, baby, it's been like three." The digital clock's battery backup showed the time as eight-thirty.

His warm chuckle excited her. "I had to shower, and then wait for these fools to get off the phone, but whatever. Call me that again." His voice held a bit of surprise.

Why would he be surprised she'd called him baby? Now that they were a couple, she definitely felt comfortable giving him a pet name. Gathering as much pout as she could, she responded, "No, you called too late."

Logan chuckled. "Is my baby drunk?"

Katie glanced at the empty bottle of wine. "I only had one flass mofficer!" Releasing a flurry of giggles, she realized just how drunk she really was. "Holy crap, I am drunk. I'm sorry." Embarrassed, she threw a hand over her face.

"What are you sorry for? Baby, you're old enough to get drunk if you want to. I just wish I was there with you." Even though she'd been drinking, she could hear the sincerity in his voice.

Katie placed a hand over her heart. "I wish that, too . . . but at least I have you." She meant that he was her man, as he'd claimed earlier, but her buzz—no, being drunk—stopped the right words from escaping her lips.

Instead, she said, "What I mean is, you and I are a thing. No, wait."

"Ha, I think I get what you are trying to say, drunkie. You want me there with you. Do me a favor." Logan's voice lowered, and the unmistakable tone of his voice told Katie he was about to ask her something he shouldn't, at least not while their conversations were recorded. "Don't drink anymore tonight."

Her eyes popped open. "What? Why?"

"Because, I won't be there in the morning to help you nurse that bad ass hangover you're gonna have," he whispered. "Who is going to help you to the bathroom when you gotta puke? Hmm?"

She was silent because there wouldn't be anyone there.

"Who is gonna hold your hair back, baby? Actually, what color is your hair?"

"Brunette ombré."

"I have no clue what that means."

Katie snickered. "Like Beyoncé when she had it dark at the top and copper blonde on the bottom."

"I have no clue who that is, but it sounds nice. So who is going to hold your hair out of the way, get you water, and an aspirin if you are there all alone?"

Unfortunately, Katie hadn't thought about any of that. Even though it was easy to nurse a hangover alone, she thought it was sad and pitiful to do so. Grateful that Logan hadn't treated her like a child or admonished her mistake, she agreed.

"Okay, I've had enough anyway." Katie pushed the empty bottle as far away as possible. "I drank a whole bottle of white wine, Logan. I think I'm going to puke my kidneys out tomorrow." She couldn't help but laugh at her own statement.

"You'll be fine. I've been drunk plenty of times. Just drink water."

"You aren't mad at me?"

"No, just mad that I'm not there. I know you're in Vermont, and I'm stuck in here."

"Yep, but not for long, right?" Katie was nervously excited for Logan's release. Her drunken brain wouldn't let her think of the consequences of meeting a convict; all she could think about at that moment was being next to him. "I can't wait to hold you in my arms, is that weird? I don't even know what you look like, but all I can think about is holding you in my arms," she lowered her voice, "and kissing you. I cannot stop thinking about kissing you," she admitted. Luckily, she'd had a full bottle of liquid courage and was more than willing to tell him how badly she wanted him.

He cleared his throat before he spoke. "And what else, baby? What else do you think of doing to me?"

"Logan, are you asking me to talk dirty to you?" she gasped in mock offense.

He laughed. "Hey, you started it!"

"I just said that I want to kiss you—"

"And I want to kiss you, too." His voice was sure and strong, as if he were challenging anyone to say otherwise.

Katie smiled, but was stricken with sadness. He was there, and she was alone in her home wishing for him to walk through the door.

"When you get out. We'll go on a date. You'll take me to dinner and a movie. Afterward, you'll bring me back home and make love to me, Logan." Katie sat up, dizziness be damned. "And neither one of us will ever be lonely again, you hear me?" She meant it.

No hesitation. "Yes, ma'am."

Satisfied with that, Katie lay back down and adjusted her pillow. "Logan?" A wave of nausea hit her so hard that she grabbed her belly. "I think I'm ready for you to come and hold my hair now." Her stomach rolled and her head ached. Why the hell did she drink?

"Go take care of yourself, baby. I'll call you tomorrow. Early this time, to check on you."

Katie appreciated that. "Okay, bye."

"Bye, baby."

She hung up the phone and lifted her head. Not as dizzy as before, she grabbed the afghan and crawled onto the couch, cuddling up for the rest of the night.

CHAPTER 14

KATIE IMAGINED LOGAN'S HANDS would be rough from the type of work he'd done before prison, and maybe even in prison. She expected a life of labor would harden any man, but when he touched her so gently, she thought she felt it in her soul. Her bed had been empty most times, so she slept on the couch, hoping to forget the emptiness of the bed made for a king and queen. She expected he'd be more experienced, but Katie was a fast learner. His hands were in places that recently Katie reserved for herself. His lips, tongue, and teeth were on her skin and . . . light. There was light.

KATIE HATED THE SUN. She hated light, sound, and scent. Yep, that damned automatic coffeepot that Teal had bought her for Christmas was going through the window as soon as she worked up the ability to move.

Most of all, she hated the dream ended without her being able to see her man's face. With a glance at the digital clock, Katie knew she had missed Logan's first call, since it was already past noon and he said he'd call in the morning.

Wait. A. Minute. The coffee pot is working. It took her brain a few minutes to work out that her power was back up and running.

Katie sat up, releasing a groan that could wake the dead. She stood on wobbly feet and headed to the kitchen for a glass of water. After downing two glasses, she filled another and headed into the bathroom. Once inside, she grabbed some aspirin and choked them down, too. She glanced at herself in the mirror, and was startled by her reflection.

"What the hell?" Her normally chocolate-brown eyes were bloodshot, her shoulder-length hair stood at odd directions and was matted in the back, and her nut-brown skin seemed a few shades lighter. "What was in that wine?"

She started the shower and jumped in as soon as the water was hot enough, hoping to scrub away the remnants of last night's wine binge.

Thinking back, Katie was embarrassed at the things she'd said to Logan on the phone. As they'd made love in her dream, she couldn't see his face and that creeped her out. Screwing a faceless man wasn't sexy, but on the other hand, the body attached to it was the type that made panties drop all across the US.

Katie shivered as her hand softly moved across her tender breasts. Her eyes popped open as soon as she realized what her body was begging for. "Nope." Snatching the two-in-one shampoo and conditioner off the caddy, she squirted a liberal amount in her hands. "I can wait, it's not that long, just a few more months," she said as she lathered her head.

It was crazy. Meeting a man from prison, falling for him, and waiting for him to get out. Never in a million years had she thought she'd be in this situation. The oddest place she'd ever met a man was in a cemetery after leaving roses on her mother's grave. She'd given the man her number, but to her relief and disappointment, he'd never called.

Rinsing her hair, she washed quickly, and got out of the shower just as the phone rang. Since it was her cell, she decided she'd call whoever it was back in a minute. Heading to her room, she sat at her desk, pulled out her photo album, and searched through it. There were hundreds of pictures, but Katie had her heart set on one in particular. It was the one when she and her mother were in Greece with her father on a business trip.

While he'd been working, she and her mother lived on the beach. The picture showed her in a light pink bandeau bikini top, covered with a white beach wrap landing just above her knees, which were submerged in the crystal clear water. She'd never been happier and her face showed it. When she finally found it, she smiled. Her hands were in the air above her as a gentle breeze blew through her long brown locks.

Katie grabbed another more recent photo of herself at a dinner party with friends. Teal had caught her in mid-laugh. She wore an emerald green sweater that stopped far above her belly button and black leggings. It took Teal four hours to convince her to wear the six-inch heels, and it'd taken her two more hours to get all the little corkscrew curls to perfectly frame her face.

She scribbled Logan's address on the envelope, and wrote a short, sweet letter to go along with the pictures. After she placed everything inside, she went to her closet to dress. She was sure the mailman wasn't working, but a two-minute walk to the corner was a blue drop box for mail. When the storm was over and the mailman ran again, Logan would get her letters.

Katie didn't have the strength to blow-dry her hair, so she towel-dried it and threw it up in a messy bun. Just then, the phone rang again, but it was her cell. Katie ignored it and left the house to her destination.

After putting the letter in the mailbox for the mailman, she ran to her living room to see that it was Teal calling on her cell . . . again. Just as she was about to answer it, her house phone rang and she knew it was Logan. With a grin, she picked up the phone while ending the call on her cell.

"Good morning, baby," Logan's warm voice came across the line.

"Yes, for me. Good afternoon to you, Logan."

"Yeah, I'm up at six every morning thanks to my damn roommate and his stupid ass rap. That damn boy can't remember he's white to save his life."

Katie laughed. "Well, there *are* white rappers."

"Yeah, and they need to stop." Logan sounded serious, but he also sounded just like Teal. Apparently, they both thought rap only belonged to black people. It was a stupid thought to Katie, but to each his or her own.

She shrugged. "I didn't puke. Does that make you feel better?"

"Honestly, yeah it does. When you told me you drank a full bottle of wine I thought for sure you were going to puke."

Katie looked down at the mess she'd left on the floor. She had opened another bottle; she didn't remember doing it, but she had. Only one was completely empty, but she wouldn't tell Logan that.

She enjoyed his concern. "You didn't have to worry, Logan. I'm fine."

"Yeah, I did." He sounded resolute.

"How was your morning?" she asked, changing the subject. While his concern and not admonition was refreshing, Katie didn't want to dwell on it.

He heaved a sigh. "I told you, baby, my cellmate thinks he's black and keeps telling me he needs to 'get his flow right' for when he gets out. I swear, if they were to keep me in here for another year, I'd kick the white back into his ass."

Katie hated when people attributed race to a person's actions. "You don't need to kick anything into anyone. Maybe he's just one of those white kids from the ghetto who picked up on what they heard and saw. It could be all he knows," Katie reasoned, but Logan didn't seem like he was trying to hear it.

"I grew up in what you could call a ghetto, yet you don't see me trying to be anything but the white male that I am. All I am asking is for that little shit to do the same."

"Wait, are you saying that you think only certain races act 'ghetto?'" Katie was confused; Logan had gone from thinking rap wasn't for white kids, to ignorant ways being reserved for non-white kids as well. Not cool. "Because—" A knock, no a banging, at her door stopped the words. "Baby, give me a sec. The cavalry is here," she said jestingly, storing their conversation in her head for later discussions. "Don't hang up. I'll let them in and take this call to the other room to tell you goodbye." She set the phone down.

As Katie went to the door, she glanced at the mess she'd forgotten to clean up and groaned. A quick glance out the window showed Teal's truck, which was good . . . her father would take one look at the place and scold her. She opened the door to a fuming Teal, who stormed into the house.

"What the fuck, chick? Your damn dad has been all up in my ass asking about you." Teal snatched off her coat and threw it on the hook by the door, before marching into the living room and glancing around. "Nice to know you aren't dead or frozen to death, while my black ass had to come all the way from my house to check on you."

Katie laughed, which only seemed to infuriate her more. "I'm a big girl, you didn't need to come all the way over here. I don't care if he asked you to, you could have said no."

She placed a hand on her hip and cocked a brow. "Oh, a big girl are you now? I think a big girl would have answered her phone and let her friends and family know that she made it through the storm alive." Teal threw her hands up in the air. "I don't know what to do with you."

Now it was Katie's turn to get mad. "Maybe you want to leave then?" Teal's gasp was so loud Katie had to roll her eyes. A loud beeping pulled then both from the argument.

"The fuck is that?" She looked around for the source of the noise, and Katie followed her eyes as they landed on the phone.

"Damn!" Katie ran over and placed it to her ear, only to hear the annoying ROH warning tone. "He hung up."

Teal moved over to Katie. "Who hung up?"

Without thinking, Katie answered, "My boyfriend." She wanted to slap herself in the face as soon as she'd said it. She had planned to tell Teal, but not just yet.

A squeal flew from Teal's mouth. "Oh damn! So you and Joe finally hit it off? I knew your dad was right about him." She sat on the couch as Katie cleaned up the mess she'd made the night before. "He was like, 'Teal, just give it time.' At the time, I didn't have the heart to tell him that shit just wasn't going to work."

"It's not Joe, and you and my dad need to keep your noses out of my personal life unless invited into it by me." Katie stood and took her trash to the kitchen, and Teal jumped up to follow.

"I know everyone you know, so I can list off names until I get it right." Teal held out her hand, lifting a finger for each name as she said, "Marcus, Anthony, Will, Carlos, Danny, Eric, Lee, Randy—"

Katie knocked her hands down. "I'm about to depend on you as my best friend by telling you this, and you can't tell a soul." For all of the things Teal was—loud, nosey, annoying, demanding, and crazy—she was more dependable than any of those other traits.

Her brow furrowed in what Katie knew was concern and intrigue. "Tell me."

Taking a deep breath, she spilled her guts. She told her friend about Logan calling, their new relationship, and their plans to meet. Halfway through, Katie knew telling Teal was a mistake. She could see it in her eyes, but when Katie was done, she steeled her nerves and resolve.

"You are one dumb-ass chick, you know that?" Teal was shaking her head. "Brave, but dumb. Come in here and tell me what this fuckery is all about, please."

Katie followed Teal. Well, so far so good, she thought, as she headed into what felt like the deep abyss known as hurricane Teal.

CHAPTER 15

THERE WAS ALWAYS SOMETHING that ruined the good things in Logan's life, or at least that's how he looked at it not too long ago. When he was a teen he'd had a good life until his stepfather had come along. He'd enjoyed Paris, Kentucky until the black kids had decided to use him as a punching bag, so he'd met the wrong people and ended up in prison. Back then, Logan would have blamed anyone except himself. He'd been a hardheaded kid who couldn't live up to his stepfather's militant standards, so he rebelled, letting his life take a turn for the worse. He couldn't blame anyone except himself, but what he could do was keep his ass away from people who would, and could, make his life hell.

Logan had decided years back not to associate with anyone outside of his race. He and Trent had decided there were just some things that made sense, and that was one of the many things they agreed on. Upon

Logan's incarceration, and being roomed with Aaron, Logan had learned that Trent's connections with the KKK were weak at best.

He believed Trent used the words KKK as a deterrent. The Mexican and black kids had kept their distance, and Logan's life had improved markedly, which he could only contribute to the lack of "color" in his life. Aaron's ties to the AB Brothers was real and deep, and Logan had learned on his first day in prison that men like Iggy ended up in the infirmary often.

Laying on his bunk, he wondered how he could convince his girlfriend of this as well. When he'd talked to her about his cellmate forgetting his color, it seemed like she was siding with Iggy. Worst of all, was that person who'd come into her home sounded like the black women that Logan had to deal with in the ghetto. He couldn't understand how a woman like Katie would even consider associating with someone who spoke like that.

He'd hung up disgusted and a bit pissed. When he got out, he didn't want that in his life, and as much as he'd grown to care for Katie, he had high expectations of his woman. Therefore, she wouldn't be hanging around anyone like that woman whose disregard for good English and her foul mouth made his skin crawl. Hell yeah, Logan cussed like a sailor, but just like a lot of men, he wanted those words reserved for him—when he and his woman were home alone in bed.

Logan silently watched as Iggy got dressed. He was always rapping, always acting so damned odd. Logan knew that he'd have to give Katie an ultimatum, because he was sure as shit not having anything like Iggy in his life when he left prison.

He was supposed to call Katie back, but he knew the provision that he was going to place on their relationship would piss her off, if not push her away. Regardless, that was the way it was going to be. There were no other options in his mind. She'd either stop seeing that friend of hers, or him. Even as he thought it, he knew it wasn't right to place that kind of ultimatum on her. However, this was his life. It was how things would be, and most likely, Logan would end up without Katie.

He closed his eyes, trying to relax for a nap, but his heart stuttered in his chest at the thought of losing her. He hadn't even known her that long, but it didn't matter; she took the stress away and made him look forward to getting out even more than he already did. It couldn't matter.

Even as Logan lay there lying to himself, he realized that he yet again was about to ruin something great . . . but the pains of the past were just too much and still cut deep.

CHAPTER 16

WITH HER FINGERS DIGGING into her temples, Teal paced the living room floor. She'd been repeating the same sentence over and over while Katie just sat there staring at the phone. It'd been three hours and no call back from Logan. It was Saturday, so she knew his day was open all day. Maybe he was giving her time with Teal and he'd call later tonight.

"Oh my God, Katie stop staring at the phone."

She looked up to find Teal eyeing her.

"You can't do this. Your dad is going to kill you . . . and Logan."

There was that sentence again. Teal had made sure to say it at least once every five minutes for the last three hours. They'd sat in the kitchen while Katie had made some lunch. She hadn't expected her friend to react this way, but she understood the concern; if the situation had been reversed, Katie would be just as worried and just as talkative as Teal.

Katie started cleaning; it was a nervous tic. Cleaning her home was something she could control while her life seemed to spiral out of control. "Stop saying that. Damn."

Teal turned to her wide-eyed. "Look, just promise me you won't send him money, okay?" The disquiet in Teal's voice made Katie stop. Even though Teal often times pushed harder than she should, she knew her friend loved and cared for her, but what she needed most was her friend to trust her. To trust the choices Katie made in her life.

"I don't give him money. As a matter of fact, he offered to pay my collect call bill." She smiled at the memory. He'd been adamant he would take care of it if she couldn't. That was weeks ago; she'd already gotten the bill, paid it, and forgotten about it.

Teal rolled her eyes. "Mmhmm, I bet he did. What else did he offer to do?" Katie didn't like her tone.

"Whatever. See, when he gets out and gets his life—"

Teal rushed over and snatched the towel out of Katie's hand. "Oh hell no, what do you mean when he gets out? You will not be meeting him!" Her eyes burned with anger, and Katie's with defiance. "Katie," her voice lowered, "you *can't* do this. These men are all criminals."

Katie agreed, "Yeah, they are. However, once they serve their time, they should be looked at as more than convicts." She wasn't a fool—she was nervous, too—but Logan felt so right, and she wasn't lonely anymore.

"Girl, a few of them are getting out due to overpopulation. So, in my eyes, they are getting off easy. Plus, you don't even know if what Logan says he did is true. We have rapists, child molesters, and monsters in there that are eligible for parole. Meaning your Logan could be one of them." She crossed her arms over her chest. "Did you think about that?"

True to form, Teal had made Katie feel like an ignorant ten-year-old child, because she hadn't thought of that. "I—I guess I was just too—"

"Lonesome?" Teal's voice lowered with care. "Since your mother and Roman, you've kept yourself, all cooped up in this house. Then you come up with this Inmate Pen Pal Program as a cover for your own solitude . . . which, in my eyes, is causing you to make some bad decisions."

"No, it's not just that." Again Katie wanted to tell Teal about her miscarriage, but she wasn't sure if Teal would use it as ammunition, not that she needed much more. Her mother and Roman would have been enough.

"Yeah, it is." Teal headed out of the kitchen. "Where's your laptop?" she called out.

Interest piqued, Katie followed behind her, pointing to her bedroom. "In there, why?" Entering the bedroom, she walked to the laptop.

"We are going to look up this Logan. What'd you say his last name was?"

"I didn't, but it's Whyte, Logan Whyte." Katie pulled her chaise lounge closer to Teal and perched on it.

"Spelled W-H-I-T-E or W-H-Y-T-E?" Teal asked, and Katie's face heated. She was embarrassed that she didn't know, so she guessed.

"W-H-Y-T-E." If Teal knew she was guessing she didn't let on.

Teal entered in some info. "Where is he from?"

"Born in Lexington, Kentucky." Katie leaned forward to see that Teal was on a site called Mugshot.com.

"What did he tell you he did?" Teal asked, turning away from the screen to stare at Katie.

She fought the urge to look away. She knew Teal well, and Teal hated a thief. "Armed robbery and assault . . . with a deadly weapon."

Teal's eyes popped out of her head. "Oh, girl, you can sure pick 'em, huh?" She turned back to the screen and continued to type. "Has he sent you a picture yet?" Teal glanced back again, and Katie shook her head no. "Okay, so. I see no Logan Whyte's, and there are only two pictures of men with the last name spelled W-H-I-T-E."

Katie leaned over and looked at the men; both were old and gray-haired. For the first time, she wondered whom she'd really been talking to. She could hear Logan's voice in her head, and it was young and gruff. Therefore, neither of those men could be Logan.

Katie stared at the screen and scanned the state. When she noticed Teal had only looked up Kentucky, she had a thought. "Maybe Logan committed his crime in Vermont?" She'd never asked him where, or even when, he'd committed his crime. "You know what? I don't want to do this. If I want to know anything about him, I'll ask. He never sent me a picture because I asked him not to, I asked him for anonymity and he gave it to me. That's respect."

Teal closed out the windows and shut the laptop. Her resigned sigh didn't signal her submission, but her disappointment. "Look, when does he get out?"

"He goes up for parole in a few months, and his lawyer said that overpopulation was making it look really good for him."

Teal's smile confused Katie. "Oh, so he might not even get out?"

Katie wanted the conversation to end, so she shrugged and nodded, trying not to let on that if that were the case she'd probably freak out. "True. See? You were getting all upset for nothing." She quickly stood and walked to the door because she couldn't let Teal see how her words worried her. Plus, now she wanted Logan to call and reaffirm his place in her life even more.

Teal smacked her lips, an annoying gesture to Katie. "Oh no, I'm still worried, but I feel better that this thief may not make it into your life."

Katie's heart stuttered at her words, but she did everything she could to school her features as Teal walked up from behind her.

"I don't know what you two have going on, but you need to be careful. You don't know what kind of shit he has in his life, and you don't know how it may spill over into yours. I'm just looking out for you, you're my girl. I love you."

Katie smiled and moved to embrace her friend. As much as it sucked, Teal was right. However, she had faith in a lot of things, and although the fear of Logan and her relationship falling apart was real, Katie knew in her heart that she'd try harder than ever to stop it from happening.

CHAPTER 17

AS A LAWYER, JAKE had done a lot of grimy shit in his life, but today was probably one of the shittiest on a more personal level. He'd lied, cheated, and even tampered with evidence. The morning Jake went into Graham's home office and stole the list of names for the Pen Pal Program, he realized that Logan's past slights wouldn't go unanswered.

Back in college, Jake had been this scrawny pothead in love, and when he met Logan, he thought he'd met a buddy. However, Logan had ended all that when he fucked his girl. Then, to add insult to injury, he returns damn near seventeen years later, and that motherfucker bribed him into taking his case for less than half his going rate.

But Logan didn't know who Jake was anymore. While Logan had changed, so had he. Jake had made contacts along the way, and finding out whom Logan was talking to, getting her PO Box, and then her address had only cost him two days, a bag of coke, and three hundred bucks. Now, Jake sat across the street as snow fell from the sky, watching and waiting.

The house was dark, but it was noon. The entire day yesterday, the warden's daughter, Katie, wouldn't leave the house. While Jake had planned to try and fuck her to get back at Logan, he realized he didn't have enough time to weasel his way in her pants. At that realization, Jake decided that planting a seed of doubt in her mind about Logan would have to do, and it'd be easy.

If a good friend of Logan's—that person being Jake—were to go to Kathryn and fill her in on the devious scheme he had in place to gather groupies while he was in jail and fuck them all when he got out, it would cause enough suspicion to hurt Logan. It wasn't the best plan, and Jake wished he didn't have to leave town in a few days, because fucking her would be the definitive payback.

He exited his vehicle and headed up the drive. With a knock at the door, he stood back and waited. He could only imagine the type of woman Logan would go for, but he also knew that the program didn't let you choose who you spoke to. As the warden's daughter, a man he'd seen before, Jake assumed that Kathryn would be a tall, hot Scandinavian blonde . . . not the slim black woman who answered the door.

"Yes?" Her voice was smooth and proper. He could hear the confusion and hesitance in her voice.

Jake plastered on a fake smile. "May I speak to Kathryn Andreassen?"

Her eyes narrowed. "Who are you?"

Hiding his annoyance that some black bitch had the nerve to ask him who he was, Jake smiled wider. He hated when the maids answered the door. "I'm Jason," he made up a name just in case she called Logan, "a friend of Logan's." Jake noticed her eyes widened a bit in what he thought was recognition. Maybe she was a maid for the Andreassen's.

Opening the door wider, she wrapped her sweater tighter around her slim body. Suddenly, Jake noticed the alarm in her eyes.

"Is Logan hurt?"

He was stunned into silence.

"Is that why he hasn't called in two days?" She ran her hands through her hair and stared at him.

"I—I, umm . . ." Jake was at a loss for words—almost. "Are you Kathryn?"

She nodded, and he almost howled in surprise.

"May I come in?"

Nodding again, she moved to the side.

Jake walked past her, careful not to bump into her. He was still in shock over the fact that Logan was dating a black woman. Jake silently took the seat she offered, as well as accepting the drink. The alarm in her voice set him on a new path for revenge.

"So what happened? Is everything okay?" she asked, sitting across from him.

"Yes, he's fine." He feigned sincerity as he spoke. "I'm just out with a list of names of women that Logan has contacted." He watched her face as he spoke. "I'm trying to get Logan to get his life straight before he gets out. Attempting to get him to stop his womanizing ways, but it seems like nothing I say to him works."

She was already shaking her head in disbelief. "No, he and I are in the Pen Pal Program—"

"I know," Jake interrupted. He knew women. Even as this one sat in front of him and tried to deny that an inmate could possibly be playing her, he could see the doubt he was placing in her. "He is actually engaged to a woman named Dawn." Jake pulled a name off the top of his head, and it just so happened to be his ex from college. He watched as Kathryn took a deep breath and closed her eyes. It took everything in Jake not to laugh.

"So, is that all? You just came to tell me he's screwing around on me?" she asked in a strong voice, but Jake heard the crack in it that she so desperately tried to hide.

He nodded, hoping his eyes held the fake sadness for her that his voice had.

She stood. "Okay, thanks Jason, but I think you should leave now."

Jake stood and walked to the front door. "I'm sorry, Kathryn. I just thought I should come and warn you about him."

She nodded solemnly and opened the front door. "Thanks for the information."

Jake gave her a sad smile and walked out the door. As soon as he reached his SUV, he pulled his phone from his pocket and dialed his secretary.

"Schuman and Blake, Marge speaking. How may I help you?" his secretary asked.

"Marge, I need you to set up a meeting at Capshaw correctional facility." As soon as Jake realized the woman who Logan was talking to, he'd added an extra step to his payback plot.

"Yes, sir, who do you need to visit there?" she asked, and Jake could hear her typing on the computer.

"Aaron Matterson." Jake remembered the name of Logan's old cellmate perfectly; he was in jail for kicking the shit out of some black guy and robbing his house. Jake knew the best way to show Logan he wasn't the little pothead he was in the past; now he wasn't someone to fuck with.

CHAPTER 18

LOGAN'S FINGERS HOVERED OVER the phone. Ordinarily, he would press the buttons as fast as possible in order to hear Katie's voice, but today his fingers wouldn't move. It was a hard thing to call a woman who'd given you her trust, only to turn around and give her an ultimatum. He'd realized shit was serious with Katie as soon as he understood that he needed her to be on the same page in life as he was. He wanted her, needed her, and would tell her . . . again. First, he had to make something clear. Yes, he was expecting for more than a good man would, but he wasn't going to accept anything other than what he was asking. Stay away from people outside of her race—plain and simple.

He dialed his code and Katie's number. They'd charge the call to his canteen, and from here on out, he wouldn't have to record his voice and wait for Katie to accept the call. As the phone rang, Logan worried that he'd waited too long to call, and when she answered the phone in a clipped, angry voice, Logan was positive he'd fucked up.

"Yes?" she answered.

He had talked to Katie long enough to interpret her temperaments, and this mood was pissed. It wasn't often that Logan was at a loss for words, but the sound of her voice stopped him cold. He closed his eyes and took a deep breath, ready to tell her that they needed to talk, but she beat him to it.

After a beat of hard silence, she asked, "Is there anything you'd like to tell me, Logan?" The accusation was there; he heard it loud and clear.

"What are you talking about?"

The calming breath she took as if she were speaking to an idiot frustrated Logan. What the fuck was she talking about? He thought as she asked the question again.

"Is. There. Anything. You. Want. To. Explain?"

Her chilled voice echoed in his head, making him think back over the past two months. Was there anything he needed to explain? "Hell no, and that's not why I called. We have a problem." He wasn't about to get off the reason he'd called. First and foremost, he wanted to talk about what happened a couple days ago. "I called to tell you that we needed to talk, Katie."

Logan adjusted himself in the seat and lowered his voice. What he was about to say was something that could get his ass kicked for, and while Logan was no punk, he was no fool either. Fighting could get Logan another year of hard time, and when he could taste release on the tip of his tongue, being stupid and getting into a fight was something only a fool would do. "Who was that who came to your house Saturday?"

"Saturday? When Saturday? You mean a few days ago. The guy named Jason?" Katie's voice escalated as she spoke, as if he was supposed to know who the fuck Jason was.

"Goddamn it, Katie, no," he hissed. "And who the fuck is Jason?" he nearly bellowed. Logan glanced around the room, and while he wasn't alone, none of the inmates that were in the room seemed interested in his conversation.

"Logan, stop playing games, please."

The hurt in her voice cut him. "Baby, I'm not playing any games with you, but what I am about to tell . . . I mean ask you, will change shit. It will really define what we are doing here." Her silence urged him to keep going. "If we are gonna keep this going when I get out, there are things that have to change. Things you need to understand about me, and what I except from the woman I plan to be with.

"I ain't saying it's going to be easy, baby. You know this shit is going to get hard. With who your father is, and my past, we are going to be fighting an uphill battle. But none of that shit will matter, if our relationship is right and steady. We have to be on the same page." Logan stopped to take a breath.

He worried that what he was going to say next would start a war between him and the woman he was falling for. It hadn't taken much. She was intelligent, artistic, and responsible, all things Logan thought he'd never find in a woman, or at least not in the women he'd pursued.

KATIE HELD HER BREATH. Something in her said that what Logan was about to say would be a game changer. There was no way he was about to ask her to marry him, was there? Her stomach dropped and she almost hung up the phone. She was not ready for something like that, nor was their relationship at the point in which marriage should have been brought up. No, Logan wasn't that careless. It was probably something else. Something about fidelity or—

"I only want you associating with our race. It's important to me, and if I'm going to continue this with you I'm going to need you to do this." His voice was stern, and it reminded her of how her father spoke to her when she wanted to buy her house by the prison, when she wanted to write fulltime, when she wanted to buy a small car instead of an SUV, or whenever she wanted to do something he didn't approve of. Logan's words created a visceral reaction in her. If Katie had to explain the emotions running through her heart at that moment, she'd end up speaking in tongues.

"Say that again." Her voice was unreasonably calm and that scared her. She knew that Logan wasn't black—he'd told her the "black kids" had constantly kicked his ass, and that he didn't like that his white cellmate wanted to be a rapper—but those two things didn't equal racist.

He cleared his throat. "My whole life I've stuck with my own kind, and the few times I didn't, I paid for it severely."

She couldn't believe what she was hearing. Her heart broke while her head told her she was a stupid idiot for not catching it before.

"Now, I am not a racist," *Katie begged to differ*, "but I've learned that keeping to my own keeps me out of trouble."

"Are you saying that about all black people?" she whispered. Her heart was in her throat, and she wanted to hang up . . . but she just couldn't. She wanted to know how deep his hate ran. Not that it even mattered since she was on a list of certain people Logan wouldn't associate with.

"Yes and no."

"What the fuck? That makes no sense." She never cursed, but today be damned. She was going to use whatever language she wanted. Logan had the nerve to chuckle; she assumed it was at her choice of word, but she wasn't sure.

"No, I mean any other race than our own." He said it as if that was the end all be all of everything.

Katie had to take a seat before she passed out. How could she have let this man into her life? When did her lonesomeness make her a fucking blind fool?

"You still there, baby?"

Never had him calling her baby disgusted her, but now the word hurt her ears. She was black, and the man that had kept her from drowning in her own sorrow didn't like black people.

Katie could hear the desperation in her voice, but was too powerless to stop it. "I can't believe what I'm hearing right now."

"It's not a big deal. It's easily done. I've done it my whole life." His words came so effortlessly and calmly, as if being a bigot was okay and normal.

She had suffered at the hands of blacks and whites, but she'd never placed the blame on an entire race. "You don't understand—"

"Don't worry, that person who came in your home acting and sounding the way she did, doesn't need to be in your life. She's a bad example, and needs to re-learn the English language."

That person was Teal, who had a college degree and was doing great for herself. Katie forced herself not to puke. She could feel it coming. "No, you don't get it—"

He interrupted her again. "I do, and I assume it's going to be rough at first. It wasn't for me, but—"

"Logan, stop. Just stop," she pleaded, tears escaping her eyes. There was nothing worse, she thought, than crying over a man who didn't want you based on the color of your skin. Teal was right, Logan had been hiding something—he was a fucking racist.

LOGAN COULDN'T TELL IF Katie was disappointed or just angry, but he didn't want to let her speak until he could explain. He was adamant that he wasn't like Trent, or his old cellmate, Aaron, when it came to other races. He didn't intentionally go after them like Aaron had, and he never used racial slurs to hurt a person like Trent had. Logan was just watching out for his own ass, and his method had been pretty successful over the years—especially in prison.

"Katie, you know I care about you, and I want to be with you when I get out of here, but it's an inflexible part of this relationship. It can't be any other way. Hell, it's not so bad, really. You know my childhood. After I met Trent and started working out, the black kids left me alone and the Mexican kids didn't have anyone to watch get beat up. I kept to my own, and I haven't had any issues since then.

"In here, every race keeps to its own and that is one of the more promising facts about this hell hole." Logan could hear her breathing into the phone, but she didn't speak. He waited, but there was nothing left to say because as he'd said before, it was nonnegotiable. "What do you think of that, Katie?"

The tears in her voice surprised him. "I think I made a big mistake when I wrote you. You are a racist, and I don't know how I didn't see it before now. Those little hints that you dropped . . ." A humorless laugh escaped her lips.

He wanted to stop her right there, but he let her get it out.

"I should have caught them, but I was so caught up in being with you . . . hell, being with anybody at that point, that I let you and your lies infiltrate my heart."

He wasn't sure where her tears were coming from and what lies she was talking about, but her next words echoed in his ears.

"I'm *black*, Logan. My mother and father are *both* black. You know, those people you hate?" she spat.

Her words sounded like a swarm of bees in his ears. Something in him told him she wasn't lying about her race, and his anger flared. His face reddened. She had the nerve to call *him* a liar when she'd lied about her race. Logan thought he was more than clear about how he felt long before today.

He knew all traces of warmth had left his voice. "You called me a liar and I have no clue what you are talking about, but I think that's the kettle calling the pot black, don't you?" He heard the irony in his words as soon as they'd escaped his mouth. "You lied to me!" he snarled, and this time the other inmates turned around, but Logan didn't give a fuck. "Your last name, the way you act and speak, all a lie, right?"

"Are you fucking kidding me? Are you kidding me right now?" she all but screamed. "That is all me, no lies, but what about your buddy Jason coming over here to warn me about your fiancée? And all the other women you write to?" She did scream this, and Logan was tempted to tell her to shut the fuck up, but something inside of him told him to temper his anger.

He glanced around. "Who? I'm not—"

She was past crying and to the point he thought she'd jump through the phone if she could. "The name Dawn ring a bell, asshole?"

At the moment it didn't. He was so incensed that he disregarded the name and went defensive.

"Oh, and I never lied, I never once gave you any clues as to my looks. I didn't think I had to tell you my race to pass your sick ass test!"

Just as Logan was about to speak, the dial tone assaulted his ears, leaving him to boil in anger without a soul to take it out on.

Katie,

I know we said we wouldn't exchange pics, but now that you're my woman, the only man I want you picturing is me and not that Colin fucker.

Logan

CHAPTER 19

MOST OF KATIE'S ADULT life she'd shed tears; she was no stranger to hurt or abandonment. She'd wept for her mother's pain and suffering, she'd cried for a man who'd left her, she'd sobbed over the death of her unborn baby . . . and now, here she sat, shedding tears for a racist son of a bitch who had her cursing like a sailor.

Yesterday, when she'd gone to make sure her PO box was clear and to cancel it, she found the letter with a picture inside. Tempted to burn it, Katie came home, gathered all of Logan's letters, and started a fire in the hearth. It was still cold out, as the snow in Lakewood seemed to last until March, and even sometimes into April. *"If you don't like the weather, wait a few minutes,"* her father used to say. It was an old New England saying. Katie had thrown in every letter, but couldn't bring herself to part with the picture.

She picked it up again. At the moment, she was a masochist. Every time she looked at the picture, she didn't see the racist Logan proved himself to be. She saw a man with crystal green eyes that sparkled in the flash of the camera. He had such chiseled features, Katie found she couldn't stop looking at him. His nose was nice and straight, his face wide, and he had a strong jawline with a bit of hair on his face. He didn't look at all like Colin Farrell; while he had the same dark hair and dark looks as Colin, Katie would liken him to Joe Manganiello, which was odd. She'd always thought Joe looked mixed a bit with Asian. Logan's skin was tan, his arms were big and wide, and she could see a few of the tattoos on his wrists from beneath his shirtsleeve.

Throwing the picture down, she placed her head onto her pillow. Katie felt like a fool, ashamed that she couldn't turn her feelings for Logan off, and she couldn't believe that it was just loneliness that had put her in this situation. She really cared for Logan and was ready to try a relationship with him when he got out. It tore her to the bone that she could look beyond his past and not judge him for his previous actions, yet he couldn't do the same for her. She picked up her phone and dialed Teal's number.

"Teal Lofton."

Teal was at work, but Katie really needed to talk to her. No more hiding the truth, and no more sitting at home in a puddle of tears. "You were right." The words weren't easy to say, but Katie was okay with admitting when she was wrong . . . and boy, had she been wrong.

"Right about what? You know me, I'm always right about stuff, so you're gonna have to be more specific." She laughed.

Katie wasn't in the mood. "Logan's secret is that he doesn't like black people. He didn't know I was black, and when he found out, he accused me of lying to him." She didn't feel like going into the Jason situation.

Teal moaned. "I was hoping I was wrong about that. I told you, you can't trust these damned crooks, not for one second." She sighed. "What now? You didn't give him your addy, did you? I mean, you can always change your house number if you have to." Katie didn't think that was necessary; Logan would never call her back.

Katie sat up, grabbed the water bottle she'd been nursing, and took a big audible gulp. The water was tepid, but there was something about crying that made her incredibly thirsty. "Not necessary, as I'm sure the yelling and cussing I did will keep him from calling again." She set the bottle down by the picture of Logan. "I just want to forget him," she lied. "Just want the memory of him out of my head for good."

Yet, as she stared at his picture, Katie couldn't help remembering the pleasant conversations they'd had, the way she felt when he called her baby, and his concern for her. Could she have been mistaken or imagining the whole connection they'd formed?

"I know what will make you feel better." Teal's voice held more elation than Katie could handle, and she prayed her friend didn't think she was dragging her to any parties. "We can go and hang out with Joe and Iris at Club 4-8. There's a live jazz band called Blue Fin playing tonight. You can get all prettied up and come and hang out. You know, get your mind off that convict."

Katie still hated it when Teal called him a convict, but what she hated more was how little it seemed Teal knew about her. "I am not going out. I'm going to rent *Oblivion* with Tom Cruise, and sit here with some popcorn and ice cream. I may or may not be mixing the two together, and eat them with my tears. You are more than welcome to join."

Teal heaved an over exaggerated sigh. "I guess. But if you start crying, I get to punch you . . . hard." Her remedy for heartbreak was pain. Not kill you pain, but focus elsewhere pain.

Katie pinched her thigh, but got nothing except a broken heart and a stinging thigh.

Dear Logan,

Here's hoping I can soon see your smile, but until then, I'll smile for the both of us!

Missing your voice,

Katie.

CHAPTER 20

LOGAN HAD AT FIRST refused to look at Katie's picture. He'd resigned himself to never knowing what the woman looked like, and almost tricked himself into thinking it was possible to ignore her. That was until a week later, when the ache in his chest still hadn't gone away and his longing for her voice had left him so tortured, he thought it was punishment for breaking his rule. He wasn't a fucking racist.

When he opened the letter and looked at the picture of Katie, he nearly collapsed. There was no woman as beautiful as she. The hazelnut-brown skin shone in the sunlight, and her curly hair fell around her shoulders in beautiful waves. Her eyes were closed, and she had a smile on her lips that spoke volumes to her happiness. Her body made his dick stir and stiffen in his pants the second he'd seen through the sheer dress-like top she was wearing to the pink panty-like bikini. Never had Logan lusted after a black woman, but he could almost feel the warmth between her legs and hear her soft voice in his ear.

The other picture seemed more current. Her hair was longer, her body fuller, and her face held time, all in a damn good way. And that smile. Her lips were lusher than any woman he'd dated, and her nose was wider. Logan could admit that those two features, and the color of her skin, were the only noticeable differences between them. However, Logan knew the issues of interracial dating, and he couldn't bring himself to accept that drama in his life.

He stood and pushed the pictures of Katie under his pillow. He had a lot of things on his mind, and lifting weights always seemed to lighten the load.

Leaving his cell, he headed past the guards to the weight room. He needed this . . . needed to let off some steam, to get his fucking head on straight. No matter what, Logan had a code he lived by. He'd learned earlier on that breaking that code would place him in a world of hurt; it always did. As much as Logan hated his and Katie's differences, he could admit that it wasn't fair to either of them that it placed a wedge between what they could have had.

Logan should have known that something wasn't right. Unfortunately, he was in his head and didn't notice how unnaturally quiet the hallway was, or how there were no guards. It wasn't until an arm wrapped around his neck and smashed his head into the wall that he knew something was terribly wrong.

"So I hear you like niggers," Aaron's unmistakable accented voice entered his head, "I hear you like to write 'em." He accompanied his words with a knee and a fist to Logan's gut.

Aaron moved away and stood somewhere to the side of Logan. He couldn't tell where, since an unidentified man still held Logan in a sleeper hold. He was losing air, and fighting back was becoming harder and harder. Another hit to the gut had Logan choking and gasping for breath. He fought harder, keeping one hand on the man restraining his elbow—hoping to get some air—and the other warding off Aaron's attacks. Blood, from the wound Logan felt on his head, was seeping into his eyes, making it hard to see. Then, he caught a fist to his nose, blurring his vision. He couldn't breathe, couldn't see, and felt like he was choking on his own blood.

Suddenly, the man behind him dropped him to the floor and both men started kicking Logan for what seemed like eternity. He mustered up the strength to grab a foot, and pulled hard enough to send an attacker to the floor. The man cursed and stood up over Logan. The racial slurs thrown at him, the punches, and maybe even an extra year added to his sentence, all stemmed from one beautiful person. One person he wanted so badly, but wouldn't bring pain or blood into her life. Finally, as Logan slipped under, the last thought on his mind was that he didn't bring this hate and pain into Katie's life only to die in this prison, unable to protect her.

CHAPTER 21

KATIE MADE THE LAST corrections to her manuscript and sent it to her editor. Her inbox was full of messages from fans, and she felt guilty once again for signing out without responding or at least reading one. She opened up her email again and sent a short message to her agent about getting an online personal assistant. Cheryl, her agent, had mentioned it to her before, but at the time Katie was caught up with her emails, writing, and promoting, and thought it completely unnecessary.

"I should have said yes," she muttered.

"Should have said yes to what?" Joe came from around the corner with a towel in his hands, drying off his shirtless chest.

Katie quickly turned away.

"No need to be shy, Katie," he crooned.

"Why are you half naked? You only had to fix the sink." She pretended to be searching through her emails even though she wasn't planning on opening anything. Her father had sent Joe over to fix her sink after she'd asked him not to. Now she was going to have to call the plumber and cancel the appointment last minute, since no one thought to tell her Joe was on his way over that day.

"Sorry," he said, sounding not the least bit apologetic, "I got wet. Can I put this in your dryer?"

She was tempted to say no, but even though the snowstorms had passed the temperature outside was still in the mid-thirties. She stood and moved past him, to get in the kitchen. "I'll do it. Where'd you leave it?" she asked, glancing away again, but not before getting another look at Joe's chocolate brown chest.

He was built in all of the ways a man should be; he had a tall, lithe body, which Katie was sure required time in the gym. Joe pointed to the wet mass on the table, and she quickly grabbed it, then scurried to the laundry room.

Joe had apologized to Katie for the things he'd said to her, but Katie wasn't trying to hear it. She could forgive, but she wasn't going to forget. His words had hurt her and he'd meant them to. Looking at the shirt, Katie could see that there was a small wet spot, nothing that actually warranted a trip to the dryer. She rolled her eyes and headed back out to Joe.

"Here." She handed him the shirt and led him to the front door.

His eyes heated in anger. "You're welcome," Joe snapped, snatching his coat and hat.

Katie quietly walked him onto the porch. "Yes, thanks for coming over uninvited and trying to strip down naked," she said sardonically, but he only smiled and shook his head. "Bye, Joe." Katie watched as he got in his truck and drove away.

Back in the house, she picked up the phone and dialed the plumber's number. As soon as Katie placed the receiver to her ear, a gruff voice filled the line.

"Hello?" The voice seemed confused.

And so was Katie. "Kirk? Is that you? I was just calling you! You sound different." Katie plopped down on the couch. "I don't need you to come by, my dad sent Joe to fix the sink. Although, I'm not even sure he did it right." She laughed, but was greeted with silence. "Damn, did I hang up on him?" she wondered out loud.

"No, you didn't hang up on me." The voice sounded a bit more familiar, but she still couldn't make it out.

"Wait, who—" She pulled the phone away from her ear and looked at the caller I.D., but it was blank. Placing the receiver back to her ear, Katie waited for the caller to speak.

"You still there?"

The voice was clearer now, and Katie knew exactly who it was on the line. A shiver shook her body and she had a good mind to hang up on him.

"You're there, I can hear you breathing."

She held her breath for a moment, and then realized how silly it was. There were a few things she wanted to know, but she started with what she thought was the easiest. "Why do you sound like that?"

Wheezing, Logan replied, "My nose is broken."

The anger fled her body, and much—to her own disapproval—worry took its place. Unable to help herself, she shot up from the couch. Even though she didn't think he deserved it, she worried for him.

THE CONCERN IN KATIE'S voice sent elation through Logan's chest, but he stamped it down. He hadn't been sure what to expect when he'd called, but her fear for his safety wasn't at the top of the list of guesses.

"Who broke it and why?" The flurry of words from her mouth came at a steady stream.

Logan wasn't sure what question to answer first, but he listened to the questions, fear, and dismay. With each word, he steadily became more scared; it was the first time in a long time that Logan had ever felt surefire fear. However, as Katie rattled on a million questions a minute, Logan realized that no matter her skin tone, if she was ever going to rise above the hate he'd brought into her life, he couldn't be a part of it. Not that he was so sure she even wanted him in it now that everything was said and done.

"Okay, that's it . . . I'll call my dad and ask him if this is the freaking kind of prison he runs. If he is okay with men running around and breaking noses." She was a bit out of breath, but Logan knew she wasn't done yet. "Oh, wait. You didn't fall, did you? Shit, of course you didn't. What happened?"

Logan could imagine her long legs as she paced back and forth across whatever room she was in, and then her words hit him. "No, don't call your dad. I'm fine; they got the two guys who did it. I'm fine." He said again a bit louder.

He heard her intake of breath, and he hoped she was settling down. The last thing he needed was her father finding out that she'd been talking to him, whether over the phone or through email.

"Okay, so . . . um, why are you calling me?" she asked, suddenly sounding a bit insecure.

Logan was going to be honest as hell, and hoped she would be truthful as well. "I need to ask you a few questions about this Jason guy."

"Oh."

He could have sworn she sounded disappointed. "I need you to tell me what he said to you." He worried that this question would rehash an old argument. He hadn't called in two weeks, and now he'd only called for answers.

"He told me that you were a player with a fiancée named Dawn. But that wasn't true, was it?" She asked hesitantly.

He shook his head as he spoke, even though he knew she couldn't see it. "No. What did he look like?" Logan believed he already knew, but he needed to be sure. If Jake had gotten to Katie, and then to Aaron, he could have easily set up Logan's beating.

"Tall, white, good-looking, bright blue eyes, and blond hair."

Logan cringed at the fact she'd found that bastard good looking. Still, he wasn't sure if it'd been Jake or not.

"Anything else, ba—" He caught himself. Not because he didn't want to call her baby, but because he shouldn't. "Katie?"

Katie sighed. "He drove a Denali, it was black."

Caught, Logan thought. It was Jake's SUV. "Okay," was all he said. He needed to think for a moment. He wondered if Katie was in danger, or if he needed to send someone to watch over her. But who the fuck could he trust enough to send? No damned body.

"Why are you so quiet?" Her soft voice pulled him back to her, but he wasn't ready just yet. He needed to think, and that would be impossible with her warm voice in his ear.

"Can I call you back?"

Her response came quick. "No."

"Okay." He said dolefully. He was set to hang up; it was what he'd expected in the first place.

"Talk to me *now*! Tell me what's happening in there with you, and who this Jason person is. Logan, you need to tell me the truth." The demand in her voice urged him to obey. He did need to tell her everything just in case she was in danger.

He rubbed the tension from his shoulders. "Jason is really my lawyer, Jake. He's pissed at me for something I did in the past. Being my lawyer, I guess it made it easier to find you. When he did, and found out that—"

"I was black." Her voice held more sorrow than he could take.

"Yeah, he used it against me in here." Logan was still pissed. If he had just taken the time to find out if she was white, this shit wouldn't have happened. Still, Logan couldn't help but want to make her feel better. "It's not your fault. It's mine. Normally, I'm more careful about the people I keep in my life. I dragged you into this, and I shouldn't have." His whole life he'd lived by a code; just one slip up, and shit was out of control.

"You're right." Not what Logan had expected, but her voice held an odd calm. "You should be more careful and keep black women out of your life. Especially ones like me: a college graduate, New York Times bestselling author, homeowner, and successful person. You should definitely keep white men like Jake in your life, since he's a piece of shit, lying asshole."

At a loss for words, Logan pulled the phone away from his head and took a deep breath. What the fuck was he doing? Pushing the receiver hand to his head, Logan said, "You're right, but at this point, it doesn't matter. I've messed up, and lost not only your trust, but also the ability to breathe through my nose." He wasn't apologizing for his beliefs, because he believed they'd kept him safe over the years.

"Logan—"

"Katie, I don't . . . I don't know how to protect you from him in here, and I feel obligated to. I feel like I have to because it's my fault you are in this shit." Logan's headache was back in full force, and there was an annoying pressure behind his eyes. Sleep in the infirmary was the best sleep Logan had had in years, but now—back in his cell where Katie's pictures were missing—sleeping was impossible. "There's more. I think I put your safety in danger."

CHAPTER 22

KATIE THOUGHT SHE HAD a boring life. If you were to ask anyone in Lakewood about her, the recluse who lived minutes away from the prison, they'd tell you she was a good, quiet girl. She would never have written to a convict, nor would she have placed her life in danger by falling hard for a racist.

No, Katie was a good girl who needed to call Joe and let him take her out. A good girl should hang up this phone and ask Logan, the convict, to stay out of her life. However, this good girl, the one everyone thought Katie was, was long gone. In her place was this new Katie. And this Katie sat on the couch in shock at Logan's words.

"Danger?" she whispered. In the two weeks that she and Logan hadn't spoken, she believed that she'd grown a bit, if that were possible, over that short amount of time. Unfortunately, she was still the same girl who would be afraid of the danger her situation presented.

"I'll do what I can from here to keep you safe." The reverent tone in his voice soothed her a bit. While Logan had told her that he didn't associate with anyone out of his race, Katie had a hard time relating Logan to the man he seemed to want her to see him as.

Fear laced her voice, and Katie didn't even think to hide it. "Do you think they are going to target me?" She wondered if it were time to call her father. Maybe this had gotten too out of hand. The thought of calling him and admitting that she'd messed up was too much. Katie was an adult who could handle her own issues without the coddling hand of her father.

"When I got back to my cell this morning, the picture you sent me was missing, so I don't know. Jake is out of town, or at least that's what his secretary is saying. The guy that did this," Logan paused, and Katie urged him on gently, "the guy who did it, he's my last cellmate, Aaron. He's with the AB brothers here in prison."

"AB brothers? What's that?" She'd never heard of them, but she was positive it had to do with some prison brotherhood bullshit, and since Logan had gotten hurt over her, Katie guessed it had something to do with a group she hoped she never had to confront.

"The KKK. Katie, I am not a part of that," he quickly explained.

Those initials sent a chill down her back and she closed her eyes, forcing tears back in. "I know." And she did. Nothing about Logan made her think that he was with the KKK, but she still thought him a racist. The word stung her to the core, and her answer must have shocked him into silence.

"Logan, I can see where you are coming from. The black kids hurt you in your neighborhood, and then Trent comes along and protects you. So then, you make a choice that you believe is necessary, and maybe that worked for a while, but how can you not see that not all black people are like those hoodlums, especially when you know me?" She couldn't reconcile him with a bigot or an idiot, so why was he so blind?

His momentary silence hung heavy in the air. "Katie, why are you doing this to me?" His breath came ragged.

She could almost feel his pain through the phone. This was not what she'd expected, but she so desperately wanted Logan. Katie wrapped her arms around herself and sat back in her chair. She missed his voice, she missed the feeling it sent through her, but most of all she missed his company. "What am I doing, Logan?"

"Making me rethink my life. I can't . . . I just—" His firm words sent a powerful current through Katie. There were so many things she wanted to say to him, but uncertainty held the words at bay. What was she feeling? It was a strange mix of fear and hope, but hope for what? What self-respecting black woman would let a man with issues like Logan in her life?

"This thing we have, I never thought I'd have it with a woman like you. I won't lie, it's thrown me for a loop, baby."

Still the word baby from his lips made her shudder.

"The thought of you getting hurt because I'm a fucking idiot is killing me. I want you. I want to hold you, taste you, and keep you, but my life won't allow it. The walls I've created, I swear I can see you knocking them down, but then I have to worry about the shit you'll find behind them."

Katie closed her eyes, silently praying for Logan to let go and accept what they could have—skeletons and all. "Tell me what you want from me, Logan. You know how I feel about you, even if I hate that I do. But I see you being so much more than some white kid that got his ass kicked in the ghetto. I see *you*."

Logan grunted. "Baby, they kicked my ass then, but never again."

Katie couldn't hold her tongue. "No, just this time white men did it. Is that okay to you? Is it okay white men beat your ass, but worse that in the past, black men did it?" Here he was with this shit again.

"I get where you are coming from, but you need to understand . . . if I make this change, it's not going to be overnight. I swear there are going to be some rough times, and that's why I think we should take it slow."

Katie agreed. She was still nervous and hurt by his previous actions. Plus, she was still scared that Jake had more up his sleeve.

"When I got your picture, I realized the color of your skin didn't matter. When I looked at it, I was angry with myself for the things I'd said to you because I'd promised when I found the woman I wanted to make a life with, I'd never hurt her."

The tears Katie had been fighting finally made their escape. They had overcome this hurdle, but she knew there were more to come. She wondered if she would be strong enough to be in Logan's life, and if he'd be able to overcome his past.

THERE WERE TIMES WHEN being honest could break you in half, and then times when it was liberating, and for Logan, this time it was the latter. He wanted to be in Katie's life, and he wasn't going to let the fear of the unknown hold him back anymore.

"Logan . . ." Her voice was soft and imploring, and there had never been a time when Logan wished he were on the outside more than this moment. "I don't know. I think . . . no, I know I need time to think. Like a fool, I don't want you to stop calling me. I missed you when you didn't, and now I'm worried that you aren't safe there."

He understood, and felt the same way. He didn't fear for his safety, but instead for his parole hearing, which was just a few short months away. He couldn't fuck that up, not now. "Yeah, I'll keep calling, but I'll give you some time and call you back later tonight. I need to talk to Iggy, and see who was in and out of our cell while I was in the infirmary. Maybe you can get someone to come and stay with you until I figure this out?" he asked. He didn't want Joe, or whoever the man was that fixed her sink, with her when he couldn't be, but having her safe was more important.

"I can get Teal over here," she said. "That might work."

"Okay, I'll call you back in a few." Logan paused. There were better ways to tell a woman goodbye, but Logan couldn't bring himself to say anything other than, "Bye."

When he hung up, he stared at the phone for a while before standing and heading to his cell. Actually, he limped. Aaron and his friend, Davis, had broken his nose, bruised a rib, and he'd needed twelve stitches—with a concussion to boot—but Logan didn't care. Katie's pictures were missing, and he was legitimately scared for her safety. He finally made it up the stairs and to his cell . . . only to find Iggy snoring on the top bunk.

"Iggy," Logan called, and the man immediately turned over and glared at Logan, bleary-eyed.

He flipped over and pushed a hand under his pillow. "I been waiting on you, muthafucka'."

Though his body was still sore and aching, Logan balled his fists and stepped forward. He'd gotten his ass kicked once, and he'd be damned if it was happening again.

Surprising Logan, Iggy laughed and raised his hands up to show he wasn't going for a weapon. "Nah, man. It ain't nothin' like that."

Unconvinced, Logan didn't back down. "It's not, is it?" The last time he didn't pay attention to his surroundings, he'd ended up a bloody mess on the floor.

Iggy threw his legs over the side of his bunk, keeping his hands in the air as a show of pacification. "Nah, man," he motioned to his pillow, "I got something for you. And I know you want this, you know what I mean?"

Logan didn't, but he nodded anyway. If push came to shove, even with his broken nose and bruised ribs, he could take Iggy.

His cellmate slowly reached into his pillowcase and Logan watched, waiting and willing to kick his ass up and down the cell if necessary. When Iggy pulled out Logan's manila folder, his heart dropped. If he'd also grabbed Katie's pictures, Logan could assume she was safe from Aaron, for now. He reached out and snatched them from the man.

Taking a calming breath, he looked inside. "Why the fuck do you have them?" he demanded, glancing up. Iggy looked offended, but Logan didn't give a damn. He wanted answers and he wanted to be sure that Aaron stayed away from Katie. Jake he could handle with one phone call, but Aaron had long arms that could reach further than Jake's.

Iggy stretched and pointed out of the cell. "I have them cause those dudes came in here and looked through your shit." He reached under the pillow again and pulled out Logan's pictures.

Taking them, Logan shoved the pictures into his folder, ignoring Iggy's knowing stare. They'd had issues because Logan had accused Iggy of not acting his race, but after meeting Katie, Logan felt like a damned fool. Like she'd said, ghetto wasn't a race thing. Logan thought about it for a moment, and was just about to ask Iggy a question, but the man spoke.

Iggy jumped off his bunk as he said, "And you better believe that I looked through it."

Logan took an intimidating step closer, forcing Iggy to retreat backward. Was Iggy going to use this as ammunition against him? Logan wondered if he was going to have to kick Iggy's ass after all. He knew he had to look like a monster. It'd been two weeks, but his face was still a bruised yellow and green mess, and he had a red eye from a blood vessel that'd burst.

"I . . . I had to make sure I wasn't hiding drugs or some shit," Iggy stuttered, causing Logan to take a small step back. "Theeeen," Iggy annoyingly dragged out the word as Logan moved back further and opened his manila envelope to make sure everything was all there, "I find out that you play a racist in here so those dudes don't beat yo' ass, but you really like that dark meat."

Logan paused. He wasn't sure what to say to Iggy, so he said nothing at all. Bringing his stuff to the plastic desk, he placed it down and used both hands to lower himself into the seat. Relief took some of the tension from his neck and back; suddenly, he was ready to lie down and take a nap.

He closed his eyes and massaged the back of his neck. "Don't ever call her dark meat again." It wasn't a request, but a threat.

"I hear you." Iggy clapped his hands together and sat across from Logan. "So, you one of the men that come in here, act the part, and do yo' time, am I right?"

Logan opened his eyes and stared at Iggy. Something was different about him, but Logan couldn't place his finger on it. It was like there was more to Iggy than he let on, because as Logan looked the man in his eyes, he saw understanding in them. He had told the man he needed the white beat into him, and here Iggy was, protecting his secret. Why? Logan didn't get it. The man thought he was black, didn't he? He walked and talked like the black kids in his old neighborhood, and because of that, Logan placed him right in the same category.

He wondered what Katie really thought of him. Yeah, she'd called him a racist, but there was so much more to Logan than his past, and he wondered if he could overcome it.

"Where are you from, Iggy?"

The man seemed taken aback. "For real? You want to know something about me?" Iggy feigned shock . . . or maybe he wasn't faking it. Logan had been a dick to Iggy since the day he'd moved in. "I'm from Chicago. Lived on State Street. Why you asking?" His brow raised in suspicion at the question.

Logan ignored the latter question. "It dangerous there?" He didn't know if State Street was a suburb or what.

"Ah, hell man, it's rough, but why you asking?" Iggy's voice was serious now.

"Because I want to know when you decided to start acting like a damned fool. If you had a good upbringing, I'm inclined to think you—"

"Stop that shit. You trying to find a reason to drop that fine ass woman of yours, go ahead and let her go. 'Cause the girl in that picture," he pointed to the manila folder on the desk and Logan pulled it closer, "don't need that bullshit you 'bout to bring to her." Iggy stood, but stopped at their cell door. "Yeah, my home was dangerous. People was always getting shot over bullshit feuds and drugs."

Logan looked him up and down. He didn't sag his pants in prison for obvious reasons, but Logan could imagine him doing it. "So you acted like a thug in order to survive?"

Iggy shook his head. "No, I am a thug. Thug ain't a skin color, it's a way of life. I do all the bad shit mommas warn they babies about. Being a thug and living in the hood ain't about color, you get me? It's all 'bout the finances. If you rich, you live up on a hill, looking down at the city below and wondering how you can get richer. If you po' you sitting in the hood, looking up that hill and wonderin' who you gots to rob to get there."

Logan didn't agree, but being in prison for armed robbery and disagreeing with Iggy on this point would make him look like a fool. "When I was poor . . . not po'— poor," he gave Iggy a withering glance, "I never wondered who I could rob to be rich. I just worked my fingers to the bone. I'm in here because I was too fucking stupid to say no to a woman who wanted drugs. We went to pick some up with her brother—I stayed in the truck—and next thing I know they got him at gunpoint, shoving him into my truck." Logan remembered that night all too well, and every time he told the story he felt like a damned fool.

Iggy raised a brow and leaned against the cell door. "So, it ain't your fault?"

Logan chuckled. "Hell yeah it was my fault. I wanted a piece of ass, and she wanted some grass, and now here I sit." Logan held his arms out in a wide gesture. "My choice, my fault, and I don't even smoke weed."

Iggy nodded. "Yeah, I get you. Maybe there are some of us out there happy with having less. But that girl in that pic ain't. She been having you smiling like a fool for the past few months, and I know you didn't take that ass beatin' for nothin'." He winked and pushed away from the frame. "Sheeeet, if that was mine, I'd take her ass and—" Iggy stopped when Logan growled. "Shit, man. You ain't no damned dog. I meant to say, I'd make her mine if I was you." He shoved his hands in his pockets and walked away.

Logan stood and limped to his bunk to lay down. His chest hurt, his face hurt, but all that shit didn't matter. When he woke up, he planned to call Katie and tell her that she was safe . . . and he was falling in love with her.

CHAPTER 23

KATIE PEEKED OUT THE window for the hundredth time. With Teal working overtime for the past week, she hadn't been able to stay with her the night Logan asked her to stay with a friend. However, she'd promised to come over after work tonight. Logan called every day just to check up on her, and though it was supposed to make Katie feel better, it only worried her more.

Logan didn't think Jake would come back, but after Logan had fired him, it left Katie wondering if he had more shit planned for them. It took a sick jerk to have a man beat up in prison over a woman from years ago, however when he told Katie that he'd gotten Jake to take his case by threat, Katie realized that Jake most likely had more to prove. Now, she waited for Teal to come over so that she could explain the shit she'd gotten herself into.

When the phone rang, Katie realized that she'd spent the last few months on the phone, or with pen to paper, talking to Logan. Luckily, he only had two more weeks left until his parole hearing. Katie answered the call with a wide grin. It was easy to forget the danger that surrounded Logan when she spoke to him. His warm voice filled the line, and the fear and stress Katie had been living with was gone . . . at least for the moment.

"Hey, baby," he said, his voice low and gruff as if he'd just woken up.

"You sound tired." Katie went into her bedroom and sat in front of her laptop. She'd left it open and needed to talk to Logan about what she'd been searching for earlier that day.

Logan yawned, confirming her thoughts. "Nah, not at all."

"Yep, because I yawn when I'm not tired all the time, baby." Katie laughed. "Hey." Her voice turned from playful to serious, and she hoped Logan noticed.

His tone was worried, and Katie thought it should be. "What's going on?"

She stared at the screen. The guns all looked the same to her: dangerous, but necessary.

"I'm thinking of buying a weapon." Katie had never considered this before. The need for protection seemed so out of her realm, but maybe she was just as naïve as her father claimed her to be.

Logan's words were soothing and reassuring when he said, "I can't imagine my baby with a gun, but it's a damned good way to protect yourself. Have you ever used one before?"

"Nope," Katie had never even held one, "but I can take a class. It's called Gun Safety, and I don't even need a permit to buy a gun in this state." That both excited and worried her. While some states had stricter gun laws, Vermont seemed pretty lax in that area.

"I hate the idea of you feeling so unsafe that you feel the need to buy a gun. If I was out, I could be there."

"Yeah." She'd thought of that too, but even that was scary. She wasn't afraid to meet Logan, more like scared out of her damned mind and nervous. "Right now that's not an option, but I do want to talk to you about that day, too."

Logan groaned like a child who was told to clean his room. "When a woman says she wants to talk about something, every man in the world cowers in a corner, thinking of everything and anything he could have done wrong." He let loose a nervous chuckle.

She ran her hands through her hair and smirked. "You've done a lot wrong, but you've done even more right. You should be thinking about your reward when you get out." The words were out of her mouth before she realized their meaning.

"Reward?" As if on cue, the tone in Logan's voice dropped a couple octaves, causing heat to bloom in Katie's chest. "What's my reward, baby? And remember, I used to be a bad boy, now I'm reformed. That should get me two rewards."

Katie laughed. "Greedy! Maybe you can have three or four. Keep up the good behavior and we'll see," she purred. Guns and danger instantly forgotten, Katie could only think about how badly she wanted her man free and clear. She didn't care how hard it would be or what people would say.

"Hell, baby, I'll be good for the rest of my life if it means I get to keep you."

"Really?" Her question was real; the flirting was over. She wanted to know where this was going because they could talk all day long, but in a month when Logan was released, all of the talking they'd done would be just that—talking. Katie wanted to know exactly what Logan wanted. "Can we talk about this? I mean, I know we're together, but what's next? We haven't really discussed it. When you get out, what are we going to do?"

Logan's voice lowered. "You mean privately?"

"No! I know what happens privately." She covered her face with her free hand and sighed. "I mean, where will you live, work, and all of that? Are you moving back to Kentucky?" The thought made her sick to her stomach. They'd turned a pen pal situation into a long distance one, and Katie didn't want that, but she knew Logan's life was there.

"Katie, I'll have to go back to Kentucky for a while, but not forever. I know that isn't what you want to hear, but if I'm going to be with you, I need to get my shit together."

"I know," she said unhappily. "I just hate the idea of you being so far away. But it's worse now. You're right up the street and I can't even visit you. Which reminds me!" How could she have forgotten? "I got your picture!"

"Damn, am I that ugly that you forgot to mention it?"

His joke made Katie laugh out loud. The man was far from ugly. She could picture his lips on her, and his tattooed arms around her, protecting her. While she had found a new independence, there was still a part of her which enjoyed the safe feeling that being in strong arms gave her.

"Logan, you know damn well you aren't ugly."

"You saw me pre-broken nose. I'm going to end up with a lump on the bridge of my nose." He laughed and Katie did as well.

She leaned back on the bed, tempted to imagine Logan there with her. He was definitely sexy and he knew it. He took pride in his body and stayed fit—two qualities she appreciated about her man. Katie would consider him branded by their love, and his broken nose would forever remind them of the battle they'd won. And she did think of it as a battle in a war they were still fighting. She knew the real war was still to come, but she was ready. While in prison, there was something akin to segregation, and in most cases it was for survival. Logan still had a war to fight against his prejudices when he got out, but Katie wanted to be at his side as he fought them. A bump on his nose wouldn't stop that.

"I'll still love ya' crooked nose and all."

Logan's laughter stopped.

When Katie realized what she'd said, she tried to back track. "I . . . I mean, a broken nose won't stop me from—""

"Katie?" Logan said softly.

Mortified, she covered her face. "Yes?" She was so damned simple. She and Logan weren't ready for an admission like that, nor was she ready for an admission like that . . . no matter how hard her heart hammered in her chest.

"Calm down. I can't see you, but I know you are panicking." His calm tone reminded her that Logan wasn't one of those men who would run at the idea of a woman earning a place in his heart. "I know what you meant."

Did he? What did Katie mean? She wasn't sure herself, but she sure wasn't about to admit loving Logan. Wait, what was she thinking? They'd only been writing each other for a few months, she couldn't possibly love Logan. Could she? There was still so much she needed to know about him. There were things a couple needed to discuss before they made it to the "love" portion of their relationship.

"Katie."

She'd been so deep in thought that she jumped when he spoke. "Yeah?"

"Get out of your head."

"Too late. I'm trapped in there now." She couldn't help but feel a little lost. Why wasn't Logan as perplexed as she was? "Logan, I just told you I love you and you aren't freaking out."

"No, why would I? That's my plan. I'll make you fall for me, then I'll marry you and give you some kids." Logan paused, and Katie was too shocked to say anything. "Look, I'm thirty-five years old and I am looking to settle down. Fuck all the partying from college and the trouble with the law. I'm not that boy, I'm a man ready to start a life with you. I know it seems rushed, and there will be people along the way who will question our relationship, but we can deal with it . . . together."

"Like my father?" She didn't add Teal to the list because she figure it'd be easy to get her to come around. She was her best friend, so she knew Teal only wanted her to be happy.

Logan sucked in a breath, as if he had a damned long list, causing Katie to shudder. "Like your father, my best friend, Trent, my mother, and that's just to name a few."

"Your mom?" This was the war she was thinking about earlier.

"Not in the way you think, but yeah. She's a pain in the ass and a handful."

Katie could hear the voices of other inmates around Logan.

"She thinks every choice I make is a bad one, so she'll see you as a mistake . . . I can guarantee it. See, this is what I am talking about, Katie. I'm a grown man, and I won't let what they say change anything. I hope you won't either."

Her heart melted at his words "I won't. I promise," she whispered, meaning every word of it. While she wasn't ready—just yet—to admit her love for Logan, she was ready to admit he was the man for her, the man she planned to make a life with.

She'd fight through the wall erected by hate and prejudices to live her life with the man she was falling in love with. "Baby, from here on out the words racist and convict are banned from this relationship. I'll admit that I'm nervous about all this, but I'm ready."

"That's my woman." And she was his, and only his, from today until forever. "I have to go, but I wanted to tell you that I need your address." Without hesitation, she rattled it off, but he stopped her. "I don't have a pen, just mail it to me, okay?"

Getting up, Katie went to her desk for pen and paper. She quickly jotted down her address on her yellow stationary and shoved it in an envelope. Rules and regulations about not sending her address be damned. While the inmates couldn't ask for it in the Pen Pal Program, Katie was allowed to offer it. "Okay, I'll get to it. I have to mail it from my house."

She couldn't believe what was happening in her life. For the first time since her mother's passing, she was starting to feel whole again. There was nothing better than the feeling of freedom accompanied with love . . . it was amazing.

5643 Hanover Lane

The little blue house on the hill, lightly shrouded by trees.

Can't wait to turn our phone calls into reality. I miss you, and am counting down the days until I can be with you.

Love,

Katie

CHAPTER 24

TEAL ENTERED HER OFFICE and slammed the door. "She is freaking insane!" she seethed. How could Katie be so naïve? Teal threw the letter on her desk and fell into her seat. She knew Katie was lonely, but she was taking this shit to a new level by sending Logan Whyte, a newly paroled inmate, her address.

As soon as Teal had realized that Katie was falling for the bullshit this Whyte guy was giving her, she started making sure Katie's letters to Logan came past her desk. However, all she had found at the time was that Katie had sent him her picture. Now, the final letter to Logan—since he was pulled from the program due to his release in the morning—had her address. Teal wasn't sure what to do, but she had to think fast. She'd even thought of telling Katie's father, but then she'd definitely lose her friend. While they hadn't been having their normal afternoon lunches together, Teal had assumed that Katie's excuse for cancelling them to finish the edits on her book was the truth. Picking up the letter again, Teal re-read it. She now knew her friend had lied to her in order to keep up with phone calls from Logan.

Teal lifted her phone and started to dial Jan-Erik's extension, but stopped. She couldn't involve him and keep herself out of it. Hanging up, she tried to calm her nerves. This shit was insane. How was she supposed to protect her friend if she kept acting up? Then, an idea hit Teal. She stood and searched her file cabinet, remembering that she had the same yellow paper Katie had. They'd bought it together, but Teal couldn't remember if she'd used it all or not.

After searching the cabinet again, she gave up and ripped a sheet of paper from her legal pad. It was yellow and had lines, whereas Katie's paper was yellow without lines, but it'd have to do. Teal sat down at her desk and scrutinized Katie's handwriting. It'd be easy enough to copy, but what was she to say?

She scribbled out a few sentences, testing and comparing her handwriting to Katie's. When she was finally happy with the similarities, she wrote a quick sentence, hoping that it would push Logan away. Teal re-read the sentence, and decided it needed more.

If Katie ever found out what Teal had done, it'd be the end of a fifteen-year friendship, and that thought was enough to give her pause. She didn't know if she was doing the right thing or not, but she was more afraid of losing Katie at the hands of Logan. She knew these men; she worked around them all day, and she didn't trust any of them one damned bit.

Add to the fact, Logan was rumored to have ties with the KKK, and he'd been beaten up as an initiation just a few weeks ago. He'd denied it, but wouldn't say why he'd been jumped. For that alone, Teal didn't understand why the man was granted parole. Other than over population, the prison was equipped to handle a few more bodies. However, Jan-Erik had said no. He wouldn't keep these men squashed together.

At the last meeting, he'd explained that handling the prison meant making decisions that would affect everyone in and out of it, and he didn't want to lose control of Capshaw. She wondered if he knew that he'd lost control of his own daughter.

Teal knew what she had to do. Even if Katie found out and hated her, at least she'd be safe and alive.

Logan,

I'm sorry, but I can't do this. I am not ready. I hope you understand. Please, don't contact me again.

Kathryn

CHAPTER 25

"**WHERE YOU HEADED?" THE** cabbie grunted when Logan tossed his bag on the dirty, cloth backseat of the cab.

To hell, Logan thought, but said instead, "Rock Mountain Inn." It was the closest hotel that had a mini bar and a diner close by. He threw his head back and closed his eyes as the cab started to move. He didn't even watch the prison disappear in the background. His head was aching and his heart had settled in his stomach, creating a home there.

"I know you are glad you got out of there."

Logan opened an eye to see the cabbie taking quick glances at him. The man was short and stout, with an unkempt beard taking up his entire face. He mulled over the fact that the man didn't seem the least bit tense about picking up an inmate alone in his cab, but a quick glance at his hand showed one of the prison tattoos Logan was familiar with. They were illegal, so inmates sometimes used mechanical pencils or paperclips as tattoo guns. Uneven lines and shading, accompanied with the excessive scarring, normally gave prison tattoos away.

He didn't answer the man's question. If he'd served time and been released, then Logan was sure the man knew how he felt. The driver kept talking as Logan stared at the back of his eyelids.

"Most guys get out of there and have me take them to Jade's." The cab made a sharp turn, and Logan reached out for the door to steady himself. Opening his eyes, he gave the driver an annoyed glare. "Sorry, buddy." Logan was sure that he wasn't. "Like I was saying . . . Jade's. You need me to take you there?"

"No, I told you where I wanted you to take me." Logan looked out the window. He wasn't from Vermont, and for all he knew the cabbie could have been taking him anywhere and he wouldn't know because he'd only spent a few weeks in Vermont before he was arrested. "What's Jade's?" Logan had a clue, but wanted confirmation.

"A strip club. It's real up-scale and all that. If you need a woman," the cabbie wiggled his eyes in the rearview mirror, "I can take you there."

Logan needed a woman all right, but the one he needed had suddenly gotten cold feet. It didn't make sense, but Logan wasn't going to push. He had enough money to stay at a hotel for a week, and that was where he was going to stay until he could convince Katie that her fears were unfounded.

"Just take me to the hotel. I can find my own woman." Logan had found her and he'd fight for her even if he had to fight her fears. Someone had told him when he was younger that he'd find the woman who would send him to his knees, and Logan believed it was Katie.

Feeling a bit of the stress lift from his shoulders, Logan gazed out the window again, finally seeing what his heart had been hiding from him. After eight long years, Logan was free. He only had to meet with his parole officer once before he was sure he'd be granted permission to head back to Kentucky to get his finances in order. Trent had hired him a new lawyer and had him working on allowing him to leave for Kentucky for good. It was something Jake was supposed to be working on, but after firing him, Logan was sure he'd left things unhandled. Still, Logan couldn't leave or even focus on leaving until he fixed things with Katie.

It was almost May, yet there was still a chill in the air and a light dusting of white snow on the ground when Logan got out of the cab to enter the hotel lobby. Logan quickly checked in and headed straight to the mini bar. He'd never considered himself a heavy drinker, but the stress of his situation with Katie and his future had him real thirsty. He'd downed the first bottle of vodka, and the second, in a matter of moments. Instantly, he reached for the third. There was no way a man like Logan—at two hundred and twenty pounds—was going to even get buzzed off the little bottles in the mini fridge.

Realizing he was hungry, Logan searched for a menu in the room, and found it neatly folded on the bed. His stomach growled as he read through it, searching for alcohol. Deciding to eat as well as drink, Logan placed an order for the biggest, juiciest steak on the menu and a mini bottle of Jack. He lay back on the bed, feeling the warm effects of the three mini bottles of vodka.

"Shit," Logan groaned. After getting the letter, he'd forgone breakfast and was released on an empty ass stomach. He may have been a big man, but an empty stomach combined with the fact that he'd not drank liquor in so long had his head fuzzy. Stubborn mule that he was, he ignored his head's plea for him to slow down. Up and at the mini bar again, Logan found that there was another small drawer to the left of the fridge. He grabbed two more bottles of liquor, and opened the small drawer.

Inside was a razor, along with some other toiletries, but what caught Logan's attention were the condoms. He pulled them out and searched through the sizes; picking out his own, he put them in his pocket and went back to the bed. Logan downed both bottles, laying back when the room started to spin. He felt like a damned fool. He needed to call Katie, needed to speak to her. However, just as he was about to lift up, his body rejected that idea and came up with one of its own. Logan tried again, and sighed in relief when he was on his feet. He reached the phone and dialed the number he'd memorized months ago.

On the second ring, Katie answered and Logan was stunned into silence. Her voice was so soft and broken that he could feel her pain through the phone. He wanted to curse and fight the son of a bitch who'd hurt her. He spoke, praying that his words weren't too slurred.

"Baby?" At least that's what Logan wanted to say. He cleared his throat and tried again. "Baby, what's going on?"

Katie's voice broke when she started to speak, and she broken down into sobs. Logan felt as if his heart had been carved from his chest. He was out of prison and his woman needed him, but he was too damned twisted to get to her.

"Goddamn it, Katie," he said in a rush. "Baby, fucking tell me what's wrong." Her sobbing answer wounded him.

"You, you asshole! You had me worried. Last night you said you'd call in the morning and you never did!" Her words cut him just as sure as if she stood in front of him with a knife and slashed him to pieces.

Logan tried to gather his thoughts, but all he could see was her letter. "You sent me a letter. You told me to stay away from you."

Katie's sobs had turned into hiccups, and Logan longed to be there with her. He'd swear on anything she wanted him to tell her that he loved her. All she had to do was ask him, that was it. Since Logan was drunk, he knew saying it was wrong, so he didn't. When he said it, he'd be sober and it'd be after he showed how much he loved her.

"I . . . I never sent a—" She paused. "Wait, are you drunk?"

Logan swayed. "Um . . . a little. I'm at my hotel." Her whimper made him regret opening his drunken mouth. "Sorry, I was pissed and angry that you'd changed your mind, so I had a little to drink."

"What letter are you talking about, Logan? I sent you my address. You are supposed to be here, with me. You promised."

He couldn't see her, but he knew she was sobbing and it was somehow his fault. "I have the letter you sent me. I swear, I'll come to you now if that's what you want. Baby, just tell me what you want, please." Logan reached out to steady himself on the wall. His heart sped up in his chest and he couldn't catch his breath. He'd felt this feeling before when he'd learned his Aunt Elma had died. It was fear mingled with heartbreak and he couldn't take it. He couldn't lose Katie to some stupid mail mix up.

"Logan, are you okay?" Her voice rang clear through the phone. Logan was no fool; he needed her, wanted her, and loved her.

Logan squeezed his eyes shut and pushed away from the wall. He was a grown ass man, but he wasn't above needing his woman. How ironic that it'd be Katie helping him nurse a hangover in the morning. "Only if you come to me. Can you do that for me?"

CHAPTER 26

OUTSIDE OF LOGAN'S HOTEL room, Katie glanced down at the tray of food. With shaky hands, she lifted up the metal top to see that he'd eaten steak and potatoes. Steak sauce spilled over the side of the container, and a piece of meat was still left on the plate beside half eaten potatoes. Also, to her dismay, the receipt showed that Logan had ordered a mini bottle of liquor, too. He'd seemed drunk when he'd called her, and Katie hoped that Logan hadn't drank any more. She was already tense as it was, and the thought of a drunken Logan made her more nervous yet shiver in anticipation.

The way he'd spoken to her on the phone made her wonder if drinking would loosen his tongue, since it seemed to make him more apologetic. In reality, she felt she was the one who needed a drink. Katie lowered the lid and took a deep breath. She was anxious as hell, so she paced the hall for a moment with the key card –he had left at the front desk—gripped tightly in her sweaty palm.

After she'd disconnected with Logan, she'd dressed in what she thought was her cutest outfit. Of course Teal would have called it too tame, but Katie thought she looked good in her skinny jeans, which hugged her hips in all of the right places. And she topped it off with her favorite white cashmere sweater which showed her tasteful, yet sexy cleavage.

Katie stopped pacing and bit her lip.

"Shit," she muttered to herself, and looked down at her clothes. Maybe they were too tame for Logan. Maybe after eight years, he'd want his woman to look sexy, and Katie felt very far from it at the moment. She placed a hand on her stomach as it quivered in nervous excitement. Her hands were trembling and her palms were wet. She didn't berate herself for the apprehension she felt; she knew what was going to happen when she went in that room. Logan wanted her, and she craved him just as much.

Months of yearning and casual flirting, plus the pent-up sexual frustration, had Katie torn in two directions. She wanted to run, but her heart and certain parts of her body demanded satisfaction, compelling her to stay. What if Logan didn't find her sexually attractive? He'd never been with a black woman before, and while Katie wanted to be his first, she wasn't sure she was up to the task.

The longer she stood outside of his door, the more her uncertainty piled up. Her reasons to run were starting to overwhelm her reasons to swipe the card and walk through the door.

Tired of letting uncertainties and trepidation make choices for her, Katie turned to the door and marched forward. There was no need to be on edge anymore, Logan was her man. "He's mine," she whispered, as if it were an affirmation. With a reassuring nod, Katie swiped the keycard, waited for the beep, and pushed open the door.

Once inside, she looked around but didn't see Logan. Good! Her hands were shaking so bad she was amazed she was even able to hold the key card in her hand. Katie closed the door and leaned into it. Her nerves hadn't caught up to her just yet and they were all over the place.

Walking further into the room, she glanced around. The king-size bed was made—nice and neat—and there was a bag on the desk in the corner. Katie moved toward it, and took a quick glance inside to see Logan's meager belongings: a wallet, manila folder, a pair of jeans, and a shirt. Feeling like a snoop, Katie closed the bag and moved away. Further into the room, and closer to the bathroom, Katie could hear the shower running. Her body told her go inside, but her fears had her moving in the other direction.

Meandering to the bed, she perched on the side, waiting for her man to come out. Her heart was beating so fast she feared she'd have a heart attack. Kicking off her heels, she scooted back on the bed, placing her feet beneath her. Her hands were shaking—hell, she was shaking—and when the water stopped, Katie nearly jumped off the bed.

She removed her coat and laid it next to her. Next, she pulled her hair out of the bun and let it fall to her shoulders. She hoped Logan liked her shoulder-length hair. Katie ran her fingers through her curls, helping the strands feather against her cheeks.

The bathroom doorknob turned and Katie pulled her hands from her hair, glancing over her body. The normal self-consciousness any woman would have in this moment, assaulted her. She looked back to see the door open, and Logan's large body filled the doorway—a towel fitted tightly around his waist, and another in his hand drying his hair—and her breath caught. Steam escaped from the bathroom behind him, and the sight of Logan brought tears to her eyes.

The fear that she'd been fighting disappeared, and was replaced with the need to hold him, touch him, and kiss him. The tattoos he'd explained covered his upper arms and chest glistened with water from the shower. Logan hadn't been lying when he said he worked out on a daily basis, cords of hard muscle confirmed his words. Katie swallowed hard as her eyes roamed over his chest.

When she finally thought to look back up at his eyes, they held her in their gaze. She was frozen, unable to move. Logan dropped the towel from his hand and walked toward her; he was so tall, he had to duck under the doorway. Suddenly, Katie could breathe again, but her breath came in crazy pants. She was dizzy and her brain wasn't functioning properly. She squeezed her legs together as soon as the warm sensation assaulted her.

As if she and Logan were so connected that he could sense her need, he moved to her in a quick and deliberate pace. Soon, he stood in front of her.

Katie released a noise that sounded like a whimper, but she wasn't sure and didn't have time to question it. Logan's heavily tattooed arm reached for her, pulling her up off the bed and to his lips with a swiftness that had her head spinning and her core clenching. His arms were around her in a quick second; his hand tangled in her hair as another found its way to her face.

Logan's touch was so hot, it burned Katie's tender flesh. Her moan was cut short as he deepened their kiss, stealing her breath . . . along with her soul. She'd never been kissed so deeply in her life, and she fought to keep up. There were no dueling tongues or clanking of teeth, yet Logan invaded her mouth thoroughly and allowed her the same.

He tasted of mint, and was so sweet that Katie needed more. She moved her hips against his now long, hardened length, but the thick towel and her jeans fought against her pleasure. Something akin to a whimper left her throat as she bucked against him, needing more, begging for more. Logan pulled away and Katie took in some much-needed air.

He placed a chaste kiss on her neck. "Hello," he murmured as he placed even more warm kisses along her neck.

Katie sighed. "I like these kind of hellos," she said breathlessly. He released her, and she slid down him—

past the massive bulge threatening to escape the towel—until her feet hit the floor. Her fears had seemingly made their way to the back of her mind. He kept his arms around her while his eyes roamed over her face. His eyes were so green, Katie couldn't believe they were real.

"Pictures didn't do you justice." Logan pushed his hands up the back of Katie's shirt and caressed her skin, causing her to shudder in his arms. He chuckled when she ducked her head to his chest. He was so damned tall, Katie feared she had to climb him like a tree to get to his lips again, and that was what she wanted—to taste him.

Swallowing hard, she pushed away her nerves. "Logan," she sighed, cuddling closer. She wasn't sure what she was going to say, or if there was anything to say at all, but when he pulled her close and whispered in her ear, Katie nearly lost her balance.

With her hands on his chest, she gently pushed herself back and gazed in his eyes. Since he'd recently taken a shower, he smelled of sweet soap and shampoo. Logan's eyes were clear as a sunny day, so Katie couldn't tell if he'd drank the liquor he'd bought or not.

"What'd you say?" She'd heard it, but damned if she didn't need that phrase repeated.

He smirked. "I said I love you."

The words echoed in her ears. She wanted to fight them, but couldn't. She felt the same way, and no matter what anyone said, Katie planned on showing Logan how much she loved him every day.

A sigh of relief escaped her lips. “I love you, too,” she admitted. She stood on her tiptoes and kissed him. “When I came into this room, I was so scared, I wanted to run. My head was spinning, but then you came out of that door and the world stilled a bit.”

Logan gave her a gentle squeeze.

“And when you put your arms around me, my world stopped. Instantly, all of the shit that was blurry and unclear, just disappeared.”

His eyes narrowed slightly. “What were you unclear about?” he asked, confusion wrinkling his brow.

Katie tucked her head into the crook of his neck, too embarrassed to tell him. She didn’t want to bring up their differences because she thought if she reminded him of them, he would want to walk away.

He softly kissed her neck and her cheeks. “Tell me what had you unclear, baby.”

Katie was glad he’d used the past tense. “I’m not uncertain anymore,” she looked up at him, “but I was afraid you wouldn’t want me. However, from the way you greeted me, I’d have to say that was an unfounded fear.” Logan’s hands roamed down to Katie’s ass and he pulled her closer.

Moving against her, he asked, “Does it feel like I don’t want you?” As his bulge pushed against her stomach, his need was made clear.

Katie’s face heated and she shook her head. Grasping his arms, she closed her eyes. He hadn’t even touched her in her most intimate spots, yet her body felt close to a release. Maybe it was because she knew what Logan was capable of. His kiss demanded things from her body that she'd gladly give, and the waiting was killing her.

She bit back a moan when he leaned down, tracing his warm tongue across her lips before she let him in without hesitation. Katie moved into him, giving all she could with her kiss. She hadn't spoken, but she prayed he could feel and taste her love in the kiss. Pulling away to breathe, she bit her lip. "I told you, unfounded."

Logan chuckled deeply. He took a step back. "I want you, Katie. Never think I don't." He moved over to his bag and searched through it. "But you do need to explain this." His voice was different, harder.

Logan removed the manila folder, rifled through it, and pulled out a yellow paper. "You asked why I didn't call you when I got out?"

Nodding, Katie walked over beside him and took the paper from him to read the words. Katie was shaking her head before she even finished the letter.

A cold fear snuck up her spine. "I . . . I didn't write this, Logan." She searched his eyes, hoping he'd believe her. "I sent you my address, and told you that it was the blue house on the hill. If you give a cab driver the address, they'd only take you as far as the driveway, but you need to go up the hill to get to my house." Katie looked away from Logan, unsure if he believed her or not. The writing was very similar to hers, but Katie didn't use lined paper.

Logan took the sheet of paper from her shaking hands and placed it on the table. Sitting down in the chair, he pulled Katie onto his lap where she nestled close and wrapped her hands around his neck. "You believe me, right? I hope you know I wouldn't play any games with you like that." She prayed he did; she'd never do something like that. She wanted him, needed him, and she thought she'd proven that to him.

CHAPTER 27

THE IMPLORING IN HER voice had Logan inclined to believe her. He was so damned surprised to get the letter asking him to leave her alone, he'd done just that. He wasn't sure why she'd pushed him away. Everything had been calm and smooth, and then he got the letter. Something wasn't right, but he knew one thing. . .

"Yeah, Katie, I believe you."

She appeared relieved. Logan rubbed her back and placed a kiss on top of her head. Her unruly curls tickled his nose and he kissed her again.

"Who wrote it?" he asked.

She was quiet for a moment. "I think I know, and this time she went too damned far. But I won't let her take this from me." Katie lifted her hand, placing it over the tattoo on his arm. She traced the outline of the shattered skull, and slowly moved to the next one.

Logan's skin broke out in gooseflesh and he reached up to touch her face. She caught his hand in mid-air and placed a soft kiss on his palm, before kissing her way down his arm and to his chest. He gently grabbed her neck and yanked her lips to his, foreplay be damned.

If she kept her lips on him, he'd embarrass the shit out of himself. His shaft was nestled between his lap and her ass cheeks. Every time she moved, she slid along him, causing a shudder up his spine. He wanted to know more about the letter, but his dick had taken over. It'd been too damn long for Logan. Eight years without the touch of a woman was a prison in and of itself.

Normally, he was the king of foreplay. He wanted to taste Katie in so many ways before he made love to her, but he was ready to explode just from the rhythmic movement on his lap. Releasing her neck, he gazed at her wet lips.

Katie reached down and grabbed the hem of her shirt. Pulling it up, she showed him her nut-brown skin. He'd never been with a black woman before. Everything was the same, yet different. There were the same soft curves and contours, but where white women were pink or tan, Katie was a warm russet brown. He marveled at the difference.

Reaching behind her, he had her bra off in seconds and on the floor. She went to hide her breasts, but he was quicker and pulled her arm away.

"They're small," she whispered, glancing away.

Logan didn't give a damn. He reached out and cupped the tender flesh. Sighing, Katie arched her back, pushing into Logan's hand. The dark nipple poked out, and the crown around it tightened, pulling taut. His mouth watered. Gently squeezing the flesh, he nipped at her peak. "More than a mouthful's a waste, darlin'."

His husky words drowned out her moan. Logan leaned forward and placed the hard bud in his mouth and sucked on it, plying it between his tongue and teeth. Katie bucked in his lap, causing the towel to shift. His shaft sprung free.

Wasting no time, she eagerly reached for his cock. Sitting up a little, she pulled it out from underneath her and stared at the length. His excitement was visible in the clear, sticky liquid pearling at the tip. Using her small, warm hand, she spread the natural lubricant over the bulbous head and moved up and down his shaft. Logan thrust with each motion. Closing his eyes, he tried to think of unsexy things, but his body wouldn't listen and kept pushing through her tight hand.

"Oh shit. I think I'm going to come," He whispered on a moan. She let go of his shaft and brought her arms around his neck, grinding her center into his arousal with hard, small circles.

"Fuck," he groaned. Squeezing her ass, he lifted her up and down against him, harder and faster. Whimpers and grunts filled the small room.

Katie's body started to tremble. "Oh my God," she cried, freezing in place, legs shaking, as he continued to work their hips.

Two seconds later, he roared, jerking beneath her in brutal spasms.

Holding onto each other, their labored breaths mingled, slowing with each exhale. After coming down a little, his brain cleared. This was not the way he'd wanted to make love to her for the first time.

Logan picked Katie up and she wrapped her legs around his naked waist. Making his way over to the bed, he placed her down, her hair fanning around her head. Lying there, legs open, he was excited to see she was so relaxed around him. It showed she trusted him.

He worked at tugging her pants down her long legs, and placed soft kisses on her upper thigh. White lace panties did little to hide her brown glistening folds, especially now that they were drenched with her juices. Logan couldn't stop himself. Spreading her legs open and holding them down by her inner thigh, he leaned in and delivered a long lick over her panties. Katie bucked and her eyes flew open. Putting her hand on his head she pushed him down and moved her center over his face. Then she used her hands to pull him up over her.

She was so innocent and sweet—yet sexy and decadent—his need for her started to push his racing blood south of the border once again. Katie reached up and caressed his face with soft, gentle strokes. Her eyes held him in such high regard he swore he'd never let her down. His chest ached as he reached for her panties, pulling them down her legs and off her feet.

Pushing her further up the bed, he crawled between her legs. Sitting back on his heels, he gently grabbed each thigh and opened her legs. He glanced up when Katie's hands moved to her breast. Logan liked the sight of her dark nipples rolling between her fingers. Bringing his attention to her brown folds, he reached up and pulled her nether lips apart and dipped a finger inside.

The tight grip on his finger worried and excited his dick. He knew it had been a while since she had been intimate with a man, and though Logan was proud of his size, he knew if he wasn't careful, he could hurt her.

Logan moved off the bed and pulled Katie down until her ass was half on and half cradled in his arms; now her legs lay open and directly below his face. The first lick was from her ass to her clit.

She jolted, "Oh my God."

Logan looked past her flat stomach and between her breasts to catch her eye. "Baby, what's my name?"

Her eyes were glossy and she was in a haze. "Logan," she whispered.

He grinned. "Good girl, that's the only name I want to hear from your lips for the rest of the night."

She bit her lip and nodded.

He dove back in, taking that little pink nub between his lips. Though he'd wanted her to say his name, it seemed Katie could only speak gibberish. He pushed his tongue into her body, and rubbed her clit. He could hear her panting, and from the amount of juices leaking from her body, she seemed ready. His shaft was now bobbing heavily between his legs and he brought a hand over it to pump it a few times.

The time was now. Logan reached out and pulled Katie up. "Come here." He helped her move to sit on his lap. Positive he'd fuck her like a beast in heat, he pulled her close and said, "Ride me." Reaching for the condom on the nightstand, he slid it on.

KATIE CAREFULLY CENTERED HERSELF over Logan and slid down his length. She held his shoulders to keep from falling, or taking too much in at once. His considerable girth had her stopping and readjusting a few times. He didn't help her. He actually didn't even touch her. Leaning back on his arms, he watched her through hooded eyes.

She loved the fact that he watched. Moving a hand from his shoulder, she reached between them, rubbing her clit until she was panting again. Logan's eyes darkened and a groan emanated from his throat, but he still didn't touch her.

His restraint was remarkable, but Katie would soon make him give in. She lifted up a little, and then came down all the way, until her ass rested against his balls. He released a puff of air through gritted teeth. She enjoyed the slight burn and stretch. She'd be delightfully sore in the morning, but it'd be worth it.

Katie sat for a moment, allowing her body to adjust. She needed him to touch her, but his eyes only bore into hers. He was waiting for her to be ready and allowing her to set the pace, but she wanted to be ravished. When had she last allowed her inner temptress free—never?

She gave Logan a small grin and then rocked her hips. He gripped the sheets and threw his head back, but she didn't move until his eyes were on her again. Continuing to move her hips on his lap, she waited for him to reach for her, but still he didn't.

Katie leaned back, placing her hands on Logan's knees. She rose and fell, harder and harder each time. Giving him a front row seat to watch his cock disappearing into her.

"Baby, touch me," she moaned.

Logan finally reached out and grasped her hips in a bruising grip. "Fuck me, Katie. This is all yours. Fuck it," he demanded.

His words had a profound effect on her; she gushed at the gruffness in his voice, and his naughty words had her close to the edge again.

"Touch me."

He shook his head no.

"Why?" Her eyes narrowed, and the lust haze seemed to evaporate. Her movements halted.

His eyes held something burning deep. "I can't. I won't be able to control myself. I think I'll hurt you." She shook her head, but he continued, "My heart wants to make love to you, but my body is telling me to break you, to shatter you into a million pieces."

Katie leaned in, allowing him deeper inside.

He bucked a little and then held her hips at bay, "There is a fucking beast roaring to get free. You give me control, and the fucker comes loose. I will fuck you into next year." His voice was so stern. Katie knew it was meant to scare her, but it didn't have that effect.

Suddenly, she hopped off him and crawled onto the bed. Laying on her back, she spread her legs as wide as she could. Her hand slipped down and she rubbed her slick folds. Her hips instinctively rose, chasing the sensation and promise of completion. Katie kept her eyes on Logan, who surprisingly didn't look down at her actions, but kept his eyes on hers.

His green eyes darkened to an almost black, his arms flexed, and his hands clenched in tight fists. Logan stood and a wave of excitement and lust broke through her. She stopped her movements.

"Don't fucking stop," he growled.

Katie placed a shaking hand back between her legs.

He moved slowly around the bed, his eyes never leaving hers. "Open it up so I can see."

She blushed so hard, she was sure her whole body was tinged pink. Reaching down, she pulled herself apart.

His nostrils flared. "That's my girl. That pretty pussy looks like a sweet strawberry dipped in milk chocolate." He stopped moving, and asked, "May I have a bite?"

Nodding, she attempted to spread her legs wider when he got on the bed. He brought his hot mouth down between her fingers and sucked and flicked her button.

"Damn it," she called. "Logan, I need you. Please," she begged.

While his mouth was amazing, there was something more she needed. As if sensing she was at the end of her rope, he crawled up, and with one sharp thrust, filled her.

Katie's back arched and a groan left her throat. Pleasure and pain zipped up her spine and settled in her chest.

With each deep stroke, Logan carefully embedded himself in her body and her heart. She watched as he fought off his orgasm, waiting for hers. What he didn't know was that his pleasure was hers. Watching him reach completion would push her over the edge.

Katie thrust upward into his downward lunges, heightening her pleasure. She leaned closer and spoke in his ear. "Come for me, baby."

Her words sent a jolt through Logan's body. He groaned, thrusting harder and faster.

"Take it, Logan. It's yours. All yours. Pound that pussy." She meant every word she'd said.

His body quaked above her and he released a deep moan. Wrapping her legs around his back, she moved with him and the first wave hit her hard. Crying his name, she begged him to follow her off the cliff.

When the second wave hit, Logan roared and slammed roughly into Katie. She gritted her teeth as pain and pleasure both took their turns deep within her. Entwining her arms around him as he shook above her, she held him until his body calmed and her breathing slowed.

He'd sworn to keep her from the bad parts in his life if it killed him. However, Katie was no longer fearful of their future. She was ready to embrace it.

ROLLING OVER, SHE FACE-planted into a big-ass brick wall. Logan lay beside her on his back, snoring like an overworked lumberjack. She turned over and snuggled into his firm, warm body, and placed a kiss on his tattooed chest. Closing her eyes, she inhaled. He smelled of sweat mingled with mild soap, the scent of her skin, and her perfume.

Last night, he'd kept their bodies close, his hands constantly floating over her skin in feather-soft caresses. His heavy body had been draped over hers like a protective veil. Katie had never felt so safe, or so desired. This was intimacy, and she needed more.

Logan stirred, turning over and placing his heavy arm over her stomach. His possessive grasp pulled her tight and squeezed her bladder. The snoring didn't bother her, but she needed to pee, bad. And, a nice long soak in a hot bath to soothe achy muscles would be amazing. Her limbs were screaming and begging for some heat therapy.

She moved from his arms and headed into the bathroom. Quickly emptying her bladder, Katie washed her hands and then started a warm bath. As the water filled the large garden tub, she went back into the room to check her cell phone. She hadn't told Logan it was her best friend, Teal, who'd most likely changed the letter. She didn't care at the moment because no one was going to ruin this for her.

Scrolling through her missed calls and texts, she saw Teal's number first, and then her father's. She could only guess that since she hadn't answered, Teal had gone to her dad. Typical of Teal, but Katie didn't give a damn. She'd stay in this hotel until she and Logan were kicked out by management, and with the way he'd made her scream last night, it was a good possibility they'd be booted out.

"Why are you over there?" Logan's sleepy voice called from the bed.

Katie placed the phone on the table and gingerly walked over to the bed.

He sat up on an elbow, eying her. "You okay?" His voice, gruff with sleep, made her insides tremble.

She nodded. "Yep, better than okay."

Logan pulled her onto him, and shifted her gently to the bed. Kissing her, he stole her breath away, along with her sanity. She pushed him back on the bed and deepened the kiss. While her body needed rest, it still craved his touch.

He pulled away. "You limped over here." Squeezing her ass, and then lightly spanking it, he asked, "Are you sore?"

She nodded and tried to get up, but he pushed her back on the bed. Scooping her up, he carried her to the bathroom, and placed her down next to the tub. Turning off the water, he got inside. Then, he helped her step in and settle on his lap.

Running his hands up and down her arms, he asked, "Who wrote the letter, Katie?"

She groaned, adjusting herself between his legs. Instead of answering, she slipped her hands beneath the water. Unfortunately, he was going to be stubborn about it, and stopped her before she could distract him again.

Katie huffed. "Fine. It was most likely my best friend Teal. She works in the administration building at the prison, and she was the only reason I was able to get in the Pen Pal Program when my dad told me I wouldn't qualify for it. I think she reads my letters. . . Well, at least I know she read the last one I sent."

She hated feeling as if Teal and her dad needed to treat her like a child. She didn't need their help. She was an adult and capable of making her own decisions. Of course, meeting a man fresh out of prison could hardly be considered rational, but Katie had faith in her choice, and in Logan. She just wished her father and Teal had more faith in her.

Logan was silent. He pressed a kiss behind her ear. "You think she did it to protect you?" If he was mad, she couldn't tell. "I think I understand where Teal was coming from. She doesn't know anything about me, other than my rap sheet."

His words rang true. What if Aaron had gotten her letter, instead of Logan? That would've ended horribly. "I'm sure she did, but she should have talked to me first. I don't know why everyone treats me like I can't make my own decisions, but it has to stop. My whole life has been this way." She reached up and pulled her hair into a sloppy bun.

The words Logan meant to say next dried up in his throat as he watched her breasts.

She peeked back at him. "I thought you wanted to talk? Keep your eyes off those," Katie said with a sexy smirk.

Logan covered both of her breasts with his hands. He leaned over and whispered in her ear, "Then stop showing them off."

She wiggled in his lap

"Katie," Logan warned in a low voice.

She pushed her bottom lip out in a pout, and he kissed it.

"You need to call her and let her know you are safe before the cops knock down my door and throw me back in a cell." His voice was light, but his words worried her.

"That won't happen." She leaned back into Logan. "And don't say stuff like that. Do you still have to go back to Kentucky?" She knew he did, but maybe she could talk him into staying for two or three weeks before he left.

She felt him nodding. "Yeah, my new lawyer is working it out with my parole officer. But money isn't tight—yet. I have a free place to stay back at home, and a little bit of money waiting for me in a trust from my aunt."

Katie nodded. She lifted her feet and propped them on the lip of the tub. "How long can you stay?" She hoped her voice didn't seem whiny, but she felt like whining.

"A few days. It's too expensive to stay at this place, plus I drank fifty bucks of vodka out of that mini fridge." His laughter rumbled through her.

"Yeah, and what about that mini bottle of Jack Daniels?" She looked up at him. The water was so warm, and her muscles so lazy, she realized moving her head was all she could muster. Logan's big body fit so perfectly with hers, she thought he'd have to drag her out of the water when it turned cold.

He kissed and nibbled her neck before answering. "I didn't drink it. It's in the room somewhere."

"Okay, we can share it," Katie said. She was just about to fall asleep in his arms when she felt fingers slide up her sides. He began tracing small circles over her flat stomach, then slowly crept his way up to cradle her breasts.

Katie sighed, arching her back. "I have no clue why you love those things so much," she whispered. Logan's chuckle vibrated through her, and his warm tongue traced a path from her ear lobe to her collarbone where he tenderly bit the flesh.

With a note of awe in his voice, he murmured, "Your breasts are one of my many favorite parts of your body."

She tried to pull his hands away, but he held on. Katie was self-conscious about her breasts. If she had to list the things she didn't like about them, she'd have a million things, but the top two were that they were barely a B cup and her nipples were larger than she thought they should be. "Why do you like them?"

Logan kneaded them and tweaked her nipples, causing her body to jolt. "Because of that," he whispered. "And because the nipples look like tasty little raisins."

She laughed. "I've never heard it put like that before." Reaching up, she covered his hands—her favorite body part.

Katie had never noticed the differences in the shades of her body, but now, she wondered if Logan noticed them. He touched her like he didn't care, and he'd made love to her as if he had something to prove.

She had to admit there were times the night before when their lovemaking was so intense, she feared she'd never come down. He seemed to understand her—gentle at times, and rough when she needed it. Her legs ached, her back was stretched in ways meant for a gymnast, and her lady parts needed a day. . . well, maybe two days of rest.

Water sloshed around the tub as Logan adjusted his big body deeper into the water, taking Katie with him. "What are you thinking about?" Logan asked, his hand tracing a hot path down her belly and over her pelvic bone.

"Wondering how long it will take me to recover from last night."

His hand stopped. After a short pause, he placed a kiss on her neck. "Are you still sore, baby?"

"A little, but in a good way. A very good way." She giggled at his gruff groan.

"I suppose we could cuddle in here until the water cools?" His hands made their way back to her breasts.

She rolled her eyes, still not sure why he felt the need to hold those little things, but inwardly ecstatic he paid attention to them at all. Most men loved her butt, and she was always less than enthusiastic about what they wanted to do to it.

Cradled in his warmth, Katie closed her eyes. "Tell me about your plans. Better yet, let's make our plans now."

"Our plans?"

She nodded. "Yeah, what's in store for our future?" She was a tad bit worried about her father's reaction to him, but she had made her mind up weeks ago and there was no changing it. She wanted a future with Logan, and no one—neither her father, nor Teal—was going to stop it.

Logan was a convicted felon, but Katie could look past that, as long as he worked hard to get his life back on track.

CHAPTER 28

LOGAN WASN'T TOO SURE what he planned to do. Katie lay snuggled against him, and it took all he had to not slip between her legs and make love to her again. Maybe he'd been a bit too rough with her last night, but in reality he'd held back . . . a lot.

Her small body shuddered in his arms, and Logan grinned in satisfaction. He loved touching her smooth skin and the way his hands glided against it.

He wanted to talk about the future with Katie, but her wet body was such a distraction, his mind couldn't settle on any one thing. Using his knees to part her thighs, he pulled a hand away from her breast to reach down between her long legs. Katie softly moaned in response.

Logan made a mental promise to be as gentle as he could, but he had to touch her. He had to hear her call his name in that reverent tone that made his chest bolster and his manhood stand at attention. Softly, he stroked her. He wasn't trying to change the subject, because after he finished—after she whispered his name and arched her back in release—he'd talk about anything and everything she wanted to talk about.

Searching for the certain little button, he lightly feathered his fingers over her flesh. Katie's breath caught in her chest and she placed her arms under his, holding tight. Logan increased the pressure, kissing and nibbling her neck, waiting for the signs of her release. He'd memorized them. No, they'd engrained themselves in his memory.

Her voice was so soft, he wasn't sure he'd heard it. She murmured his name on a sigh and Logan gingerly bit her neck, applying enough pressure to cause her to cry out.

Water sloshed out of the tub and onto the floor, but he didn't care. The sound of his heart beating roared in his ears, and the sound of Katie's gasps and moans urged him on. Her warm body moved steadily across his lap, but this moment wasn't for him, it was only for her. He clenched his teeth and his body begged for its own release.

Logan shoved his face into Katie's back, never releasing her center from his hands as he fought his own need. Her body rocked against his erection, and Logan was so damned turned on from her scent and the way his fingers easily danced with her slippery nub, that Logan thought he might finish when she did.

Katie's body pulled tight and her nails scored his skin. Logan plunged a finger inside of her, listening as she came apart in his arms. The sound was amazing; his name had never sounded so beautiful. He would be content to hear her scream his name from now until forever.

Removing his finger, he rubbed the little nub until Katie's body twitched and jerked. Her breaths came in short pants and her beautiful brown eyes glazed over. He leaned in and tasted every inch of her mouth, before pulling back with a satisfied moan.

He wanted to take her past the twitch, past the overly sensitive jerks and groans, so he kept rubbing. Katie moved her hips, trying to escape his greedy fingers, but he applied more pressure and rubbed harder.

"Oh shit, oh shit, oh shit." Her body jerked and her head flew back. "I'm gonna. . . I. . .baby!" she screamed.

Logan's chest puffed with pride. There was nothing better than seeing her come apart in his arms. "Now, I'm ready to talk about our future."

She chuckled and shook her head.

He pushed her legs together and started talking. "I have a few things to handle in Kentucky." A disappointed groan came from Katie. "It won't take long. I just need time to talk to a lawyer about Elma's will and find out what Trent's been up to."

"What about after? Does your probation mean you have to stay in Vermont?" She turned her head and gazed up at him. Her curls were dampened from the water, and her eyes were still hooded.

Logan thought there was no way she could ever look sexier than she did now.

"Are you going to stay here in Vermont?"

He thought about it for a moment. He didn't want a long distance relationship, and he couldn't ask her to move with him to Kentucky with his turbulent past there, nor did he want to barge into her home by moving in with her so soon into the relationship.

He could afford his own place, and they could date like normal couples did. Rushing always fucked things up. His lawyer had told him he had options. There were a few rules that'd allow him to leave the state while on parole, and even a few more that allowed him to return home for good.

"I guess I could get an apartment out here, but I'd have to find a job first and my lawyer is handling the fact that I need to leave the state. I just need to meet up with my PO and I should be good." He didn't think there were many places willing to hire an ex-con, but it wouldn't stop him from trying. "Finding a job up here will be hard. I already have a place to stay and a job lined up in Kentucky." He kissed her nose when she frowned.

Her voice sounded lost in disappointment. "Sounds like you have more reasons to go than to stay."

She was right. There were many reasons why Logan should go home.

"Hmmm . . . that may be the case, baby, but the one reason I have to stay trumps everything." Many people would tell Katie she was too good for Logan, but he wouldn't leave her side unless she asked him to.

"Good." She reached up to pet his face. "You want me to go down with you? I've been to Kentucky before."

Logan licked his lips. He wasn't sure how to tell her about Trent and his connections to the KKK. He also didn't want her to worry that going back home would put him in danger, or back on the wrong path. However, he couldn't lie to her. "No, Trent isn't the type of man I want to bring you around." He kissed her, hoping to soften the blow.

Coming back up for air, she asked, "Is he racist?"

Logan could only nod and watch her think on his words.

"Okay then, you go home and get your life down there in order, and then you come back to me." She sat up, and Logan's eyes instinctively dropped to her dark, puffy nipples. Katie hooked her finger under his chin and lifted until his gaze was on hers. She was serious as hell. "You have one week, and only one week, to come back or I am coming after you, Logan Whyte."

He nodded his agreement, and she gave him a peck on the cheek before lifting out of the water. Logan patted her ample bottom as she got out of the tub.

After she found a towel, she held it out for Logan. "When you are gone, I'll talk to my dad. It might go over better if you aren't here."

Logan raised up out of the water and took the towel she offered. "Sounds like a plan. I'll leave the day after tomorrow so we can spend some more time together."

When he'd finished drying off, he flung the towel over the railing, picked Katie up—even though she was in the middle of drying herself off—and chuckled at her surprised squeal. He felt lucky. His life was coming together, and Katie was an integral part.

TWO DAYS OF ISOLATION with Logan in his hotel room seemed to be just what the doctor ordered. While he'd only left once for a meeting with his lawyer and PO, Katie had used that time for some well-needed rest. She didn't want to leave, and she'd even offered to pay for some additional days, but Logan had flat out refused her money saying he wasn't going to cost her a cent—ever. Katie was pleased and disappointed by his declaration, but he was right. He needed to get back home, and the faster he did, the faster he could come back to her.

Her phone rang as she was getting in her car. Logan looked at the display before he handed her the phone.

"I hate that you are lying to your father, Katie." His voice sounded dejected. "This is starting off wrong."

She took the phone. "Logan, I can either tell him I needed to get out of the house to write, or that me and my boyfriend, who happens to be an ex-con, were at a hotel where he made love to me so thoroughly that I'll only have fifty percent usage of my legs for the rest of my life." She placed her finger in a shushing gesture over her lips when Logan started to laugh.

"Yes, Dad?" Katie started the car as she answered the phone and adjusted the heat. April's in Vermont still offered frost, and a chill was in the air . . . as well as in her father's voice.

"Have you left the hotel yet?" His voice was short and clipped.

Katie could hear in his voice that he was upset about something. She'd talked to him yesterday and told him she was working on a deadline and needed a change of scenery to get her creative juices flowing. She hated lying to her dad, but she couldn't imagine telling him the truth at the moment. On top of that, Katie was an adult, she wasn't sure why she always felt the need to explain her actions to others.

"Yes, I'm heading back now." Unsure of what was happening with her dad, Katie forced pep into her voice even though dread filled her heart. She glanced over to Logan and gave him a look that she hoped conveyed her nervousness.

"Good, I'll head over after this meeting. I need to discuss something with you."

Katie's heart jumped into her throat. There was no way she was going to hide Logan in her house, she was too old for that, but she wasn't ready to introduce him to her father yet.

"Um . . ." She searched her brain for an excuse. "How about Mel's Bistro in an hour?" That was their normal spot. She didn't think he'd mind meeting there.

He cleared his throat. "I need to speak to you in private, Katie." Her heart dropped, and she cursed Teal in her head. Her best friend had betrayed her trust and told her father. She wouldn't put it past her—it'd happened once or twice before.

"Uh, okay. Is everything okay?" She grasped the steering wheel. Logan reached for her hand, placing it in his, and she loosened her grip.

"I sure hope so, but I'll have to talk to you about it when I get there in an hour and a half. Love you, Katie." Her father's voice softened.

"Love you, too, Dad," Katie responded before disconnecting the call. She turned to Logan and said, "Looks like you'll be meeting my father sooner than expected." She was freaking out inside, but Logan seemed calm. Bees buzzed in her head and her stomach ached. "You aren't nervous?" She pulled the car from the parking spot and headed out of the lot.

Logan pulled her hand into his lap. "It is what it is, Katie. I really don't want you lying to him anymore. I don't want him to have any excuse not to accept me in your life."

Katie knew there was one big reason why her dad wouldn't accept him, but she planned on convincing him to give Logan a chance. How she planned on doing that was beyond her, but she would try.

Driving up the hill, she parked in front of her house. They stepped out of the vehicle and walked up to the front door.

"Looks like my baby is pretty successful."

She glanced at Logan looking over the house. She saw the awe in his eyes and smiled. It was a modest home in her opinion; not too big or too small. Everything was brand new when she'd moved in, and there was a large front and back yard. Her dream was to get a dog, but she hadn't gotten around to it yet.

"I do all right," she said humbly as she put the key in the door and pushed it open. Stepping inside, she looked around. Ordinarily, Katie worried about what her guest would think about her home—like, was there a funny smell, was her furniture nice, or did they see an ant crawling on something—but with Logan, Katie had none of those concerns.

He glanced at her pictures on the wall, and then sat down on the couch and patted his lap. Katie threw her keys on the end table and perched herself on his strong thighs.

"When your dad gets here, I think you should tell him the truth."

Katie hated when Logan took a disapproving tone with her; it made her feel so young.

"And what would you have me say, Logan?" she retorted hotly. "He isn't going to understand, and I just don't want to disappoint him." Katie knew that being an adult meant making your own choices, but that didn't mean the choices you made only affected you. If you screwed up, the backlash might fall onto others, and Katie knew her father would say just that to her.

He shrugged. "I don't care." His voice was cold. "I'm not going to be some dirty little secret, Katie."

She turned in his lap and took him in. She hadn't thought of it like that. Kissing him, she apologized. "I'm sorry. You aren't a secret to me. I guess I'm just trying to avoid the stress of an argument."

He huffed. "An argument that will be so much worse if you keep lying."

Katie agreed, but was still looking for ways to push this meeting back. She stood from his lap even as he tried to pull her back down.

"I need to change my clothes and do something with my hair."

Logan followed her into her room, watching as Katie picked out a shirt and a pair of jeans, and changed her clothes. "I was thinking about something." She motioned for Logan to follow her into the bathroom, where she plugged up her flat iron.

"Maybe Howard could hire you over at his auto repair shop?" Katie knew that Logan wanted to work and make his own money, but if he couldn't find a job, she was worried he'd move back to Kentucky to work with Trent.

Long distance wasn't something Katie had ever done, but she was almost positive it'd kill her. Maybe that was a bit dramatic, but her heart cracked at the thought of not having Logan next to her.

He came into the bathroom, placed the lid down, and sat on the toilet as Katie straightened her hair. "Maybe. It's the work I used to do, so I have experience." Logan stood and pulled the flat iron from Katie's hand. "What are you doing?" His brow crinkled when he picked up the small section of hair that Katie had straightened.

She looked at him in the mirror. "I'm doing my hair."

"Stop. Whatever you are doing, stop." He chuckled and patted her bottom. "I love the curls."

Katie glanced at her head in the mirror. "No way, look at how frizzy it is!" She pointed to the top, where the frizzies rose in all directions. The past two days without a proper comb had worked its voodoo on her head.

Logan ran his hands through her hair. "Well, I like it curly."

She picked up a bottle of moisturizer and shook it. "I guess I can add some moisturizer to it. Normally it takes the frizz away."

Logan moved behind her and kissed her neck. "Good. Now, I am going to catch a quick nap before your father comes over. I have a feeling I'll need all of my wits for this."

Katie frowned and started working on her hair. Unfortunately, she felt the same way.

CHAPTER 29

WHEN HER DAD'S SUV pulled into the driveway, Katie felt a bit faint. She'd thought about what she was going to say and how she was going to say it.

Logan was seated on the couch with a magazine on his lap. He was this large, tatted man looking through a Cosmo. If Katie hadn't felt like she was about to puke, she'd have laughed at the humor in it. When her father knocked on the door, Katie took a deep breath and opened it.

"Hey, Dad," Katie said cheerily, but her eyes were drawn to the folder in his hand, which was stuffed with paper. Those papers could be anything, she rationalized. She knew that Logan still had her letters, so the previous fear of her father having read them was tenuous.

"Katie," he responded, stepping past her to enter. She'd never been so happy that she hadn't let Logan convince her to spill her secret in her letters. She followed her father out of the foyer and into the living room where Logan sat. Katie crossed her arms over her belly as her dad eyed Logan. Suddenly, he turned to her and handed her the folder. "I'd hoped that Teal was playing a joke, but it seems she wasn't."

She took the folder and opened it; inside were her envelopes sent to Logan with the name Kristen on the front. Katie looked up at her father, and his eyes held what she had worked her whole life to never see. His disappointment burned deep, and she didn't know what to do. She'd thought of a million things to say, she had her reasons lined up and ready to go, but as soon as her father looked at her as if he'd given up, something in Katie broke . . . and not in the way she thought it would.

She placed the folder on the table. "You and Teal have spent too much time controlling and micromanaging my life." Katie wondered if it was really their fault. After all, she'd allowed them to do it. She'd never stood up for herself, and the times she did, she acted as if her actions needed explaining when in reality they didn't. She was an adult, and even when she made choices that others didn't understand, she had wanted the support of her friends and family.

Her dad ran a hand over the back of his neck. "I'm not sure what I'm supposed to do with you. When your mother was alive, I never worried, but now?" He shook his head.

She moved to him and took his hand in both of hers. "What is it that you are worried about?" she asked.

There were many things she could guess at, but she wanted to address the more important things first.

Her dad tugged her close. "First, the lies. Teal went to the hotel looking for you, but you weren't checked in there," he motioned to Logan, who was silently waiting to be introduced, "he was. That's when she came to me." Jan-Erik palmed Katie's face. "I don't like lies. I don't like my daughter in a hotel with an ex-con, I don't like the fact that you entered the IPPP without my permission, but what I don't like the most is that you are an adult and my words don't hold as much stock as they did when you were a little girl."

Katie's eyes burned with tears and her chest ached. Her father's words meant the world to her, and she hated that her lies made him feel as if she couldn't be trusted, but the fear of letting him down was so great, she thought she'd buckle under the pressure.

"They still do, but there will be times when I don't agree and you'll have to accept that." And Katie meant it. She wanted to be in control of her life.

Her dad looked back over to Logan who stood. "I don't like this."

Katie didn't think he would.

"If I don't support it, it'll push you away, wont it?" her father asked in a resigned voice, but Katie was dazed. She thought he would take it much worse than what was happening.

"Yes, I want you to give him a chance." Katie moved away from her father and walked to Logan. "Dad, this is Logan Whyte." Logan extended his hand, but Jan-Erik only nodded.

Logan dropped his hand. "Sir."

He pointed to his daughter. "You know she's black, right?"

Mortified, Katie closed her eyes and fought the urge to curse.

Logan rubbed her back. "Yes, I noticed, sir. I can only guess you know my past and there are things you heard that happened while I was in prison." He looked down at Katie, and she offered him a sweet smile while taking Logan's hand in hers. "I fucked up plenty of times in there."

Jan-Erik scoffed. "You placed my daughter's life in danger by being affiliated with that hate group, and you place her in danger as long as you stay with her."

Katie and Logan both worried about that, but she couldn't imagine letting him go out of the simple fear that some skinheads wouldn't like it.

"No, it's not enough that I have to worry about my daughter with an ex-con, but now I have to worry that the color of her skin will get her hurt."

"I wouldn't let—"

Jan-Erik took what Katie felt was a menacing step forward. Her nerves were rattled as the situation gradually heated up. "It's not like you have control over what those hate mongers do, Mr. Whyte," he spat. "You couldn't even keep them from kicking your own face in. How the hell are you planning on protecting her?"

Logan tensed, and she knew her father was purposely rubbing salt in a still healing wound. Katie stepped forward and between the two men. She didn't think the argument would come to blows, but she hoped if both men saw her it'd stop them from arguing further. Unfortunately, she wasn't so lucky.

Logan grunted. "Sir, I was jumped," he stabbed a finger toward Jan-Erik, "in your prison. One you should have control over. I spent my whole time there doing whatever the hell I was supposed to do and I stayed out of trouble until that moment. I won't have you throwing that shit in my face."

"This is getting out of hand." Katie placed her palm on Logan's chest; his face was red and anger radiated off him. She turned to her father. "We'll handle this together, right?" She blinked rapidly, hoping to clear away the blur that was her tears. When her dad didn't answer, Katie asked again, "Right?" She turned to Logan, hoping he'd jump on board. However, when he looked at her, she wasn't so sure he cared to have her father on their side anymore.

He rubbed his stubbled jaw and took a step back. "Right," he muttered, but Katie was far from convinced.

"Dad?" she pleaded.

"What the hell kind of choices are you giving me, Katie?" her dad growled. "If I say no it'll push you away, and if I say yes I'm helping place you in danger. What exactly is it that you are asking me to do?"

Katie didn't know what it was, other than a chance to be happy without losing either Logan or her dad. "I'm just asking for you to give him a chance." When her father shook his head, she suddenly felt deflated and so damned tired.

"Okay, so now what? You'll never speak to me again?" Tears made their way down her cheeks. How the hell could he make her choose? "You'll just walk out of my life? Is that the choice you are offering me?" Katie couldn't hide the hurt in her voice. She never once believed her father would take it this far.

He reached out and pulled her into an embrace. "No, Katie. I'd die first, but I can't agree with you seeing him. I know you'll continue to, but as a father, being so damned helpless to protect your kid is a horrible feeling. You aren't the only one here who's afraid of having to sacrifice a person you love."

Katie pulled away to look at her dad. "I won't give either of you up. I can't." She placed her face in her dad's chest. She wanted both of the men in her life, and she wasn't willing to sacrifice either for the other. Katie understood her father's fears better than he even knew. She was scared to death when she had thought Aaron had her photo and address, but that still didn't squash the feelings she had for Logan, and she was sure nothing ever would.

CHAPTER 30

LOGAN OPTED TO TAKE a bus back to Kentucky to save money, and Katie let him know that it bothered her he wouldn't let her buy him a plane ticket.

"Why don't you just let me buy you the freaking ticket? It's not expensive, and you'll get there faster."

Katie and Logan stood at the bus station. It was too late even if Logan changed his mind. He had his ticket in his hand, but more so he was sure that if he went back to Katie's, he'd never be able to leave the state.

Threading his hands through her hair, he tilted her head back. "No." He placed a kiss on her forehead, cheeks, chin, and then to her pouty lips. Logan hated to leave. Her relationship with her father was shaky, and she wouldn't even return Teal's phone calls. Logan was worried that Katie was placing her friendship with the girl in jeopardy.

In the week he'd had spent with her, he could tell that Katie was a little hermit. She was content in his arms on the couch all day long. Logan never considered himself one to soak in a tub, but Katie often had him in there with her until the water turned cold.

At first, he thought it was Katie's way of spending time with him before he left for Kentucky, but soon Logan realized she had a total of one close friend, and her father. Her phone never rang unless it was her agent or editor, she never had visitors unless it was a package from Amazon—he had to admit he was a little annoyed with the delivery guy's flirting—and Katie never wanted to do anything outside. Granted it was still chilly, but Logan vowed to get her out of the house in May when he came back.

"Fine, remember you have one week, seven days, and however many hours are in a week to come back, and that includes the two day travel time. Or I will come get you."

He nodded. "It might not even take that long." He was sure it would take about six days total, but he didn't tell her he'd planned to either fly or take the train back. Logan had been locked up for eight years, so he didn't mind traveling the East Coast by bus.

"What have you decided to tell Trent about me?" She ducked her head away, apprehensive about him telling Trent his girlfriend was black.

Logan was nervous because just as Katie was torn regarding her dad, he didn't want to have to choose between Katie and Trent. Even though he would always choose love over hate, he still had a hard time with the thought of his best friend not accepting Katie. "I'm going to tell him I fell in love with you long before I'd ever seen you, and when I found out you were black, I acted like an asshole until I realized you were the one." He moved his hands down Katie's back and rested them over the swell of her ass. "I'll tell him the truth."

"You'll tell him love is color blind?" Her brow arched.

"Something like that." Logan wasn't sure he could convince Trent of that; Trent was set in his ways and had always hated any race that wasn't his own.

"You don't have to convince him of anything, Logan." She peeked around him as the announcer called his bus number. "All you have to do is let him know that you are happy, and if he is really your friend, he'll be happy for you whether he approves or not."

Logan felt the same way about Katie's friend Teal, but in that area he kept his mouth shut. Walking with Katie to his bus, he stopped next to it and kissed her goodbye. He watched as she waited for the bus to pull away before he turned around. For some reason, she seemed concerned that he would take longer than a week, but Logan only planned to get his inheritance, and talk to Trent and a few old friends. It would probably take him less than four days if he flew back. He and Trent didn't have much to catch up on since they'd kept in touch over the past eight years.

ARRIVING AT THE STATION in Kentucky, Logan was tired and annoyed. His quiet East Coast bus ride was supposed to be relaxing, but thanks to a man named Donald and his twenty-year-old girlfriend, Logan spent more than half of the time pretending to be asleep or answering questions about his tattoos. The twenty-four hour trip had all but guaranteed he'd be buying a plane ticket back.

Logan hoped off the bus and headed to the parking lot in search of Trent. He wasn't sure if the man had gotten his truck back, so Logan scanned the parking lot, spotting him leaning against an old, yellow pick-up truck. Though it'd been eight years and Trent had come up to visit him a few times, Logan was surprised by how much his friend had changed. He'd grown his hair out, gained more muscle than Logan, and had twice as many tattoos, giving him a full sleeve on both arms and a few tattoos on his neck. When Logan reached him, Trent moved off the truck and engulfed him in a manly, but welcoming hug.

"About time," Trent said as he pulled back. "I've been out here waitin' for your ass," he joked.

Logan jerked his head at the truck, and tossed his bag in the bed. "What's with this piece of shit?"

Trent kicked the tire. "I told you that crazy-ass bitch took my Dodge. I swear, if I could kick her ass without ending up in jail I would." Trent laughed, but Logan raised a brow.

"You've never laid a hand on a woman, and even if you could without consequence, you wouldn't," he said as he opened the passenger side door. He knew Trent and the women he dated. All of them were the kind that were used to getting slapped around, but never by Trent.

"Nah, shit ain't worth it. Plus, you know I love me some little short women, too. I'm too damned big to be pushin' 'em around." Trent jumped in the driver's seat and started the rough sounding truck.

Logan listened to the struggling engine as it roared to life, and heard a knocking noise. "That sounds like a clogged air filter, or you need a damned tune-up." He listened carefully as they headed down the road. "Although, it could be the timing is set improperly. I'd have to get under the hood and look at it."

His buddy waved off his concerns for the truck. "What I want to hear about is why it took you two whole weeks to get down here, and who is this new girl you met?" Trent glanced at Logan in disapproval. "Is it that bitch that sent you looking for weed?"

"Hell no," Logan grumbled. "Someone new." He hadn't meant to sound elusive, but he was waiting for a better moment to confide in him about Katie. Trent had never expressed hate for just one race. Gang violence had taken his father's life, and Trent had attributed that to the fact that illegal immigration was on the rise. There was also something about a girl in his past, but Trent never explained more than a few words like, *"never trust 'em"* or *"they'll take your pride then run and hide."* He'd taught Logan every racist word there ever was, and even though Trent seldom threw them around, there were times when he did and Logan wasn't interested in the backlash that would cause between him and Katie.

"Someone new, eh?" Trent scratched his scruffy beard. "The girl you were calling on the phone?"

Logan glanced over at him. He hadn't told Trent about Katie, and now he was searching his memory for any information he could have let slip.

Trent reached over and slapped Logan on the back. "I'm just guessing. You needed a big ass credit for your phone bill, and I don't know many men who sit around all day chattin' it up with other men on the phone." Trent took a sharp turn. "Except maybe them gays."

"It's a woman." Logan felt the need to set the situation straight.

Trent laughed. "I bet she is." His laughter faded and he got serious. "So, you want to head by the shop and see the job I got lined up for you when your PO gets you the waiver to move back?" He was at a light. If he went straight, Logan knew it'd take him to Trent's, and with a right turn they'd end at Lou's Automotive Repair. Trent's hand hovered over the turn signal.

Logan shook his head. "Nah, man. I'm good for now."

Trent tapped the steering wheel and said, "So, home it is."

He didn't have the heart to tell Trent that he was about to create a new home.

After waiting for the light to change, Trent spoke. "Logan, you planning on living with me or getting your own place?"

He thought for a moment. "What if I told you I planned on going back to Vermont?"

"I'd tell your ass there ain't nuttin' up there for you," Trent huffed. "You got a place to stay and a job here, and if this is about that girl, tell her to come and visit for a while."

"For a while," Logan repeated. "I have to tell you, man, it's more serious than that." He had already made his choice.

"Yeah." Trent threw one hand over the back of the seat, and continued driving with the other. "So was the chick that got you locked up, and the one before, who lied and said she was pregnant to try and scam you out of three hundred dollars for an "abortion". Oh, and don't forget about the one who said she didn't have the clap." Trent glanced at Logan for a second, then turned his eyes back to the road. "Need I go on?"

Nope, he got the message loud and clear. "Point taken, and I never slept with that one with the clap." He rolled his window down and propped his elbow on it. He thought of Katie in the morning when they woke up; her hair in a sexy disarray of curls on her head, the sweet noises she made as she stretched her limbs, and the blood-boiling kisses she placed on his tattoos to wake him up. Logan knew she was different, and while he didn't have to convince Trent, he wanted to try. "What if I told you this one was different?"

"Ha! What if I told you that I've heard that from you before?" Trent thumped the steering wheel again. "And what always ends up happening?"

"Not this time. This woman doesn't need me in her life, but she accepts me in it." Trent's laughter started to piss Logan off.

"Sentimental fuck," he muttered. "And it always gets you into trouble. Always. Last time it got you locked up. What the hell, Logan? Drugs? You don't even smoke cigarettes, and you took some chick to pick up weed?"

As Trent's voice rose, so did Logan's temper. "I don't need the goddamned lecture. How do you feel about that? I served my time, and now we won't bring it up again, agreed . . ." It wasn't a question, and the tone of Logan's voice was a friendly reminder that he wasn't playing around.

Trent sucked his tongue. "You know I only say this shit 'cause it's true. If it wasn't, I'd keep my fuckin' mouth shut."

Logan didn't agree or disagree, and as Trent's house came into view, he turned to him and punched him in the shoulder, causing the car to swerve.

"Fuck, man!" Trent bellowed good-naturedly. He pulled into the driveway and turned the engine off. Turning to Logan, he said, "Just think about it, man. You have a life here—a place to stay and a steady income. Don't fuck that up over some chick in another state." Trent decked Logan in the arm with a powerful—yet playful—punch, and then jumped out of the truck.

Shit hurt like hell. "Dick!" he called after Trent, who threw a middle finger up over his shoulder, heading up the driveway and into the house.

Logan got out of the truck and grabbed his bag from the back. While Trent was right about him having a steady job and a place to stay here, small piece of shit town that it was, he was wrong about Katie. He had a few days to convince Trent to give her a chance . . . because whether Trent liked or accepted it, Logan would be leaving to start a life in Vermont with Katie.

CHAPTER 31

LOGAN WOKE UP TO screaming. Having been in jail for the last eight years, waking up to screaming, yells, or the occasional moaning wasn't unusual. However, Logan wasn't in jail; he was asleep on a cot in Trent's extra room. The sounds of a screaming woman had awakened him, so he stood and went to the door. Trent was coming around the corner with a big pot of what Logan thought was water. His mind was fuzzy with sleep and he was confused.

He momentarily froze, and then kept walking to the door, ranting, "Got a phone call from the cops. They found my truck at the park, but no bitch in sight. Seems like she walked here and wants to raise hell about the warrant on her ass." Trent chuckled, and Logan came out of the room to see what he was up to. "Crazy bitch!" He screamed as he went to unlatch the door.

Logan ran to him and placed his hand over the latch. He shook his head no; it was more to clean the cobwebs of sleep from his brain, but he'd meant the "no" part, too. "What the hell, man?" He glanced at the pot in Trent's hands and saw that it was water.

"It's three a.m. and that psycho ass bitch is banging on my windows, tellin' my neighbors I'm a pig. What the fuck do you mean, 'what the hell?'" Trent's voice lowered. "I swear, if she doesn't leave I'm callin' the damned cops," he raised it again at the door, and Logan was sure Trent wanted his ex, Shayla, to hear, "and have them drag her fat ass off to jail."

The flurry of curse words hurled at the front door from Shayla had Logan cringing. He wasn't sure why Trent had called her fat. While Shayla wasn't thin, she wasn't fat, and if Logan recalled right—and he did—Trent liked his girls on the plump side.

He cleared his throat. "How about you let me handle this?" Logan said, regretting the words as soon as they'd left his mouth. He didn't want to get involved, but wanted to go back to sleep, and if Trent doused Shayla with water, that'd never happen.

Trent sobered up a bit and lowered his hand from the latch. "Tell her to get the fuck out of here," he said. Turning his back to Logan, he headed back to his bedroom, and placed the pot on the floor outside of his door.

Logan unlatched the door and slowly opened it. "Shay, you out there?" he called. She was probably waiting around the corner with a rock in hand, ready to pelt Trent in the skull first chance she got.

"Logan? That you?" Shayla called in an awestruck tone.

"Yeah, Shay, it's me." Logan opened the door further. "Can I come out there without getting my ass kicked?" he asked, and wasn't entirely sure if he were joking or not. He'd never called Shay a crazy bitch like Trent had, but he'd thought it on a regular basis.

Her girlish giggle belied her crazy ass ways. "Yes, Logan. Get your ass out here. It's been too damned long."

Logan carefully pushed the door open and eyed her. He placed a sexy smile on his face to hopefully discourage her from bum rushing the door. "Hey." He opened it further to make room for his big body, ducking his head as he stepped outside.

She was standing on the porch with her hands on her hips. Logan looked at her face to see ruby red lips in a smile and her long, blonde hair in a braid over her shoulder. He thought back to when he'd first met her, and compared her to a Coca Cola bottle. She had a full chest, hips, and ass. She was sexy as hell, and Logan didn't have a hard time understanding why Trent had put up with her shit for so long.

Shayla's eyes widened and she gave him a once over. "Shit, Logan. When'd you get so damned big?" She moved closer and placed a hand on his bicep.

Logan glanced down, just then realizing that he hadn't put a shirt on.

Shayla squeezed and caressed his arm. "And all of these new tattoos. I don't remember seeing these on you before you went away."

He didn't know what she was talking about; he'd had the same ones when he left as he did now. Logan moved away. "I've always had these, but let's talk about what we can do to get all this settled." He softened his voice. "Shay, I'm tired and I need to sleep."

Shayla batted her eyes playfully. "Logan, from where I'm standing you don't need any beauty sleep."

Before Logan could speak or even push her away, Trent burst through the door.

"You damn stupid slut!" He barged past Logan. "See? This is why I can't stand you. Logan doesn't want your slutty ass," Trent growled. He turned to Logan. "I got this, brother." Patting him on the back, he took Shayla's arm and guided her away from the house.

Logan looked to a seething Shayla, and realized there was nothing he could do to help and he really didn't want to. What he wanted to do was call Katie. She was an hour ahead him, but he still needed to hear her voice. Logan went inside and picked up the phone. He knew Trent had long distance on his plan, so he dialed Katie's number and waited.

Her sleepy voice made him long for her. "Hello?"

"Hey, baby." Logan heard the rustling of sheets as she shifted on the bed.

Unease filled her voice. "What's wrong, baby? Why are you calling so late or early or whatever?"

Logan felt like an ass for making her worry. "Nothing, I just needed to hear your voice and tell you how much I missed you," he said honestly.

Her voice lightened. "You are such a softie. My big two hundred and twenty pound bear is missing his baby, huh?"

He sure as shit was, although he wouldn't admit it to anyone else. Katie made him feel like his soft side was her favorite side, unless they were in bed. He smiled at the thought. "Yeah, sorry I woke you."

Her voice held a hint of annoyance as she said, "You should be sorry you didn't call to let me know you'd arrived in one piece!"

"Babe, I'm sorry, but I got to talking with Trent. Then some of the boys came over and we drank a little." Logan didn't explain what happened because Katie demanded it, but because he was truly sorry that he'd made her worry.

"Okay, but you'll have to make it up to me when you come home." The word home sent heat up his back. He wanted to think of Vermont with her as his home, a place he was welcome and a place where he'd keep his woman safe and happy.

"Oh, I will." The front door opened and Trent stormed in. Logan glanced up and saw his face was contorted in anger, and if he were any other man, he'd be worried about Shay's safety.

"That bitch wants to stay the night. Can you believe that?" Trent sounded outraged, but disappeared down the hallway . . . only to come back with an armful of sheets and a pillow. He threw it on the couch by Logan. "Bitch thinks she can lick my dick and flick my balls and all is forgiven." He headed to the door. "Hell no! She burned her bridge when she stole my girl." He slammed the door on his way out.

"Uh . . . so I guess that was Trent?" Katie asked.

"Yeah, that was him." Logan went silent.

"Sounds . . . *charming*," Katie said sardonically. "So, did I hear that right? His girl stole his girl?"

He chuckled. "The first girl, Shayla, stole his truck, his other girl." Katie's silence, and then laughter, made him laugh as well. "Yep, she stole it and now he's ready to dump her." Logan didn't think that'd happen. She'd come in and weasel her way back into his life like she always did.

"And now she wants to, and I quote, 'lick his dick and flick his balls?'" Katie clarified.

Logan burst into laughter. Hearing his woman repeat the words made him forget the turbulent relationship between Trent and Shayla, and smile at their own semi stress-free relationship.

Katie lowered her voice into a sexy whisper that had Logan's dick twitching. "Baby, if I licked your dick and flicked your balls, would all be forgiven?"

Without hesitation Logan said, "Hell yes."

Instantly, Katie burst into a fit of giggles.

Shayla and Trent's voices were at the front door, and Logan didn't want Katie to hear the crap he was sure would come from her mouth. "Baby, I'll call you tomorrow, okay?"

Disappointment flooded her tone. "Okay. Bye, baby."

More than anything, he wanted to tell her exactly how he wanted her to do the things she had just said she'd do, but as the doorknob turned. Instead, he said, "Love you, baby."

Hanging up the phone, Logan stood and adjusted his crotch as he headed back to the bedroom. Trent and Shayla's voices followed him down the hall, and he shut his door. He didn't think he'd be able to sleep even if they were quiet.

The thought of Katie home alone, in bed—coupled with her sexy words—had him hard and aching for her touch. After turning the lock for privacy, Logan lay back down on the bed and shoved a hand under his basketball shorts, grasping his dick. With his other hand, he pulled the shorts down just beneath his balls.

Logan had masturbated a few times in prison, but the lack of privacy had taken away the urge, and oftentimes left him with a case of blue balls. But not tonight. Licking his hand, he rubbed the moisture on his shaft and started to pump hard. He worked his cock over, sliding up and down, again and again, until his breaths came in ragged pants and his hips rose from the cot.

Closing his eyes, he thought of Katie in those tiny black panties she loved to wear. Her skin had been so warm when he pulled those panties off and nestled between her legs. Logan could almost taste her and smell her sweet scent. Using his other hand, he pinched his nipple a couple times, before traveling downward to tug his sac.

A zing of pleasure raced up his spine and caused his ass to clench. Logan was close, and never had he wanted a feeling to last forever more than he did now, imagining his baby's warm body engulfing his shaft, her tight sheath stretching over his skin and her soft moans in his ear.

Logan let out a gruff moan as warm liquid coated his hand, slickening his grasp. With another few pumps, his body jerked and thick jets of come shot all over his lower abdomen. Heart pounding, he fought to catch his breath. Again and again he pumped until his body shook and he'd gone dry.

Looking at his spent cock, Logan vowed the first thing he would do when he got home was show Katie how very much he'd missed her.

CHAPTER 32

KATIE WAS BORED...MORE like bored as hell. With Logan gone, her book finished, her father barely speaking to her, and Teal's apology was neither desired nor required, she didn't have a damned thing to do with herself. It was May, the sun was shining and the birds were chirping while Katie sat in her house, counting the days until Logan's return. She felt pathetic, and at this point she was. Katie stood and stretched her limbs. She didn't need a man to keep her busy, although she loved how Logan kept her busy. Katie blushed at the thought.

"Maybe I'll get my hair done," she said to the empty room. Katie patted her head. She didn't need anything done to it, so she skipped that idea. Her stomach growled, and at that, she decided to go to Mel's.

Normally, she'd meet her father there for lunch, and the urge to call him hit her like a freight train in the chest. Katie almost sat back down, but the thought of missing Logan and moping around the house was too much. She headed toward the door and grabbed her phone, keys, and a light jacket.

In the car, Katie turned on the radio and headed to the bistro. Her stomach growled again, and she tried to remember the last full meal she'd had. As an author, oftentimes she'd snack the entire day as she spent hours in front of her laptop. Pecking on snacks from chips to dried fruit kept her need for a full meal at bay, adding hours of more writing time to her schedule. It was an unhealthy, silly habit, but it worked. Minutes later, Katie pulled into the bistro and parked. Her mind on food, and food only, Katie tunnel-visioned it to a table inside and sat down.

"Katie?" her father's voice called. She glanced up quickly to see her father one table over.

"Dad?"

He narrowed his eyes in what looked like confusion. "Forget me already?" he asked with a smile. Katie's heart melted and she stood, heading toward her father's table.

"No, I haven't." She sat down in front of him.

His eyes brightened. "Good! Join me for lunch, please."

Katie looked around and signaled a waitress. She wasn't sure if she was waiting tables in the section she was sitting in, but she didn't care. The waitress came over, pen and pad ready.

"Turkey club with asiago cheese and a water please." She glanced at her father for his order.

"Club sandwich and a Caesar salad, please."

She and her dad never got menus. Even though it seemed the servers changed week to week, the food and its quality remained the same, and for that she was grateful.

"When were you going to call me back?" Katie asked. She'd called her father twice, and his secretary had said he was in meetings. Her father wasn't one to use avoidance as a tactic, so she believed he was truly busy at work.

"When I had a chance to break away," he answered.

Katie looked around. "This seems like you've broken away." She pinned him with an icy glare. "You've never avoided me before, but it seems like times have changed." Katie was hurt and confused.

"I'm sorry, Katie. I didn't know that I'd moved, changed my cell number, or made myself totally unreachable." He retorted.

Duly chastised, Katie backed down. She didn't want to admit it, but she hadn't tried to reach her father as hard as she could have. "Sorry, I miss you."

Her dad huffed. "You are the one who has isolated yourself in that house with that man, so if you miss me, it's of your own accord. You know where I am, Katie." He looked away from her. "This is ridiculous," he murmured.

"Excuse me? What is ridiculous?"

He turned back to her with his own cold scowl. "This isolation you want to blame on the world when it's your own fault. You want me to treat you like an adult, but you act like a petulant child when you don't get your way."

Katie wasn't sure whether to be offended or angry, so she opted for both. "Petulant?" She shook her head in disbelief. "I don't even know how to respond to that." Heartbroken, she wanted to leave, wanted to get up and pretend that this day never happened, but that solved nothing and she couldn't leave it this way.

"Dad," his eyes softened at the word, "I need you to give Logan a chance. Let him screw up before you judge him." Katie was only asking her father to do what he'd taught her to do. "I love him."

"Oh, Katie." Her father seemed to be at his wits end, and Katie couldn't blame him. He reached past his ice water and took her hand in hers.

Tears forming and fleeing from her eyes, she repeated her words and poured every bit of truth into them. "Please, Dad. Just give us a chance." Her dad caressed her fingers and pulled her hand to his lips for a sweet kiss.

Releasing her, he reached and ran his hands through her hair, ruffling the bone straight locks. "If he—I swear."

Katie smiled. He was softening.

"I can't guarantee a damned thing, but, baby girl, I love you and losing you would kill me." Her dad's eyes glistened.

She felt her heart break for what she was putting him through. However, Katie wouldn't give up . . . not on Logan, or her father.

LOGAN SAT AT TRENT'S computer and stared at his new account balance. His Aunt Elma had left him twenty grand. Combined with Logan's ten grand, he was sitting in a nice position to start his own shop back in Vermont. He'd called Katie earlier that afternoon to learn she'd personally vouched for him with Howard, and had gotten him a job just doing oil changes until Howard felt comfortable allowing him to do anything else.

A ruckus from the other room made Logan log out of his account and turn off the screen.

Shayla entered the room in a pair of shorts and a bikini top, which couldn't support the weight of her cleavage. "Logan, Trent wants help out on the grill." She handed him a beer and perched on the edge of the desk beside him. She sat with her legs open and her back bent.

Logan wished she'd save the show for someone else, but the last thing he wanted to do was call her out and start an argument between her and Trent. He used his keys to pop the cap. "Oh yeah?" he asked, and took a swig.

Shayla bit her lip and nodded.

Logan supposed it was meant to be sexy, but it just came off as needy. What kind of woman flirted with her ex's best friend? "I'm more than positive Trent can handle burning coals and meat all on his own."

Shayla leaned back even further, and he was surprised she hadn't fallen over yet. "Good, he can handle that 'cause I got a question for you."

Damn. Please be something reasonable. He could imagine Katie's reaction to this ludicrous display of flirting. Logan took another sip of the beer. "What's up?" he asked, trying to sound as casual as possible. He didn't want her thinking he was flirting with her.

Shayla lowered her voice and whispered, "The other night, were you and," she pointed at his lap, "hand-jelina going at it?" With a smirk, she eyed his crotch.

Logan was too damn old to be ashamed of masturbating. He'd abused his dick on a regular basis as a teen, and was sure as fuck not reluctant to admit to it now. The issue was, it wasn't Shayla's business what he did, or didn't do, to his dick.

He stood and headed to the door. "Shay . . ." He shook his head. While searching for the right words to set her ass straight, he had paused too long.

She hopped off the desk, sliding past him and out of the room. "It's okay, Logan. I heard every bit of it." She winked before leaving.

He blew out a frustrated breath. Between Shayla flirting with him and Trent trying to convince him to leave Katie, Logan was planning on shortening his trip. He headed down the hall and out the back door to see Shayla and Trent laughing. Trent's head popped up when Logan made it to the plastic table and chairs he'd set up earlier.

"Shayla told me she was ribbing you about beatin' your meat." Trent popped her hard on the ass and smiled when she let out what sounded like a delighted squeal. He flipped a burger, and pulled a few pieces of barbeque chicken off the grill.

Logan eyed Shayla. "Your walls weren't so thin when I left," he said. He suspected Shayla had had her ear pressed against the door.

Trent looked away from the grill and to Shayla. "They aren't." Trent eyed her until her smile disappeared. "Logan, you want some slaw?"

He stood and grabbed a plate, wondering how long Trent would put up with Shayla and her crazy ass ways. Either way, he wouldn't be around long enough to find out. He took his half empty beer bottle and plate to the table to eat.

Trent picked up another plate, but froze mid-action. Logan watched as he turned to Shayla. "Will you go get us some more beers, Shay?" he asked.

Logan was shocked she didn't put up a bit of a fight. As soon as she left, Trent sat in front of him. Setting his fork down, Logan gave him his full attention.

"You going back to Vermont?"

His answer came quick. "Yes." Then he chortled. "Why, you planning on coming with me?"

Trent seemed to think over Logan's question. Logan was both petrified and excited by that scenario. He was positive his friend wouldn't last more than a few month's during Vermont's winter. On top of that, Logan's black girlfriend would have him thinking Logan was insane, and he was . . . insanely in love.

Standing, Trent went back to the grill. "Nah, I just hope you're making the right decision." He plated some food as Shayla came out with the beers. "What time you want me to take you to the airport tomorrow?"

He wasn't sure whom Trent was talking to, until he looked directly at Logan when he glanced up.

"Huh?" he and Shayla said at the same time. "What are you yapping about?" Logan added.

Trent sat down with a plate and Shayla placed the beers in front of them. "You've been distracted." He shoveled some food in his mouth.

Logan searched his friend's eyes for anger, but was met with understanding.

"And this bitch," he pointed his fork toward Shayla, "can't keep on her pants when it comes to you." Shayla smacked him on the back of his head and Trent shrugged. "Hell, the truth is the truth."

And it sure as hell was. Logan would miss Trent, but before he left, he needed to confide in him. He thought to ask Shayla to leave, but he really wasn't interested in her opinion, nor did he care what she thought about Katie's race.

Logan placed the fork down. "Her name is Katie."

Trent nodded. "Nice name."

"Normal name," Shayla added, her tone full of jealousy, but Logan ignored it.

He watched Trent as the next words came out of his mouth. "She's black."

Shayla laughed, as if he'd told a joke, and he guessed with his past, it'd seem like one. However, neither he nor Trent laughed.

Trent placed his fork down and leaned back. When he spoke, his voice had hardened. "Every now and then a man is gonna want some chocolate, you get my drift? But we don't go having serious relations with them."

This was the response Logan figured he'd get.

Shayla came to the table and sat down. "Shut the fuck up, you're not serious are you?" She sat wide-eyed, her blonde hair moving in the wind as she glanced between Trent and Logan.

"Yeah, Logan. You're joking, right?" Trent's voice changed again. "You ain't fucking thinkin' about leaving here for no black bitch, are you?"

Logan had the sudden urge to make Trent swallow his words and his teeth, but he sat back and calmed his nerves. "Don't call her that," was all that he could utter.

Trent smirked. "What'd prison do to you?" he asked. Slanting his head, he eyed Logan as if he'd grown two heads.

Shayla smacked her lips. "Nah, Logan. That shit ain't right." She pushed back from the table and headed into the house.

Still, Trent watched Logan.

"It is what it is," Logan stated, unsure of what else to say.

"Yeah, it is. Go on to her. I want to say you won't have a place here to come back to, but here's what I'll do . . ." Trent took a long drink from his beer. "When that shit fails, you can come home and I'll piss the words *told you so* all over the backyard."

Logan thought about defending his choice, but what would it matter? He didn't need Trent to approve. He placed his elbows on the table. "And if it doesn't come to that? If Katie and I make it work?"

Trent mulled over Logan's words, but smiled. "It won't, brother. It won't." Trent stood and picked up his plate. “Get yourself a flight for tomorrow. Quicker I get you to Vermont, the faster I get you back here like a dog with his tail between his legs.” Trent walked into the house, and Logan couldn’t help but think that it’d gone too well.

CHAPTER 33

LOGAN FLEW BACK. MINUS a few hiccups, he was on his flight and back to Katie. Even though the bus trip was a shitty experience, so was the damned plane. First, Logan's flight was delayed due to maintenance issues, causing him to miss his connecting flight. He ended up having to wait four hours for the next flight. Then, Logan lost his damn ID in his luggage and almost missed his second flight.

Now, boarded and in his seat, Logan leaned his head back and closed his eyes. Since he was flying Southwestern, there were no assigned seats, but the back hadn't packed out. He hoped the last few passengers would skip past him and move to another seat. While a few eyed his empty seat with interest, only a small-framed, pale faced, brown-haired girl was brave enough to join him. She didn't speak, and Logan was glad. She pushed her carry-on under the seat in front of her and opened her book to read.

Logan opened the slider to the window and gazed out. The weather seemed nice enough that he wasn't worried about it affecting take off, and Logan watched as the baggage handlers carelessly threw luggage on the conveyor leading to the plane. Luckily, he didn't have anything valuable in there other than an old bottle of Kentucky Whiskey.

"Shit," he groused.

"You got something important in there?" The girl's voice pulled his eyes from the window. She was staring in the same direction he was when he cursed.

Logan glanced back and said, "No." It wasn't a lie; the whiskey didn't mean much to him, but he did want to share it with Katie when he got back home. Home. He was starting to enjoy that word.

"You sure?" the girl asked again. Logan looked back at her. She wasn't a girl, she was a woman . . . just very small and petite with a tattered notebook in her hand, pen in place over the page. She'd already written some words in it, but Logan couldn't make them out. Her thin limbs and frail-like body probably had men running the other way her whole life, but when Logan looked up at her face, he saw bright eyes and a welcoming smile.

He adjusted himself in the small seat to turn his body toward her. "No, nothing at all. You?" he asked. Making small talk wasn't his thing, but Logan had loosened up. He'd bought an iPod and headphones in

Kentucky, which he could use as a sign that the conversation was over if he needed.

Casually, she said, "My meds are in there, but I won't need them until tomorrow. My guitar is in there, too."

His eyes widened. "You sing?" Logan hadn't meant to make is sound like that, as if he were surprised or something.

She closed the notebook, and lifted it in the air a bit. "Yup, my words, my heart and my soul, are all in this little notebook. I have a gig coming up soon and I'm kinda stuck on this song I'm writing." Her nose wrinkled in annoyance.

Logan nodded. He couldn't help her with that. "What's your name?" he extended in greeting.

"Call me E, and you?"

Logan took her small hand in his and gently shook it. "Logan."

E's nose scrunched up and she pulled her hand back. "That was the weakest hand shake I have ever received from a guy your size."

Logan laughed. "I was trying not to crush your hand." He peeked down at her long, slim fingers.

"Oh, I see. I look weak to you?" She raised a brow.

Logan wondered if he'd offended her until she cracked a smile.

"Where are you headed, Logan?" She lifted a leg and tucked the notebook under it.

"Home." Logan loved the way the word sounded and everything it meant. He and Katie were creating a life together and he was itching to get home to her.

E poked him. “Ah, I know that look. You are headed home to your woman, yeah?” He nodded. “Awesome.” Her voice took on a soft tone. E turned back to her notebook and started to write.

Reaching into his pocket, Logan pulled out his headphones. The flight attendant came on the overhead with her announcement, and as the plane pushed backwards, Logan closed his eyes, listening to the attendant list the emergency exits and yadda yadda . . . He was asleep before that plane even took off.

LOGAN FOUND HIS BAGS at the carousel and headed out the double doors. Katie was walking toward him, just as he opened them. At that moment, she looked up and squealed, and took off at a run. He dropped his bags and caught her as she flew into his arms and buried her head into his neck.

While Logan was excited to see Katie, he felt as if he was being watched. In order to not alarm her, he kissed her cheek and casually checked out their surroundings. Logan’s eyes landed on a black man standing not ten feet away from them. He kept his eyes on the man even as Katie pulled away and placed her lips on his.

Katie moved back and reached for his face. “Babe, what’s up?” He looked down at her, and his face must have set off alarms in her head. She appeared panicked and nervous. “What is it?”

Logan closed his eyes and shook his head. “Nothing, baby, that flight messed me up,” he lied. Glancing over at the man again, Logan noticed that he was still staring in their direction. *What the fuck was he looking at?*

Katie's eyes still held worry as she took his light carry-on. Grabbing his hand, she started to lead him to the car. "You're acting odd. Is everything okay back home?" she asked, but Logan wasn't paying attention. They were walking past the man who had been staring at them . . . no, who was *still* staring at them and it was pissing him off. Why was this motherfucker eyeing him? Was it 'cause he was white and with a black woman? As they got closer, Logan had it in his mind to ask the man.

As they approached, the man stood and Logan lunged forward. "What the fuck you been staring at?" Logan yelled. His heart beat heavy in his chest; he was used to stares like that leading to fights. No one needed to be staring at him and Katie for so fucking long. The man shrank back, and Katie jumped in front of Logan, her face marred with lines of confusion and then anger.

"What the hell?" she whispered. She turned and was about to go to the man, who had moved so far back Logan wondered how he'd gotten there so quickly. Logan's arm darted out and grabbed Katie's, yanking her back to him harder than he'd planned to, which caused her to trip over her feet and land in his chest. Logan moved his hand to grab her again, but he was trying to right her this time.

Katie snatched away from him. Her eyes blazed with anger and her chest rose and fell rapidly. She turned away from him and marched over to the man cowering.

Logan thrust his hand through his hair as Katie spoke to him. He realized he might have overreacted—okay, he did overreact—but who the hell was that man and did she know him? He assumed not as he watched her awkward posture. When she reached out and touched the man soothingly on the shoulder, Logan's anger exploded again.

"Katie!" Logan bellowed. The man raised his hands in surrender and headed off in the other direction. When she turned around there was fire in her eyes. With each step she took toward him, his anger grew as well. Other passengers had gathered around, eyes on the couple, and as Katie made her approach, Logan's anger crested.

Her voice quavered, and he could tell that she was on the verge of tears. "Who the fuck do you think you are?" Her body was taut with fury, her eyes tearing in anger or sadness. "I don't even know what to say."

Logan stepped forward reaching for her.

"Don't you even think about hurting me again," she hissed. The words shocked Logan out of anger.

"Hurt you?" He took a deep breath and stepped back. Her hands were out in front of her, demanding space, and Logan's brain finally registered what he'd done when he glanced at his fingerprints forming on her skin. "Fuck!" He pushed his fingers through his hair and gritted his teeth. "Who was that guy?" he demanded. Logan still felt as if he needed to defend his actions. "He was staring at us like he fuckin' wanted to do something."

However, she was shaking her head and walking away. Logan took a second to catch his breath before he picked up his shit off the ground and followed her to the car. He let her have all of the space she wanted; not just for her benefit, but because he was so pissed he was scared he'd say something he wouldn't be able to take back. Katie clicked the FOB and popped the trunk. After Logan threw his stuff in the back, he got in the front seat.

It was still chilly outside, and Logan reached up to adjust the heat. Katie kept her eyes on the road, yet he kept his eyes on her. What was she thinking? He thought to ask, but was she even speaking to him? He sat back and watched the road. It was a thirty minute drive from the airport, and Logan thought that time would help him cool down, but all it did was give his anger and insecurities time to grow and fester.

He wondered if the man was a boyfriend from the past, if he was staring at Katie because he wanted her, or was he staring to ask her out? Did he think she needed a black man over Logan's hillbilly ass? The fact that Katie had gone to him and not stood by her man had pissed him off. He grunted at the thought.

Katie's eyes left the road and narrowed in question. "What was that?"

Logan rolled his neck, listening as it popped. The tension loved to make a home in his neck and shoulders. "Oh, now you fuckin' speak?" His tone was sharp and mocking.

He watched as Katie's hands tightened on the steering wheel. "Fuck you, Logan! Do not act as if I am the one in the wrong here! You did this, and why? I want to know why?"

"Why what? Why did I ask that guy why he was staring at me like he had a fuckin' issue? I saw his shady ass as soon as we walked out the door, Katie. I stay aware of my surroundings. The better question is why the fuck did you go over there and comfort that man in the first place!" Logan's voice echoed throughout the car. When he looked at Katie, he saw in her eyes what he'd hoped he'd never see again.

KATIE'S GRIP ON THE steering wheel tightened even more. Logan's face changed as his rage grew; it reddened and his jaw clenched. She had a hard time concentrating on the road with him beside her.

As his anger grew, her fear of him grew as well. Her stomach dropped and Katie fought the urge to cry. She wouldn't show him that weakness, she refused to, and when she got the nerve, she planned to tell him that if he ever touched her that way again, she beat him with a brick. Her arm throbbed from his earlier crushing grip, and her heart and head ached as well. Maybe she had made a mistake.

Katie swallowed nervously. "Did you happen to see the outfit that man was wearing?"

Logan looked at her. His face crumpled in confusion. "What?"

They were about four minutes from her house, and Katie was thinking of dropping Logan off at a hotel and spending the evening alone. She was livid, hurt, and she hated to say it, but a bit afraid. "The black guy." She glanced over at him. "Did you see that he was wearing a chauffeur's uniform?" Katie had talked to the man. His uniform had a yellow and black emblem on it, indicating that he worked for Goldman's chauffeur service. The man was only coming toward Logan because he thought he was his client.

Logan shrugged. "No, I didn't see that. I was just looking at his beady little eyes." His clipped tone incensed her even more. Katie pulled up to the house. How was she supposed to tell him she didn't feel comfortable with him around her tonight? She was amazed by the feeling herself because even when she'd met him fresh out of prison, she'd not once worried about him yelling at her or hurting her the way he did earlier. Logan was out of the car and at the back in seconds, but Katie just sat there. Finally, when he noticed that she wasn't out of the car, he walked around to her window and tapped it.

Katie pushed the button and the window rolled down. She didn't look at him as he leaned in.

"What now?"

Her anger flared. "He was a *chauffeur.* He thought you were his client, who happens to be a tattoo artist coming here for a convention, and then driving to Canada." She finally looked at him. "But all you saw was some black guy looking at you, huh?"

Logan didn't speak, nor did he look the least bit ashamed of his actions. Katie felt like an idiot. What kind of self-respecting black woman . . . no, what kind of woman would accept these actions from the man she was dating?

"I saw a man—" He paused and stared at her hard, his lips in a grim line.

"Say it, Logan. You saw what?" He stood, pushing away from the door. Katie opened it and got out, walking to the house and listening as Logan followed behind her.

She was searching for the words to tell him to go away when he said, "You want me to change, but it ain't gonna happen overnight." There was something in his tone she didn't like. It sounded like defiance or maybe even denial. She didn't know, but she didn't like it. When she got to the door, she pushed the key in and turned.

"Logan—" She was tired. It was like after a long fight and your body finally sagged in exhaustion. "I think you should just—" Her words were cut short as his hand wrapped around her waist and his lips flew to her neck. She wasn't sure what he was doing, but she reached behind him and threaded her fingers in his soft hair. His rumbling voice sent shivers down her spine. She hated how her body bent to his will. She hated how easily he could turn her brain off yet turn her need for him on.

"I'm sorry, I fucked up. I looked at him and judged him. Baby, I'm sorry," he whispered against her lips.

Katie tried to pull away, but Logan pushed her in the house and slammed the door behind them. She turned and pressed her back to the wall, trying to keep her balance. His apology wasn't enough. He wasn't admitting to it all. Had that been a white man, he wouldn't have even cared, and Katie wanted him to admit to it.

She put her hand out, trying to halt his movements, but Logan stalked closer. "Logan—" He slammed his lips against hers, and his tongue filled her mouth before she had a chance to finish. She tried to push him away, but Logan was this colossal unwavering brick wall, leaning into her and suffocating her with his sweet breath and needy hands. Her body leaned into him as her brain withdrew. It was so hard to think rationally with Logan so close. Every part of him touched her in some way, confusing her yet heating her to her very core.

Logan reached down and yanked Katie's skirt up, the fabric cutting against her skin. She gasped at his roughness, but he kept her mouth occupied with his lips and tongue as he abruptly yanked down her tights. She threw her arms around Logan's neck and her nails scored his skin, causing him to shudder in her arms. When he pulled away to unbutton his jeans, Katie fought to catch her breath. She still wanted to scream at him, to punch him in the face—anything. Instead, like a fool, she kicked off her heels and stepped out of her tights.

Logan's jeans were down around his ankles in seconds. He hadn't bothered taking anything else off, and his erection in his hand made Katie tremble with need, but she needed more time. Logan normally prepared her for this part, but this time he wasn't waiting. Yanking her panties to the side, he spit in his hand, but it was far from enough.

Katie cried out when he entered her rough and deep. Her pleasure from pain had never felt so great; they mingled together and pulled her away from her rage to a pleasure induced haze.

As Logan pressed deeper with each thrust, Katie fought to match his intensity. Wrapping her legs up around his waist, her body screamed in sweet agony and he thrust her into the wall. Her back ached and her body burned for more. She whispered things—dark things—in his ear, surprising herself with the dirty words escaping her mouth.

The angry monster he had been in the car was gone, and in his place was the man who made her scream and beg for more. He was back, the man she loved, and while she still had a smidgen of fear tucked away in the back of her mind, Katie came apart in Logan's arms.

She was a screaming, shivering bundle of nerves, so sensitive and needy, that as Logan came, Katie felt her stomach quiver and her body break into pieces once again. When Logan's body stilled, Katie unwrapped her legs from his waist and settled on to the ground.

His breathing slowed and evened out. "I'm sorry. I didn't mean to take you that rough." She wasn't sorry one bit, but his voice was so small that Katie's heart shattered.

She placed a hand on his chest; his heart was still thundering even though his breathing had slowed. Logan placed a hand over hers and moved it directly over his heart. "I know."

She wasn't worried about how he'd fucked her against the wall half clothed like an animal—that she could get used to—but there was another problem. Katie knew there was so much for him to overcome. Yes, he was wrong, and yes, he needed help, but she'd known that from the start. She said she'd be there and she wasn't holding up her end of the bargain.

Katie's legs wobbled a bit, so she used the wall to hold herself up. To her dismay, warm liquid seeped from her settling on her thighs. "Oh my God, Logan." She gently pushed him away and placed her fingers between her legs. His eyes widened when he saw the creamy substance on her fingertips.

He moved away, nearly tripping over his pants, which were twisted around his ankles. "Shit . . . fuck . . . shit." He pulled them up and buttoned his pants. He faced her, his eyes wide and bright. "Please tell me you are still on birth control." Katie nodded her head, and the color that had drained from his face returned. He placed a hand over his chest and exhaled.

Katie wasn't upset that he was relieved. A baby in this situation would only serve as a problem, and while she wanted kids, she couldn't see having one anytime soon. Picking up her tights, she wiped her fingers. She was more concerned with something else than a baby at the moment. "Yeah, but that's not the only thing we have to worry about." She eyed him. STDs were real and deadly.

When he got her drift, he said, "Oh, I'm clean. I got tested in prison." Logan moved to Katie, kneeling down to help her right her clothes. He placed a kiss on her thigh and stood. Looking her in the eyes, he added, "And I think that since you're on birth control, we should both get checked again and then maybe we won't need condoms at all?" It was a good suggestion, one she'd think about—well, getting tested was a definite yes—they were both getting tested as soon as possible.

Katie pushed that thought away and wondered if she and Logan would even last that long. It pained her to think that. She wanted him more than he'd ever know, but his past was threatening to ruin their future, and as much as Katie wanted to believe they were strong enough to prevail, a small voice questioned her strength and Logan's ability to change.

CHAPTER 34

IN A RELATIONSHIP, FORGIVENESS wasn't guaranteed, and love in the real world didn't always last forever. Logan knew that, he'd seen it and lived it. At thirty-five, Logan had been in what he thought was love a few times, but later realized as those women walked out of his life that he was actually happy to see them go. The stress left with them, leaving him feeling free and alive.

Katie came out of the bathroom wrapped in a fluffy white towel, with another wrapped around her head. Water clung to her brown skin, causing it to glisten. He was sure those russet colored ringlets were soft, springy, and damp under the towel she wore on her head. She was always complaining about her hair frizzing, but Logan loved it. Especially after he'd made love to her and it looked as if she'd narrowly survived a tornado.

Logan could smell her vanilla and lavender body wash all the way from the other side of the room, and a part of him was upset she'd washed his scent off her as he sat in the chair in the corner, still smelling of her body and perfume. He watched as she dried herself off and dressed in a shirt that barely covered her bottom, and hung from one shoulder. She kept the towel on her head and walked over to the bed.

Katie pulled the covers back and sat down. "You coming over?" she asked as she pulled a bottle of lotion from the nightstand. Logan silently stood and removed all of his clothes, heading to the side of the bed she was sitting on. He removed the lotion from her hands and motioned for her to sit back in the bed. When she did, he squirted some of the lotion in his hands and rubbed them together.

"What are we going to do, Logan?" Katie's eyes held a sadness he'd never seen in them before.

He sat on the bed and placed her leg over his, gently rubbing the cream into her velvety skin. How did he tell her that he wasn't sure he'd ever trust black men? Common sense told him they weren't all bad, but personal experience from the past kept him right there—in the past. Logan had been confronted with plenty of stare downs or whatever they were called by plenty of men, and no matter what Katie thought, the man who'd stared at them had more on his mind than just thinking he was a client. The man had watched as Logan held Katie, touched her, and his eyes had narrowed as Logan kissed her, which had pissed Logan off. He wasn't imagining things; Katie was just too kindhearted to notice.

Still silent, he rubbed the lotion into her skin until it gleamed brighter than before. Katie reached out and stilled his hand. "Baby, look at me," she whispered, but Logan couldn't.

He hated letting her down, and she'd never know how it tore him up inside, how he literally felt as if he was being ripped in two. His past held him by the neck while Katie's love wrapped gently around his heart, begging him to follow her. Logan was a strong man. He'd taken beatings, seen death, and dealt with men in prison determined to fuck him, yet he'd always prevailed.

However, tonight he felt so fucking weak and completely lost. He was supposed to be her guiding light. In addition to that, he was supposed to be more than his past . . . yet, for some reason he held on to yesterday when his future was right there in front of him.

Her hand was firm over his, anchoring him to her in the here and now. "How do I make this right without falling apart in the process?" he asked. Never had he felt so lost, but when Katie reached out to him with her other hand, her touch stopped the spinning and pulled him back to her. "I love you, but this is . . . I am—" Katie placed her fingers over his mouth.

"We can do this, I know we can." She leaned forward and placed her head on his shoulder. "Together we can fix this."

Logan wasn't so sure. For the first time in a while, he was afraid. Losing Katie would kill him.

WARMER WEATHER BROUGHT NEW night sounds, and they were currently keeping Katie awake. She slipped out of bed and went to the kitchen. She needed time to think, and what better way to think than over some ice cream, wrapped up in an afghan? Normally, she'd call Teal, who'd actually stopped all of the texts, emails, and phone calls, but in Katie's mind they were still on bad terms. Still, she picked up her phone and then glanced at the time. It was well past three in the morning and Teal was asleep. No, that was an excuse, Teal would answer the phone for Katie no matter what time she called.

Katie dialed the number she knew by heart, but didn't press send. She placed the phone on the counter and scooped out a big scoop of coffee flavored ice cream. Placing the top back on the tub, she used the spoon as a makeshift cone by licking the large glob of ice cream. She and Teal had been friends for so long, but right now she felt like she was a stranger. Katie completely understood the concern, but that had turned to interference when Teal changed the letter from her to Logan. Katie's heart hurt at the thought, but more so at the idea of losing Teal.

She cleared out the phone and went to her messages. Selecting the first one she found from Teal, she responded. Fighting tears, she left a message she was sure might cause more problems, but what Katie said needed to be said. No one else had any issue telling Katie how he or she felt about her actions, so she thought she'd try the same thing.

> *I love you, but I no longer trust you and I don't know how to deal with that. I need time and space. I love you, Teal, but what you did was wrong. Not unforgivable, but wrong. I miss you. –Kay*

Katie read the message again before pressing send. She knew there might be backlash, but in this case, honesty was in fact the best policy. If she wanted her dad and Teal to treat her like the twenty-five-year-old woman she was, she needed to demand it, but she also needed to be able to handle her issues without running to them for help. Katie powered down her phone and pushed it away. She nearly jumped out of her skin when Logan cleared his throat.

His warm chuckle echoed in the room. "Didn't mean to scare you," he said as he moved further into the kitchen.

Katie rolled her eyes at her jumpiness. "You want some ice cream?"

Logan picked up the container and read the ingredients on the back. After he placed it down, he pulled the spoon from her hand and took a large bite. "What are you doing up eating ice cream?" he asked softly.

Katie wondered if her feelings were tattooed on her face as he eyed her. Taking a bite of the ice cream, she smirked. "I was thinking about Teal and my dad."

Logan nodded and pulled a chair up to the bar.

"Maybe the reason that they treat me like a kid is because I let them." She handed him the spoon and watched as he ate some more.

"Maybe, Katie. I can only assume your father is nervous about losing his only daughter. I'm not what he expected you to—" He paused and shook his head. "This isn't about me. You've felt this way about them before me, right?"

Katie nodded.

"Then it's your past you need to delve through. Maybe it was when you were left out as a kid because you weren't white or black enough for the other kids." Logan took another bite of ice cream.

Katie pulled her legs up in the chair and wrapped her arms around them.

"I'm here for you. Just tell me what you need." Logan placed the ice cream in front of her face and Katie took the final bite.

"I know you are." She smiled, leaned forward, and reached for the spoon.

Logan snatched it away. "Enough of this, let's go back to bed." He stood and threw the spoon in the sink, and then placed the ice cream back in the freezer.

Katie stood and wrapped her arms around his back.

"Ready?" he asked, turning in her arms.

Maybe his words had a hidden meaning, or maybe he was just talking about going to bed, Katie didn't know. She was worn-out and grief-stricken, but still, she took Logan's hand, followed him to the bedroom, and snuggled close to his side. Katie closed her eyes and tucked her head into his chest. She could no longer think of the day's events or her past; as Logan caressed her hip, she was lulled into a deep sleep.

CHAPTER 35

FOR A FIRST DATE, Katie thought Logan would take her to a movie and then to dinner, but when they pulled up to the Country Western bar she was confused. Logan may have been a Southern man, but she knew for a fact that he didn't listen to country music. One, he'd told her so, and two, whenever they drove in the car, he blasted mostly classic rock. He was surprised that Katie knew the bands he liked. Though she steered more toward bands like Pink Floyd and The Beatles, she could also appreciate some of the metal bands he listened to.

Looking over at a smiling Logan, she asked, "What are we doing here?"

He pointed to the sign on the moniker. "There's a live band playing tonight. I thought since you'd never been to a concert, it'd be a great stepping stone to getting you more comfortable with crowds."

Katie took a deep breath. She didn't want to go into the bar with loud, obnoxious drunks. She'd enjoyed the last few days with Logan cooped up at home. As the frost of winter thawed and May's warm weather brought out flowers and singing birds, she couldn't keep Logan inside any longer. They'd gone on picnics in the park, the Pascal Timbre Sports at the Botanical Gardens, and they'd eaten at every restaurant in Woodbury. Now Logan was starting to ask about the neighboring town and its cuisine.

Katie placed her hand on the door and turned to Logan. "I don't love crowds, but if I'm with you it'll be fun." She opened the door and hopped out. Walking around the car, he grasped her hand.

"It's some female singer. I read about it online last week. Looked her up and she sounds like that girl you blast when you're writing. Lela something."

Katie walked to the door at Logan's side. "Lela? No, Lana Del Ray. You think she sounded like her?" She entered through the door when Logan opened it.

He gently pulled her inside. "Yeah, I guess. At least they sounded the same to me." Katie looked around for a seat by the stage. Either they were late, or the singer was just popular. She scanned the room for two seats that were at least together.

Next to the stage, in the corner, Katie spotted a small table with a tea candle burning dimly in the corner. There weren't any drunks or fools wandering around the bar. Light music played from the speakers in the corners of the room, a waitress offered them a friendly smile as she hustled past them to the drink station, and a few couples sat at the bar holding hands. Katie smiled and pointed at the two seats in the corner. "How about there?"

Logan led her over and pulled a chair out for her. Soon after she and Logan sat down, a waiter came over and they placed their order; a beer for Logan and sweet tea for Katie. The lights dimmed, and Katie was excited that they'd gotten there just in time. Logan wrapped his arm around her and pulled her close as a small woman stepped on the stage. She spoke her hellos, introducing herself as L.E. Banks, and she sat down with her guitar and started singing. This woman sounded nothing like Lana Del Ray, but she was great. The singer had a genre-crossing mix with indie rock, electronica, and hip hop beats and Katie felt herself moving to the music.

Logan whispered in Katie's ear, "I think I know her." He leaned forward. Katie watched as Logan eyed the woman. His green eyes sparkled. "Yeah, that's the woman I sat next to on the plane over here.

Katie smiled. "No freaking way." She looked to the stage as the woman sang. She was pale, small, and beautiful with fragile features

"No kiddin'. She was writing in this little journal and she asked me where I was heading and—" He looked at her. "And I told her 'home to see my girl.'"

Katie's smile widened and her heart warmed. She was his girl and always would be.

"You want to dance?"

She stilled and almost burst into laughter, until she glanced up at the seriousness in his eyes. Katie looked around. The empty dance floor made her stomach drop. There was no one there for her to hide behind, and she and Logan would be exposed to the crowd and any other onlookers.

"There's no one on the dance floor right now," she squeaked, but that didn't stop Logan from standing and holding his hand out to her. Katie's heart thundered in her chest. It wasn't that she couldn't dance, just that she was nervous to be the only couple dancing. Logan didn't seem to mind, and she didn't have the heart to tell him no. Still, Katie took Logan's hand and he led her out onto the dance floor in the middle of the tables and in front of the stage.

Her face burned in embarrassment as other couples watched her with Logan. "Logan, I . . . I . . ."

He ignored her hesitancy and wrapped his arms around her waist. Sliding his hands over Katie's ass, he pulled her close until she could feel his warmth through her clothes.

She reached up and bound her arms around Logan's neck. He looked down at her with such devotion, Katie decided to ignore the crowd and focus on his warm embrace. When the chorus hit, Logan slowly started to sway with the music and Katie rocked with him.

Keeping her body close to his, she softly threaded her fingers through his hair. Logan shuddered when Katie's fingers moved over the soft skin on the back of his neck; she could feel the gooseflesh that'd broken out over his skin and she grinned. She loved when her touch affected him that way because the same thing happened to her with even his gentlest caress.

Katie kept her eyes on Logan; his gaze was so intense, she couldn't look away. He pulled her body closer and the gentle sway of their hips calmed her nerves. Removing her arms, Katie wrapped them around Logan's waist. He leaned in and brushed his lips against hers.

Releasing a sigh, she leaned in and joined their lips in a sweet yet stomach trembling kiss. Logan's lips tasted of mint and beer, such an odd yet seductive taste that she softly sucked his bottom lip between hers. Slowly exploring Logan's mouth, the music suddenly stopped and quiet chatter disappeared, leaving Logan and Katie alone on the dance floor. She could hear nothing but the beating of her heart and the rush of blood in her head.

Logan moved his lips away from hers and placed a kiss on her cheek. Opening her eyes, she listened as the noise from the club gradually seeped back in. Being with him was always so intense and at times it scared the hell out of Katie. He pulled from her emotions that she'd never felt before and he encouraged her to explore a part of herself she never knew existed.

He leaned away a bit. "What were you worried about?" he asked in a gentle tone.

Katie shook her head. She wasn't worried about anything anymore. She couldn't be. He kept her head filled with fog and he kept her close to him as he moved with the music. She bit her lip. They were already swollen from his kiss and she could still taste his mint on them. "Nothing, it was silly," she admitted, and glanced around to see that others had followed their lead to the dance floor. Now they were cuddled up and swaying to the melodic tones and the singer's voice.

Logan leaned down and kissed Katie softly on her lips. He lingered for a bit, and then pulled away. "I like these lyrics," he said as the song wound down and came to a natural end. Katie and Logan stopped dancing and clapped.

"When she said, 'change can be amazing' I thought of us." She used to hate change, but since meeting Logan a lot of things had changed. Some for the better, and some . . . well, not so much. Luckily, there was time to work on that, and she believed that they could do it together.

Logan took her hand and guided her through the crowd and back to the table. He took a sip of his beer. "Yeah, that's a good lyric. I think we've figured that one out, yeah?" He smirked. "I was thinking about the one where she says, 'Say it, you should say it. If you want it, ask for it and I'll give in.'"

He looked back up at the stage and Katie followed his gaze. A new song with new lyrics had started. This one was a bit more on the hip-hop side with hints of electronica. "What do you think she's wanting him to ask her?" Logan finished off his beer.

Katie took a sip of her tea in thought. She wasn't sure what the woman wanted. She replayed the lyrics over in her head only to receive no clue. "I don't know. Maybe she's looking for honesty, or an answer to a question?" She shrugged. "What do you think?"

He ran his hand through his hair and leaned back. "Maybe she wants more than he's willing to give. I don't know."

She narrowed her eyes in confusion. "What are you saying, Logan?" Katie reached out and took his hand in hers. He flipped it over kissed her palm.

"Nothing, but I think that—" He thought on his words for a moment. "I think that this is probably the best relationship I've ever been in." He bent forward and kissed Katie again. When Logan moved away, she fought to catch her breath, and placed her fingers over her lips.

The rest of their date night went on, and Katie couldn't wait to get Logan home. He'd made her dinner earlier, taken her for ice cream, and finally to the live show. She could admit that in her lifetime, this date so far was her best one ever.

WHEN THE DATE WAS over and Logan and Katie left the bar, he took her hand and headed toward the exit. She clung to him like a warm glove, and she couldn't wait to show him just how happy she was to be with him.

Katie patted Logan's right pocket. "I'm gonna drive, okay?" She held her hands out for the keys, and Logan handed them to her.

"I'm not drunk. Being as big as I am, I can handle a few more beers than a man of average weight. However, I'm also not stupid. After six beers, I'm not chancing a DUI charge."

Katie nodded in agreement. At the car, she hit the FOB just as her name was called behind her. She glanced around, looking for the person. She squinted to see that it was Shea and her boyfriend, but before she could respond, Logan grabbed the keys from her hand.

His body stiffened and his eyes darkened. "Get in the car, Katie." The characteristically soft tone he'd used with her was gone; his eyes were narrowed and his hand gripped her arm, seemingly ready to pull her out of danger, yet there was no danger, just her friends from her old job.

"What?" She looked up to Logan, noticing that harsh lines spread across his face. She reached for his face and placed what she thought was a soothing hand on his cheek. "What's wrong?"

Logan motioned over her shoulder, and Katie followed his eyes over to the group of people who now seemed too nervous to make their approach. She could see the look in their eyes, and she was sure she had the same damned confused look in hers. "Do you know those people?" he asked, but Katie didn't like how he spat the word, "those people."

She glanced back over, realizing for the first time that not only was it all men, except Shea, but they were all black as well. Katie moved back from Logan, who suddenly seemed too close, too overbearing.

She couldn't have hid the anger in her voice if she tried. Shit, she wasn't even going to try. "That's Shea, and I used to work with her before she got married to Joe's brother." Katie guessed that Shea and her friends had taken Logan's sudden change in attitude as a warning. They waved and walked back in the direction they'd come from.

Logan tracked their every movement, until they were in their cars and driving off. He turned back to her, and Katie was shocked to see that he looked angry with her . . . or maybe it was the situation.

"What the hell was that, Logan?" He reached for her, but Katie pulled away. There was no way he was going to touch her after that. They'd been doing so well tonight. "Are you going to act like that every time a black person approaches us?"

"It has nothing to do with color!" he shouted.

She marveled at how unapologetic Logan seemed, as if it were normal to tense up around other races and then lie about it . . . because he was sure as shit lying. She knew that it was a work in progress, but she couldn't let this go. It had to be addressed, so Logan understood it was unacceptable. She felt like a damned fool being with him sometimes. She was black for goodness sake. Though it seemed his main problem were black males, Katie still felt like a fool for being with someone who had issues with people of her own race.

His features hardened and he crossed his arms over his chest. "It wasn't just that they were black," Logan confessed.

Katie wasn't sure. What the hell was it then, and why did he ask if she knew them? Of course she knew them, Shea had called her damn name. Clue number one!

Logan started to speak again, but she held up her hand to stop him. "It shouldn't have mattered at all that they were black. What the hell, Logan?" She was astounded at his comment, but she shouldn't have been. She knew he had his issues when they first met, but it was another thing to see it up close and personal. It was embarrassing, and most of all it was hurtful.

Katie moved around Logan and got inside the car. She wasn't going to have this conversation out in the open for any stranger to see. Actually, she didn't want to have this conversation at all.

As Logan slid in the car, Katie glanced over at him; he kept his head turned slightly away from her. How could a man be so perfect for her, yet so different in every other way? Why was it race? It could have been anything else, but Katie couldn't change the color of her skin or of those around her, and even if she could, she wouldn't. She would let Logan go for good before she ever let him make her feel like the kids did back when she was growing up. Logan had told her it wouldn't be easy, but he hadn't told her that it would cut her to her very core.

WHEN LOGAN TOLD KATIE that changing his attitude wouldn't happen over-night, he was serious. He'd spent weeks in the hospital, then hiding from all groups of black and Mexican kids whose main goal was to kick his ass on a daily basis. Logan thought of it like this: If for a straight year a dog bit you on a daily basis, over time you'd be wary around dogs. Logan didn't explain it to

Katie that way. He wasn't stupid enough to compare black kids to dogs, but it was the best he could come up with at the moment.

Still, when they arrived at home, Katie went straight to the bathroom and readied herself for bed. Logan sat on the couch, waiting for her to come out of the bathroom, but when she did, she walked into the bedroom, ignoring him completely. Logan played with the idea of sleeping on the couch in order to avoid the shit storm sure to come, but Logan couldn't let Katie go to sleep angry.

Kicking off his shoes, Logan pulled off his shirt and left them in the living room as he headed into the bedroom. How did he explain that even as a grown ass man he worried about black strangers in large groups? He had to be aware of his surroundings at all times, and not doing that had gotten his ass kicked plenty of years ago . . . not to mention just a few months ago in jail. He entered the room to find that Katie hadn't gone to bed, but was in fact on her laptop, browsing. Logan pulled the lounge chair up to where she was and sat down.

Katie shut the laptop, turned to him, and offered an unconvincing smile. "I think you should know that how you acted tonight really hurt me." Tears threatened to fall from her brown eyes and Logan felt the knife slide into his heart. She was beautiful, so soft and sweet, yet here he was tearing her down piece by piece. He kept his eyes on hers as she spoke. "It worries me. I'm the same color as those men." She held up her hand and flipped it over. Logan longed to kiss every inch of her brown skin. "What do you see when you see me?"

Logan gazed at her deeply. "I see the woman I love, Katie."

"And when you look at a man of another race, what do you see then?" Her voice was gentle and clear, but Logan her the tremble beneath. She wanted honesty, but she was afraid of the answer she'd get and she was right to be.

"I see a person that can cause me a lot of trouble," he answered honestly. Her eyes closed, and the tears that brimmed the edge of her eyes fell. Logan reached for her hand, but Katie quickly pulled away. "No, don't do that," he demanded. His chest ached when she refused his touch and he just couldn't handle it.

Katie opened her eyes and Logan was greeted with a flash of anger. "When my dad called you a felon and a convict, you asked him for a chance. You asked my dad not to see you for what you used to be, but for who you were working toward being: a good, law abiding man." She wiped her tears away. "Now, you refuse to do the same. If you stay in the past, you're a fucking hypocrite."

Logan leaned back in his seat. "You want me to change overnight, Katie, and I'm telling you right now that it's not going to happen. You want me to forget years of abuse in a matter of days." He was getting angry. What the hell did she want from him, a miracle? He wasn't above saying how he was acting was wrong in some ways, but he was trying and that's all he could do. "You have to work with me here. I'm not like you. I can't just look the other way and pretend that my past never happened." He reached for her again, and she hesitantly let him take her hand, but Logan was happy with that. He pulled her in his lap and kissed her on the cheek.

Katie settled in his lap. "I know you're trying, but I wish you could feel the way I do when you act like that. I mean, it hurts, and I feel like you'll someday start looking at me like that. Like I'm not good enough or the color of my skin will cost you your friendship with Trent, and I know how you feel about him."

Logan did have that fear. Trent had told Logan that his relationship with Katie was destined to fail, and he promised to have a home for him when it happened, but what if it didn't? That was Logan's goal, to make it last, and although he was failing, he still had hope.

"You worry too much," he said, knowing she had good reason to. "I'll never leave you for Trent, I don't swing that way." He nudged her with his chin. Katie smiled, but Logan knew it was forced. Her eyes still glistened with tears and he wasn't sure how to make it better. He only knew he loved her and in his mind that should've been enough. "Katie, I will do my very best to never make you feel that way again. I promise." She nodded, but Logan wanted to see her eyes. He lifted her away and turned her face toward his. "I love you, and even though it's hard I'll make it happen. You will never feel that way again. It's hard, not impossible. Baby, I can't lose you."

She smiled and kissed his cheek. "I trust you," she said with conviction. "We'll make this work."

He kissed her again and pulled her onto the lounge. Logan pulled the afghan over himself and Katie. He wanted her in his arms forever and he'd do whatever it took to keep her there.

CHAPTER 36

LOGAN FELT LIKE AN ass. Actually, he was an ass. He'd snooped through Katie's belongings when she was sleeping in order to find two phone numbers, but worse, he'd gone behind her back and contacted her father. They planned to meet at a place called Mel's Bistro, and convincing Katie that he should go alone had taken what seemed like an eternity, but she'd finally forgiven him for snooping and thrown in the towel. Now, Logan sat in the bistro waiting for Jan-Erik to arrive. Logan had arrived over an hour early and ordered a large cheeseburger, which reminded him he needed to hit the gym soon.

Jan-Erik entered the bistro and greeted a few of the servers before stopping at the table where Logan sat. He removed his coat and placed it on the back of his seat. "Logan," he greeted.

"Jan-Erik."

"Call me Erik, most people do," he stated as he unbuttoned his suit jacket and sat down. Erik placed his hands on the table and leaned forward, his eyes narrowing as he spoke. "Are you here to ask me what I think you're going to ask me?" Logan sure as hell was. He figured in order to show Katie's father how much he loved her, if he was going to ask Katie to marry him, he'd at least talk to him first. She was about to turn twenty-six and he found the act of asking her father's blessings archaic and ridiculous. Still, he was here looking like a damned fool in front of her father.

Logan nodded. "Yes, sir, I am."

"How do you plan to do this?" Erik sat back. "You can't even provide for her."

"Katie provides for herself . . . she doesn't need me to, but I'll try." Logan understood that Katie was Erik's only daughter, and any man worth his salt would want the best for her. Logan wasn't naïve. He knew that Katie had money, probably more than he'd ever make, but he had plans and the funds to make it happen.

"And you think you'll ride the cash cow?" Erik countered.

Logan scratched his head. "I get it. No man is good enough for your baby girl, and especially not a piece of shit ex-con." Logan understood that was what the problem was, and if Katie were his daughter he'd be scared shitless, too. "You want me to walk away?" He wouldn't, but he needed to know where Erik stood.

Erik laughed. "And have my baby crying in my arms?" Erik sobered at his words. "Hell no. I want her happy, but you have to comprehend where I'm coming from. I deal with people like you every day in Capshaw."

That incensed Logan. He'd tried his whole life to go unnoticed and to do right, but one bad choice would have everyone he ever met thinking the worst of him, scared of him, or unwilling to hire him. "Have you checked my record? In prison I was the model inmate. I did my time, and now I want a life outside of that hell." The waitress came up and placed water in front of Erik. Katie told Logan this was her father's favorite place to eat. After the cheeseburger Logan ate, it was now his favorite spot as well.

"You think it's that easy?" Erik took a gulp of his drink. "I should just take your word about my only child's safety and heart? What's the rush, Logan? Why do you want to marry her so fast?" Erik eyed him.

"I want her as my wife now, not later. I want to be the shoulder she cries on, the man who she comes to for advice, the man whose last name she signs as her own. I love her, and I want her as my wife now," Logan answered honestly. There were a million more reasons, but he didn't have time to sit here and explain love to another grown ass man. "I understand your worries, and I'll tell you this . . ." Logan leaned forward. "When the time comes, I'll be as big of a dick to the man who wants to date my daughter as you were to me. You think you are an asshole? You have nothing on me, sir. I'll break the little bastard's neck before I let him hurt her."

Erik raised a brow, and Logan meant every damn word of it. He wanted kids someday. That was why he'd worked so hard after he left school. He wasn't sure, but Erik still seemed unmoved. Logan leaned back and blew out a frustrated breath. Erik wanted honesty, and he'd given it to him . . . there was nothing left to give.

Erik looked just as tired as Logan felt. "When I met her mother she was ten. She was heartbroken about her parents' divorce, and she needed a father in her life. I was that man, and I still am."

"I'm not trying to take that from you. I don't want to be her father. I want to be her husband and the father of her child. Erik, I'm not letting her go. I got the shit kicked out of me, I think I lost a longtime friend, and I have to live with the fact that she could most probably do ten times better than me. Still, I'm not giving up. I love her and I'll marry her with or without your permission, but I know what it means to her to have you in her life and more than just phone calls.

"When we come here to eat, I know she misses the times she spent here with you. She acts like she's okay, but she isn't. She cries when she thinks I can't see or hear it. You just said she needed a father in her life and you're right. As much as I'd like to be everything she'll ever need, I'm not. You and Teal have to let her be the woman she's grown into and you need to get back in her life."

Logan needed a father when he was younger, and instead of letting his stepfather in, he pushed him away, feeling as if he were an imposter. If Logan was honest with himself, he would've realized that long ago, but he didn't regret any decision that'd led him to where he was with Katie.

Erik rubbed his forehead and Logan knew the feeling. A headache was looming on the horizon. "I'm not going to make this easy on you. I never will." His eyes held sincerity, and Logan hoped to hell that he didn't take it easy on him. He hoped that Erik kicked the living shit out of him if he ever messed up. "Choices," Erik muttered.

"If it makes you feel better, Katie didn't give me a choice either. It was fall in love with her or fall in love with her. She's amazing, and I think she makes me better. It ain't easy, but she makes it worth the struggle." He smiled at the thought of his future wife. "You did a damn good job, sir." Logan had never given a more sincere compliment in his life.

Erik grinned. "She's a pain in the ass and you know it."

Logan agreed in a way, but he wouldn't admit it to her father. "Well, she . . . she is something."

Erik's eyes sparkled as they talked about his daughter. "Have you got a ring?"

"Not yet." He wasn't sure what to get her. He wanted to get her the biggest damn rock on earth, but he was still saving and Katie would probably admonish him for spending so much.

Erik looked away pensively. "And she's not already pregnant?" he asked with a clenched fist.

He almost laughed. "No, sir," he said with certainty.

Her father nodded stiffly.

Logan wouldn't marry a woman for just that reason anyway. Shit like that was asking for a world of trouble and the wrong side of broke.

Erik pulled a tissue out of his pocket and pushed it toward Logan. "For a father, this day brings feelings of dread and joy." Logan picked up the tissue and unfolded it to find a wedding set nestled inside.

He looked to Erik. "What's this?"

"It was her mother's." His eyes stayed on the set in Logan's hand. "I wanted to bury her with them, but she said they should go to Katie." Erik cleared his voice.

Logan was grateful, and though he'd never been so ready to ask a woman a question, he had one more person to talk to first. "Sir, I appreciate how hard this is for you and this." He held up the rings. "Means a lot to me." He folded the rings up and placed them in his jeans pocket. He was a bit relieved, too. As much as he wanted to buy Katie a ring, he needed to save his money until he could afford to put a down payment on his own shop.

Erik pulled his suit jacket on and stood. "Just—" He ran his hand through his hair. "Be everything she expects you to be and more." He reached out to shake Logan's hand. Surprised by the gesture, Logan stood and took Erik's hand in his.

In the case of Katie's father, he'd only managed to pull him to his side because Erik knew Katie had made her choice in Logan and he was afraid to lose her. As Erik left, Logan considered the fact that Teal wouldn't be nearly as easy. He sat back down and opened his cell phone. It was after five, and he knew she'd be getting ready to leave work. He dialed the number and waited.

"Hello." Her voice was the same as he'd overheard the day he'd called Katie months ago.

"May I speak to Teal Lofton?" Logan knew it was her, but didn't want to seem rude.

"This is she, may I ask who is calling?"

Logan noted that her voice sounded a bit different; she didn't sound as uneducated and loud as she had when she spoke to Katie. Maybe he'd rushed to judgment. As Katie had pointed out to him, it wouldn't have been the first time he'd done it.

"Yes, this is Logan Whyte." He waited a beat, then added, "Katie's boyfriend." At her silence, Logan started talking. "I'm at Mel's bistro and I just had lunch with Jan-Erik."

He heard the frustrated breath she released. "Why are you telling me this, and why are you calling me? No, better yet, how did you get my number?" Her voice was rushed, as if she were getting annoyed.

Logan opted for the truth without sugar coating a thing. "I'd like to meet you for a drink at Mel's if that's okay? I want to ask Katie to marry me, but before I do that, I need the people she loves back in her life and there on her wedding day." The laughter that bubbled from the other end of the phone had him ready to hang up on her.

"Logan, Katie won't speak to me, not the other way around. She sent me one text."

Logan hadn't known that.

"I assume she's mad about the letter and then me telling her father on her, but honestly, what did she expect?"

He would guess that she would expect Teal to respect her privacy, but he didn't say that solely because he understood her worry.

"She gave her address to a man in prison, what if she had given it to the wrong person?"

"Everyone keeps saying that, and I get it, but she didn't, she gave it to me and things have worked themselves out. Do we still have a long ways to go? Yeah, but what man and woman doesn't? A perfect relationship doesn't and will never exist. I get that you were worried about her meeting me, but that time has come and gone."

Teal smacked her lips or took in air. He couldn't tell which.

"You think that's the only concern?"

"I'm sure it's not." He would forever be forced to jump through hoops for Katie's family and friends, but even though he had nothing to prove to them, he wanted to do whatever it took to make Katie happy, and that meant have her loved ones back even if she pretended to be okay without them. "I'm sure you are worried about me hurting her or my past coming back to bite me in the ass, but I'll tell you something . . . I worry about the same shit. I'm worried she'll wake up one day and realize she can do better."

Teal was silent. He assumed she'd ignored him and the tension headache that loomed on the horizon slowly crept down to his neck and shoulders.

"Back when Katie was with Roman I thought she could do better. I could see that he wasn't ready to settle down, but Katie wouldn't listen. I told her that a woman could never do better than a man who loved her despite her faults. If you love her like that, if you are offering her that, then she can't do better."

Logan loved Katie and had yet to see any faults in her other than being as stubborn as a mule, but part of him loved that about her. "I love her and want to marry her. Granted, I know you are pissed that she lied to you, but—"

"No, not pissed, hurt. The times we used to hang out she would lie to me so that she could talk to you. I think if she could have trusted me more it wouldn't have played out this way, but whatever. I've tried to call Katie, but she isn't trying to hear it, and I'm not begging for a chance to apologize, you feel me?"

"Is this your way of saying she needs to meet you halfway?" Logan asked.

"This is my way of saying I want to apologize and I want my friend back, but she has to talk to me. I won't beg her. I love her, and looking out for her comes like second nature to me," she responded.

Logan wasn't sure how he would make that happen, but he knew he had to. He needed Teal and Erik in Katie's life. She didn't have many people around, and the ones she did were overprotective, and not without good reason. She had lost a lot and needed their strength when she couldn't find her own; however, over the years she had grown into this amazingly strong woman. How they didn't see it was beyond him, but she was there wrapped in a tall, slim, and sexy body.

"Will you join me for a drink so we can discuss this more?"

"Hell no." She laughed. "Two reasons: one, I have a date tonight, and two, I'm not brave . . . or should I say fool enough to meet up with a stranger."

"Well, I wouldn't be a stranger if you'd taken the time to get to know me," he reasoned. He'd been out long enough that she could have talked to him.

"Hmmm . . . and how would I have done that when your soon-to-be fiancée won't even answer her phone?" she countered.

Logan smirked at the comment. "True, she's stubborn as hell, but now you have my number."

"Mmhmm, so now you think I'm the type of girl to be calling her best friend's man?" she joked . . . at least he hoped she was joking.

"I—I meant, so you can call and get an answer," he sputtered in reply.

Teal didn't laugh, but he heard mirth in her voice when she responded, "Yeah, I get what you're saying. How's tomorrow at noon? It's Saturday, so I'm off."

"Okay. And then I'll take you to Katie's and you can talk to her."

"More like ambush her."

"Yep," Logan chuckled. "Thanks, Teal." He was surprised with how easy it'd been to convince her, and it'd also convinced him that Teal wasn't the mean ass he'd thought she was. She wanted her friend back in her life and he was going to try and make that happen . . . for Katie.

CHAPTER 37

KATIE PULLED THE COVERS over her head when the alarm screamed. She reached out next to her, feeling for Logan; his spot was empty but still warm. She listened for the shower or noises from the kitchen, but all was quiet. She popped her head up and looked around.

"Logan?" she called out, but nothing. She laid her head back down and yawned.

They had stayed up until two a.m. watching T.V. and eating chips. Katie had patted her tummy, complaining that she was getting bigger, but Logan had only replied by leaning in and kissing her belly button.

Then she remembered he had said he was going to join a gym in the morning, but he'd let her sleep in. She stretched and headed into the bathroom and took a shower and washed her hair.

"I need a haircut." She said as she looked in the mirror taming her mane with a wide toothcomb. She wanted to blow dry and flat iron it straight, but she knew Logan would complain. He loved the springy curls and their puffy ways. Katie wrapped the towel around herself tighter and left the bathroom. Checking the clock in the hallway told her it was well past noon and she was tempted to call Logan. He said he'd be back before lunch. Katie went to the kitchen and pulled out some stuff to make soup and sandwiches then headed back to her room to get dressed.

The front door opened while she sat on the couch with a book in her hand. Logan came through the door in a wife-beater and a pair of mesh basketball shorts. Katie stood and went to him.

"You sleep well?" he asked before placing a kiss on her lips.

Katie wrapped her arms around his sweaty body and squeezed. He smelled like sweat and a hint of cologne. "Yeah, next time wake me up with a kiss before you go." She pouted and was rewarded with another kiss.

Logan let her go and dropped his gym bag down by the door. "Babe, I told you last night I was going to the gym."

Katie picked up his bag and placed it in the hallway closet. "Yeah, you did. I think I should start going too." She lifted her shirt and peeked at her belly. It was still flat, but she'd been snacking on chips and cookies more than veggies and fruits. Logan came over and kneeled in front of her. "At this rate, I'll be a blimp in the next few months." He kissed and nibbled her belly.

"Do you want to come with me? Logan reached up and pulled Katie's shorts down a little. "I lift weights, you can start with something a little bit easier like, the treadmill or elliptical machine?" He kissed a trail down her belly that ended just below her belly button.

Sighing, Katie placed her hands on the sides of his face. "I should, yeah? I mean, me and Teal had planned to go, but—"

Logan looked up at Katie. He pulled her shorts up and pulled her into an embrace. "I need a shower, and then I have a surprise for you," he whispered into her hair as she hugged him back.

"And what, may I ask, is the occasion?" She gazed up at him with a pleasant smile, and Logan tapped her nose.

"My baby just deserves something special every now and again, don't you think?" Logan kissed Katie on her forehead and she swatted him away.

"I think you need to kiss me!" She stood on tiptoes and placed her lips against the warmth his offered. Logan threaded his fingers through Katie's hair and tilted her head to the side. The fluttering in her belly and tingling in her spine increased when Logan tugged her strands a little harder.

With a moan, Logan pulled away. "Baby, I need a shower before your surprise." He smiled with swollen lips, pecked her cheek again, and moved away.

He headed to the bathroom, but not before stating, "Make sure you get dressed."

Katie looked down at her clothing; she was wearing her 'lounging around the house' clothes. "Are we going somewhere?" she called, skipping down the hall and into the bedroom.

Logan stuck his head out of the bathroom door. "No, we have company coming."

Katie paused in the middle of taking off her shirt. "Huh?" She pulled it over her head and flung it on the bed. Pushing her shorts down, she waited for an answer from him. As she impatiently waited for his reply, she rummaged through her closet and removed a summer dress. It was nice out, and the pale yellow looked good against her skin. She pulled it over her head, and then went to join Logan in the bathroom.

Opening the door let out a puff of steam, and Katie stepped back; her hair would turn into a puffball of cotton if she went in there. Logan stood in the shower, covered in suds. He turned around and winked at her.

"I'm not telling you the surprise," he teased, and Katie narrowed her eyes. She crossed her arms over her chest and leaned against the wall facing the bathroom. "What time is it?"

Katie glanced at the clock in the hallway. "It's almost two." Logan rinsed off and opened the door, drying off quicker than Katie liked. She enjoyed watching him with rivulets of water rolling down his chest; his tattoos damp and glistening. The flutter in her belly was back and in full force. Logan watched her as he tugged on his boxers.

"I know that look, baby. Trust me. If we had time—" A knock on the door made him pause.

Katie's brow furrowed and she pushed away from the wall. "Should I get it?"

"No, wait a bit." He pulled up his pants and threw on a shirt. "Come with me," he said, reaching for her hand and leading her into the living room. "You look good in that dress, sorry I didn't say it sooner." He kissed her cheek and motioned for her to sit on the couch.

Anxiously, Katie sat down, a worried noise escaping her lips. "Okay, now I'm anxious." Logan's face was serious as he left her and headed to the door. Opening it, Katie heard his greeting and her father's voice. Beyond perplexed, Katie wondered why her father was at the door and what he had to do with her surprise.

Then she heard it; Teal's voice was soft and sweet when she greeted Logan, which flabbergasted the hell out of Katie. She leaned forward and looked around the corner as Logan, Teal, and her dad walked into the room. She felt like she might puke.

A nervous chuckle escaped her throat. "Is this some kind of intervention?" Katie asked, not too sure if she was joking or not. Her father sat beside her, placed his arm around her, and kissed her cheek.

"An intervention?" He patted her back. "No, baby girl." Katie's apprehension somewhat dissipated and she leaned into her father, glancing at Teal.

Teal waved and smiled, and Katie nearly burst into tears. She stood and ran to her, wrapping her arms around her friend, who was already crying. She was suddenly angry and embarrassed by her own actions; no matter how justified she believed they were, Katie regretted them. She missed her friend, and the isolated life she'd created for herself could be destroyed by forgiveness.

Teal hugged her tighter. "You pigheaded brat," she whispered.

"You overbearing jerk," Katie retorted. "I missed you." She pulled away to look in Teal's eyes.

LOGAN WASN'T SURE IF the insults were the girls way of apologizing, but it seemed to be the case. He and Erik stayed to the side as Teal and Katie held each other, uttering sincere words of apology.

Katie was the first to come up for air. "I was angry at you, but I didn't handle it right," she said. Logan agreed, but Katie had needed to figure that out herself. "I wish I would have just called you and explained."

Teal shook her head, her eyes darkening with regret. "I wouldn't have listened. I didn't trust your judgment, and as your best friend I should have, or at least let you explain it to me instead of trying to force my opinions on you." Teal placed her hands over her face. "I'm sorry, Katie. I should have handled it better, and that big ass dude over there helped convince me of it." She pointed to Logan, and he felt like he'd committed a crime of some sort.

When Logan stepped forward, he was blushing like a damned fool. Katie's eyes were full of tears, but her lips were in a smile.

"We said we'd create a life together," he folded his hands behind his back, "and we have to start with the broken relationships before we can make a healthy one of our own." Logan had read that in the same book he'd read about creating real connections with others. That had been a day he was bored and there was nothing to do but read.

"That's right. When he called me I almost didn't show up," her father said from the couch. "I'm glad I did." Her father nodded in approval to Logan.

Logan stepped forward again and took Katie's hand. His stomach was in knots and he felt dizzy, but nothing was going to stop him from giving Katie her surprise. "So, are you ready for your surprise?" Katie looked baffled and Logan enjoyed it.

"This isn't it?" She waved her hand, motioning to her father and Teal.

"No, that's not it." Logan kissed her nose and swallowed a ball of nerves before kneeling down on one knee. Katie swayed, and Logan reached up to steady her. Tears flowed down her cheeks, and Logan could tell from the look in her eyes that he was gazing upon his future wife. Suddenly, he couldn't remember why he had even been nervous about her answer.

"Katie, will you marry me?" he asked. Still, he held his breath, waiting for an answer.

She fell to her knees in front of Logan.

At eye level, he could see the woman he loved, the woman who had saved him from the hate in his past. They still had a long way to go, but it was a journey he couldn't wait to take with her.

"Yes, Logan. I love you so much, yes!" she whispered.

He yanked her into his arms and kissed her as if they were alone, not caring that her father and friend were there or that he was crying like a damned fool. In that moment, all he cared about was his fiancée in his arms. The woman he loved and planned to spend the rest of his life with.

EPILOGUE

LOGAN ENTERED THE ROOM and the heads popped up at his arrival. He glanced at the podium to the tall, white male standing behind it. The man smiled and waved at him, motioning for him to come further into the room. A black man stood and walked toward Logan, and he tried not to tense; Katie told him he always tensed when someone from another race, or rather a *man* of a different race, came near him.

The guy handed Logan a pamphlet. "Here you go, man. You can find a seat anywhere you want." Gesturing to the rows of chairs, he sat back down. Logan could admit that he was nervous, and he could admit that he wished his fiancée was there by his side, but he needed to do this himself.

After taking a seat in a chair in the back, he opened the pamphlet. It read, *New Hope: For the support of racial equity and positive change.*

The night after his and Katie's first date, he realized that she was on the internet looking up support groups for women who were dating men with issues about race. He was mortified that his future wife needed a support group for his issues, but he was determined to get help. Logan continued to read the pamphlet, *Helping to break down barriers one step at a time.* He took a breath and glanced around the room. Men and women both sat listening to the speaker at the podium.

He was in the middle of a sentence when Logan started to listen. "—at this time, I'd like at ask if there were any newcomers who would like to come up and introduce themselves?" The tall white man, with a white beard and odd-looking black eyebrows, looked around the room. "Don't be nervous, and don't be ashamed. Please, do not be worried about speaking honestly. This group is here to help you move past your issues for a healthier, happier life."

That was what Logan was there for, but he didn't want to get up in front of a room of strangers and tell his business.

"We can't help you, if you keep it in." When no one stood, the man nodded and said, "I'll start. My name is James, most of you know me already." The group didn't greet James in unison like Logan had always thought they did; he'd been watching too much T.V.. Logan's phone beeped and Logan pulled it from his pocket to read the text message.

Love you and can't wait to spend the rest of my life with you.

We'll get this right. Love, Katie, the soon to be Mrs. Whyte.

The text meant the world to him, and her support lent him strength.

Logan raised his hand just as James started to speak again.

"Yes?" James gestured in his direction.

He stood. "My name is Logan, and I'm here because my fiancée is black and I have trust issues with black men. I can't have my past hurting her, and I need help figuring out how to understand that all black men aren't the black kids who harassed and kicked my ass on a daily basis in the past." He glanced around; there was only one black man, but he showed no signs of anger or judgment.

Maybe he was here because, like Logan, he was wary of other races. The world was full of men like Logan—people with troubled pasts, chips on their shoulders, and much more—but he refused to live like that anymore. He wanted a new life, a life with Katie, and in order to do it, he had to face the demons of his past. Luckily, Logan knew he could face anything with Katie by his side. Just like James had said, 'one step at a time.'

James clapped and said, "Welcome, Logan, welcome to the beginning of your new life."

THE END

coming soon…

INEVITABLE

A Love and War stand Alone

I crashed and opened my eyes . . . there you were, fierce and protective, and I knew . . . I just knew it was you all along.

Ex-Marine Trent Reed has been shot at, in a coma, and placed in war zones, but when his best friend calls in a favor, he is faced with the most dangerous situation yet—to be the best man. Trent's turbulent past with races other than his own taints his view on the interracial marriage, and he's none too happy to deal with the ill-tempered maid of honor. To accept the position means understanding that his friend is soon to be out of his life—for good.

Tough-girl Teal Lofton has struggled all of her adult life, from her weight to the color of her skin holding her back in work and love. When she agrees to be the maid of honor in her friend's wedding, those struggles are amplified by a hormonal bride and a jerk of a best man who she is strangely, yet wildly, attracted to.

As tensions and tempers rise, Trent disappears with the wedding rings and Teal braves a snowstorm to bring them back, determined to fix yet another problem. But a tragic accident brings together the unlikely pair, forcing them to face the prejudices of their pasts. In doing so, Trent and Teal embark on an inevitable course of self-discovery and passion like they've never experienced before—until a secret from Trent's past threatens to destroy it all.

ACKNOWLEDGMENTS

The hardest part about writing a novel is the sacrifices you have to make to get the work done. For instance, whether it is your time, sleep, or money, it all counts. I want to thank everyone who stuck with me when I "hermitted" and busted butt to get this novel finished. To my mom for missing me, yet letting me stay away to work, to my sister for her encouragement and faith in me, and to my friends who love me and put up with my shit. This is a heartbreakingly hard job, and there are times when authors fall into this deep abyss of character's voices and plot twists. Understand that we love you and have not forgotten about you. We just . . . we are just so different, but to those who stand by our side: WE LOVE YOU! Thanks so much.

A special thanks to: Brianna & Christian, Anthony Fusco, Denise Bolen, and Carma Delany! The prison info you gave me was amazingly helpful. TO MY MUSE, BRIANNA J Madden: THANK YOU SO MUCH!

P.S. Victoria from Crimson Tide Editorial:
YOU ROCK!!!

ABOUT INGER

Inger Iversen lives in Virginia Beach with her tree-hugging boyfriend, Joshua, and her overweight lap cat, Max. When not reading or writing, she spends her time watching reruns of True Blood and Walking Dead, or killing zombies in Call of Duty. Of course, if the world were to change into some World War Z type of situation, she'd probably be the only chick running around searching for a Ray Gun!

@kris10inger
www.ingeriversen.com

More work from Inger includes:
Paranormal Books:
Few Are Angels Series:
Immortal Heart
Few Are Angels
Awakened

Crushing Hearts and Black Butterfly publishing:
In the Dark Series:
Goodnight Sam (short)
Running in the Dark
Sinners in the Dark

A FEW OF MY FAVORITE CONTEMPORARY READS:

Dark Trade | Miranda Kavi

Torch | Cambria Herbert

Corporate Ties | E.L. Loraine

Mangled Hearts | Felicia Tatum

Hit | Rebecca Ethington

Forever | Mary A Wasowski

Written in the Stars | Jennifer Martinez

Alyssa's Redemption | Karly Morgan

5 Miles | Nadège Richards

Take A Gamble | Rachael Brownell

Three Days of Rain | Christine Hughes

Shady Bay | Casey Bond

Turn the page for an exclusive look at Cambria Hebert's new adult contemporary novel TORCH and Casey L. Bond's SHADY BAY!

TORCH

By Cambria Hebert

I

The pungent smell of gasoline stung my nostrils and my head snapped back in repulsion. I opened my eyes and lifted my hands to place them over my mouth and nose to hopefully barricade some of the overwhelming scent.

Except my hands didn't obey.

I tried again.

Panic ripped through my middle when I realized my arms weren't going to obey any kind of command because they were secured behind me.

What the hell?

I looked down over my shoulder, trying to see the thick ropes binding my wrists. The lighting in here was dim.

Wait. Where was I?

My heart started to pound, my breathing coming in shallow, short spurts as I squinted through tearing eyes at the familiar shapes around me. A little bit of calmness washed over me when I realized I was in my home. Home was a place I always felt safe.

But I wasn't safe. Not right now.

I sat in the center of my living room, tied to my dining room chair. I was supposed to be in bed sleeping. The boxers and T-shirt I wore said so.

I started to struggle, to strain against the binds that held me. I didn't know what was going on, but I knew enough to realize whatever was happening was not good.

Movement caught my attention and I went still, my eyes darting toward where someone stood.

"Hello?" I said. "Please help me!"

It was so dark I couldn't make out who it was. They seemed to loom in the distance, standing just inside the entryway, nothing but a dark shadow.

My eyes blinked rapidly, trying to clear the tears flowing down my cheeks. The gasoline smell was so intense. It was like I was sitting in a puddle of the stuff.

"Help me!" I screamed again, wondering why the hell the person just stood there instead of coming to my aid.

The scrape of a match echoed through the darkness, and the catch of a small flame drew my eye. It started out small, reminding me of the fireflies I used to chase when I was a child. But then it grew in intensity, the flame burning brighter, becoming bolder, and it burned down the stick of the match.

The dark shadow held out the matchstick, away from their body, suspending it over the ground for several long seconds.

And then they dropped it.

It fell to the floor like it weighed a thousand pounds and left a small glowing trail in its wake. I watched the flame as it hit the floor, thinking it would fizzle out and the room would be returned to complete blackness.

But the flame didn't fizzle out.

It ignited.

With a great whoosh, fire burst upward, everything around that little match roaring to life with angry orange flames. I screamed. I didn't bother asking for help again because it was clear whoever was in this house wasn't here to help me.

They were here to kill me.

To prove my realization, the dark figure calmly retreated out the front door. The flames on the floor grew rapidly, spreading like a contagious disease up the walls and completely swallowing the front door. The small side table by the door, which I'd lovingly scraped and painted, caught like it was the driest piece of wood in the center of a forest fire.

Smoke began to fill the rooms, curling closer, making me recoil. How long until the flames came for me?

I began to scream, to call for help, praying one of my neighbors would hear and come to my rescue. Except I knew no one was going to rush into this house to save me. They would all stand out on the lawn at the edge of the street and murmur and point. They would click their tongues and shake their heads, mesmerized by the way the fire claimed my home. And my life.

I wasn't going to die like this.

I twisted my arms, straining against the corded rope, feeling it cut into my skin, but I kept at it, just needing an inch to slip free.

I tried to stand, to run into the back of the house. If I couldn't get loose from the chair, I would just take it with me. But my ankles were crossed and tied together.

I called for help again, but the sound was lost in the roaring of the flames. I never realized how loud a fire truly was. I never realized how rapidly it could spread. It was no longer dark in here, the flames lighting up my home like the fourth of July, casting an orange glow over everything. The entire front entryway and stairwell were now engulfed. I could see everything was doused in gasoline; the putrid liquid created a thick trail around the room. Whoever had been here completely drenched this house with the flammable liquid and then set me in the center of it.

I managed to make it to my feet, hunched over with the chair strapped around me. It was difficult to stand with my ankles crossed. But I had to try. I had to get out of here. I took one hobbled step when a cough racked my lungs. I choked and hacked, my lungs searching for clean air to breathe but only filling with more and more pollution.

I made it one step before I fell over, my shoulder taking the brunt of my fall, the chair thumping against the thickness of the carpet. I lay there and coughed, squinting through my moist and blurry vision, staring at the flames. . . the flames that seemed to stalk me.

They traveled closer, following the path of the gas, snaking through the living room, filling it up and rushing around me until I was completely circled with fire. The heat, God, the heat was so intense that sweat slicked my skin, and it made it that much harder to breathe.

It was the kind of heat that smacked into you, that made you dizzy and completely erased all thought from your brain.

I was going to die.

Even if I were able to make it to my feet, I wouldn't be able to make it through the circle of fire that consumed everything around me.

I pressed my cheek against the carpet, not reveling in its softness, not thinking about the comfort it usually afforded my bare feet. Another round of coughing racked my body. My lungs hurt. God, they hurt so bad. It was like a giant vise squeezed inside my chest, squeezed until all I could think about was oxygen and how much I needed it.

My chin tipped back as I writhed on the floor, making one last attempt at freedom before the flames claimed me completely. I heard the sharp crackling of wood, the banging of something collapsing under the destruction, and I blinked.

This is it.

The last moments of my life.

I'm going to die alone.

I started to hallucinate, the lack of oxygen playing tricks on my fading mind, as a large figure stepped through the flames. Literally walked right through them. He held up his arms, shielding his face and head as he barreled through looking like some hero from an action movie.

My eyes slid closed as my skin began to hurt, like I sat outside in the sun for hours without the protection of sunscreen.

I heard a muffled shout and tried to open my eyes, but they were too heavy. Besides, I preferred the darkness anyway. I didn't want to watch as my body was burned to death by fire.

Pain screamed through me and the feeling of the carpet against my cheek disappeared. My first thought was to struggle, but my body couldn't obey my mind. I felt movement, I felt the solidness of someone's chest, and I could have sworn I heard the sound of a man's voice.

"Hang on," he said.

The shattering of glass and the splintering of wood didn't wake me from the fog that settled over my brain. The scream of pain at my back, the extreme burning and melting that made a cry rip from my throat still wasn't enough to get my eyes to open.

And then I could hear the piercing wail of sirens, the faraway shouts of men, and the muffled yell of one who was much closer.

I really thought heaven would be more peaceful.

And then I was sailing through the air, the solid wall of whatever held me ripped away. I plunged downward, and with a great slap, I hit water, the icy cold droplets a major shock to my overheated system.

My eyes sprang wide; water invaded them as I tried to make sense of what was happening. I thought I was burning. But now I was. . . drowning.

The water was dark and it pulled me lower and lower into its depths. I looked up. The surface rippled and glowed orange. I almost died up there. But I would die down here now.

I wanted to swim. My arms, they hurt so badly, but they wanted to push upwards, to help me break the surface toward the oxygen my body so desperately needed.

But I was still tied to a chair.

The chair hit the ground—a solid, cold surface—as my hair floated out around me and bubbles discharged from my nose and mouth.

It wasn't hot here.

It wasn't loud, but eerily quiet.

It was a different kind of death, but death all the same.

The ripples in the water grew and the chair began to rock. I heard the plunge of something else coming into the water and I looked up. Through the strands of my wayward hair, I saw him again. My hero. His powerful arms pushed through the water in three great stokes. He reached out and grabbed me beneath the shoulder, towing me upward toward the orange surface.

When my head cleared the water, my lungs automatically sucked in blissful air. It hurt so bad, but it was the kind of pain I had to endure. Another cough racked my body, and as I wheezed, the man towing me and my chair through the water said, "Keep breathing. Just keep breathing."

And then I was being lifted from the water, the chair placed on the cement as I coughed and wheezed and greedily sucked in air.

"Ma'am," someone was saying. "Ma'am, can you hear me? Are you all right?"

I looked up, blinking the water out of my eyes, but my vision was still blurry. I tried to speak, but all I could manage was another cough.

The ropes around my wrists were tugged, and I cried out. The pain was so intense that I thought I would pass out right there.

"Stay with me," a calm voice said from behind. It was the same voice that instructed me to keep breathing.

When my arms were free, I sagged forward. The pain splintering through me was too much to bear. And then there were hands at my ankles; I heard the knife against the rope. When I was completely untied, my body fell forward, sliding off the chair and toward the ground.

But he was there.

I slid right into his arms, my body completely boneless.

A low curse slipped from his lips as he yelled for a medic. Yeah, a medic. That seemed like a good idea. I hurt. I hurt all over.

I cried out when he shifted me in his arms, bringing me closer to his chest. I pressed my face against him. He was wet, but his clothes were scratchy against my cheek. I tried to look at him; I opened my eyes and tilted back my head. I caught a flash of dark hair and light eyes, but then my vision faded out, pain took over, and I passed out.

SHADY BAY

By Casey L. Bond

JAXON

I

ONE YEAR AGO . . .

MY BROTHERS SAT across the table from me. Can't believe I'm here again. I came home waggin' my tail behind me like a scolded dog. Castrated dog. She'd reeled me in, chewed me up and spit me out. The worst part was I'd let her. I should've seen her coming from a mile away. Starla. Stone cold bitch. I thought she loved me. I followed her all the way to Fort Lauderdale. Life was good, the sex was great, and for a while, she treated me like I was the only man in the world.

But it had been a bunch of bullshit. She didn't love me like she said, like she moaned. She didn't want to spend the rest of her life with me, like she'd cooed as she raked her long painted-red-fingernails through my hair. No. Starla was a liar. My brothers referred to her as "the cougar."

They were right. She was twenty years older than my twenty-four. And she'd sunk her claws in deep. The wounds were still fresh. My blood was still pooling up in them. I took a deep draw off the long neck in front of me and slammed the bottle back onto the mahogany bar.

Parker stiffened and then grinned. "Dude, we tried to tell you. You had those rose-colored glasses on." The neon lights across from us made his face glow orange-red.

"Shut up, Park."

He laughed. Parker was older than me, married to his perfect wife, Amy. They had adopted their perfect daughter, Maddy, a couple of years ago. He had nothing to complain about. That was for sure, and I didn't feel like listening to a lecture or his bullshit right now. Easton remained quiet, and I was thankful that he was acting as a buffer between Parker and me.

Raking my hands through my hair, I growled. "I can't stay here." Easton had his wife, Melissa. Parker had perfection. Hell, even our cousin Gabe had gotten lucky and had married Aislin, the girl he'd loved forever and was too pussy to admit it. I'd have loved to have gotten a hold of that one. Maybe if I'd spent more time chasing her, I'd have beat Gabe to the punch. Maybe I'd never have met Starla. Maybe my life wouldn't completely suck.

"What do you mean you can't stay here? Surely, you aren't going back to Florida?" Parker quirked an eyebrow at me. The bartender replaced our empty bottles with full ones and we started sipping. Guys' night out never tasted so good.

"I don't know where I'm going, but I can't stay here. I don't want to be here. I quit the mines. I can't go back. Hell, I don't want to go back. And I don't know what I'm going to do, but it isn't gonna be in or near Devil Creek."

Easton looked over at me and held his hand up to stop more from spewing out Parker's mouth. Parker closed his trap. Easton looked me over, turned to Parker and said, "What about Shady?"

Parker narrowed his eyes. "Seriously?"

Easton nodded once. "Yep."

"What's Shady?" I asked.

Easton answered first. "A business venture that we're working on. My company is building a bar in Myrtle Beach. Parker and I are partners; joint owners. If he agrees, you could go down and work for my guys to build the place. Spend some time away from Devil Creek, see if you like Myrtle. Then if you want to stay, you could manage it for us."

"When did this happen?"

"While you were hunting cougar, Jax." Parker laughed.

Keep laughing, assbag. I took a deep draw of beer. Tasted like freedom. "I'll go."

Parker stopped laughing and took a quick swig looking from me to Easton, worry etched on his brow. Easton just chuckled at him and nodded once at me. "You start Monday. I own a small townhouse complex and can hook you up. One of the units is vacant. Better get packed and on the road early tomorrow. I'll text you with the details."

Grumbling, Parker muttered, "Looks like guys' night out is over."

As we finished our drinks, excitement began coursing through my veins. This could be fun.

Mercy
still one year ago...

I SAT ON the hard wooden bench directly behind the defendant's table in the generic courtroom. White ceilings bled into white walls. Those drifted into wooden paneling, which was stained a warmer color than the worn wooden floor. I'd never been in a Federal building before the trial, let alone been wanded, scanned and patted down.

Now, I knew the drill and knew to arrive early so that I could sit behind my dad. I'd had his back at every hearing. He'd never contested his guilt, so the rest was all a formality—the government had to cross its T's and dot its I's. If protocol wasn't followed to perfection, they would run the risk of losing an appeal if Daddy ever filed one, not that he would.

When he was arrested, he turned to me after they slapped the cold-looking, metal cuffs on his wrists. He said, "Mercy, I'm not gonna lie. I'm guilty and I deserve what I get. Tell your mama I'm not coming home." I watched them lead him out the front door, down the walkway and shove him into the back of an unmarked black Crown Victoria. Worst day of my life, and his.

It took me a long time to realize that he wasn't talking about not coming home that night. He meant he was never coming home again. Six months later, I cried myself to sleep with that epiphany. It must have sunk in with Mama, too. She started dating shortly after that. At first, I was shocked. I was angry. She was betraying him, I was sure of it. But then I realized that she was just trying to cope in her own way. It was a crappy way, but it was hers.

People filed in and claimed seats along the long pew-like benches. Redemption wouldn't be found within these walls. Penitence, yes. Redemption? Not a chance. The cacophony of mindless chatter, shuffling papers, and high-heel clacks along the polished white-tile floor was almost overwhelming. The door on the left side of the room opened and a guard stepped through it. I could see the signature, bright orange-colored jumpsuit that Daddy was dressed in. His eyes met mine and he smiled, relief relaxed the tense muscles of his face and shoulders.

The officer behind him escorted him to his seat, and he settled into the seat behind the wooden table right in front of me. His face and body had thinned over the past year. His short, once chestnut-colored hair had receded, thinned and was mostly gray. Crow's feet rimmed his eyes and the wrinkles on his forehead had deepened. I mouthed the words, "I love you, Daddy."

He grinned and mouthed back, "Love you, Mercy-girl."

I wanted to run to him, throw my arms around him and cry. I knew what was coming. Today was his sentencing hearing.

MAMA AND HER flavor of the week had finally passed out in her bedroom. Frantically, I thumbed through the clothes in my closet, grabbing only the essentials: my favorite jeans, a few shirts, and a light jacket. It was the only one I owned. Moving on to the dresser: bras, panties, socks. I stuffed a few of each into the same black backpack I'd had since my freshman year of high school and then pulled on my favorite electric blue tennis shoes.

I'd gotten them at a neighbor's garage sale and it had been love at the first sight of the bright pink swoosh on the side. What was even better than their aesthetic appeal? They fit! Perfectly. After wearing them for sixteen hours a day for the past few months, the soles were worn almost through at the balls of my feet, but they were the best I had. They were all I had.

I looked around the room that had once held so many hopes and dreams. Those had begun to disappear little by little after Daddy was gone. Now all that was left was the memory of them. An enormous multi-colored, ugly-but-warm afghan stretched over my bed. Mama taught me to crochet when I was eight and I'd been doing it ever since. Mostly for necessity. It was cold in the winter here, and even in the summer my feet stayed cold as icicles.

I walked over to the dresser and grabbed a gilded memory. Displayed in a delicate golden frame, ghosts of my past smiled back at me. It had been taken right after my high school graduation. Mama on one side and Daddy on the other, with me donning the crimson and white of the Knights. This was the last picture I had of normalcy and I was taking it with me.

I blinked back at the blank walls as I eased my way out the door and padded to the bathroom down the hall. The fluorescent bulb overhead flickered frantically, as if sending out the alert. Stuffing my hair brush, toothbrush and paste, deodorant, and a small bar of soap into the small pocket of the bag. I flicked that stupid light out and crept down the stairs.

Each step that creaked underfoot made me wince. I don't know why it bothered me. When they were out, they would usually be out for a long time, sometimes days, but I didn't want to chance it. Not today. I just wanted out of there, and it would just be my luck for them to wake up as I was making my escape.

From the kitchen, I snuck the only things I could find that would be easy to carry, which amounted to two bottles of water, a can of peaches and three blueberry granola bars. I hated blueberries.

The schedule on the fridge indicated that the city bus would be here any minute, so I zipped up my bag and out the door I went, leaving all those worries behind. I'd gladly traded them in. Last night broke the camel's back and I was tired of being a damn camel anyway.

Sure enough, the bus rolled up to the street corner just as I got there. Its tires deflated with a whoosh and I climbed aboard and took a seat in the very back of the bus on the left side, the side furthest from my former house. It hadn't been a home for a long time. Soon, the beast's engine roared to life and the bored faces looked away from the newcomer to the world outside again. Ashland would be the first stop on my journey. I needed to see Daddy.

Half an hour later, the bus pulled up just outside FCI-Ashland. It looked more like a nursing home from the outside than a Federal Correctional Institution, or low-security prison, as most people knew it. Daddy called it the slammer. I'd been here once a week, every week since he was sentenced. We were lucky. He could've been sent to any prison in the U.S.

I shoved my backpack into some nearby shrubs, making sure to conceal it. I didn't need to be locked up with him. The Correctional Officers wouldn't appreciate its contents.

The judge said that due to the extenuating circumstances regarding Daddy's case, the fact that his crime was classified as non-violent, and that he had a child nearby, he would pull for Ashland. And we were lucky. He was sent to Ashland, only twenty minutes away. So I tried to never take that blessing for granted and visited him like clockwork. In the past few years, I'd only missed one week, when I had the flu and couldn't drag myself out of bed, even for work.

Rust-colored bricks lined the walls of the prison's entrance. If it wasn't for the razor-wire atop the chain link fences, one would think it was just another doctor's office or something. But that wire was a harsh reminder of reality. If someone felt like challenging that reality, it would slice right through their delusion. Literally.

As usual, I signed in, waited, walked through the metal detectors only to be met with wand-wielding correctional officers and then was patted down. Twice. I rolled my eyes. Did people actually try to sneak stuff in? How stupid could someone possibly be?

Once cleared, I was given a visitor badge to snap onto my shirt. I wore a long-sleeved, black V-neck and jeans. Last summer, in ninety-nine degree heat, I'd made the mistake of wearing shorts and the cat-calls from the other inmates almost made Daddy snap. Jeans it was.

The visitation room was a large, sterile, white rectangle filled with circular tables that seated four to five people in chairs that reminded me of first grade, for some reason--all plastic but the metal legs. I waited patiently in one of those chairs while the guards ushered in the other visitors, and we all sat eagerly to see our loved ones. Fifteen minutes later, the guards began to usher in the prisoners.

All were met with hugs and kisses, tears and smiles, all the time aware of the watchful eyes of the COs. We were allowed to hug at the beginning of the visit and at the end, but had to stay separated in between to prevent the transfer and smuggling of contraband to prisoners. Daddy's smile met mine as he stepped into the room and shuffled along behind the guard who ushered him in. His cuffs were removed and as soon as the metal chink confirmed their freedom, those wrists and hands wrapped firmly around me.

I choked on my tears. How would I tell him? Daddy pushed me back and hugged me quickly again before we settled across the table from one another. That circular piece of wood felt like a thousand miles separating us. Soon, we would be separated by distance, by five hundred miles of land. "How are you, Mercy-girl?"

"Good. I'm good. How are you, Daddy?"

"Same old. What's wrong?" His brow furrowed and his eyes grew wide taking me in. How did he know?

I smiled lightly trying to meet his eyes. "I have to go. I came to say goodbye. I'll visit you when I can and I'll call and write all the time, but I can't stay with Mama anymore. I just can't."

"Did something happen with her 'friend'?" His words dripped with disgust.

"Sort of."

Fisting both hands, he growled low and cursed under his breath. "Nothing like what you're probably thinking, though. Chill." The last thing we needed was for him to get a behavior warning.

He released a deep breath. "Tell me."

"I work two jobs. You know that, right?"

He nodded. "Yeah."

"They take all the money I make and shoot it into their veins or snort it up their nose and I just can't do it anymore. They got high on our rent money. I don't know what they're gonna do."

"That's not all, is it?"

I picked at my cuticle. “No.”

“Tell me.”

“Her, um, ‘friend’ tried to stick his dirty needle in my arm last night. He was high and I don’t do drugs, Daddy. I just. . .I just can’t live there anymore. They’re sucking me into their black hole and I don’t wanna go with them.”

“That dirty son of a bitch!”

“Shhh.” The nearest CO took notice and shifted his feet, pinning his eyes on Daddy. Crap! “I just wanted to tell you that I’m leaving. I’ll call you when I get there. You know I’m smart. I can do this.” I plead with him, using my eyes, body and spirit.

“Where are you going?”

“I’m going to the beach. Myrtle Beach. There’ll be plenty of seasonal work there in a couple of months. I can work hard. I’ll save up and get a nice place, maybe take some classes in the fall at a community college. It’ll be great!” I tried mask the worry and terror that I felt inside with more pep than should be allowed in one person. Daddy saw right through it, but he didn’t let on.

“You’d better call me. Be careful.” He leaned forward. “Got protection?”

I nodded. “Remember how I showed you to use it?”

“Yes. I remember.”

“Good. Just be careful. Do you have money?”

“I had a little stash that they hadn’t found yet. I have enough to get down there and get set up.”

“You sure?”

“Yep.”

He looked at me and gave a weak smile. "I'm sorry, Mercy-baby. It's my fault you're in this situation."

"It's not. It's life and I'm about to take control of mine."

He smiled genuinely, his hazel eyes warming. "I'm proud of you. Just please, please, be careful, Mercy. Call me when you get there. I'll worry till I hear from you."

"I will, Daddy."

The COs looked at one another. "Time's up!" one barked loudly. I stood up and rushed around the orb and threw my arms around him. I knew it would be a long while before I would be able to afford to visit him. "Love you, Daddy!"

"Love you, baby."

A guard moved behind him and he surrendered his wrists. The dull brown sweatshirt and pants hung off his body. "Be careful. Call me."

"I will. I promise."

I TOOK THE local transit authority bus to the furthest point west on their route: Charleston, West Virginia and walked to the nearest truck stop. I had $43.52 to my name. That wouldn't buy a Greyhound seat to the beach, so I was forced to find an alternate means of transportation: I would hitchhike. I knew it was dangerous, but I felt more comfortable with the metal packed just inside my bag. The Go-Mart parking lot was full, packed with truckers, commuters and soccer moms who'd just finished grocery shopping on this fine Monday morning.

It was beautiful for early March. Sixty degrees and sunny at eleven fifteen in the morning. Between the long walk from the bus's last stop and the light fleece jacket around me, I was getting warm by the time I entered the convenience store. The bell attached to the glass swing doors pinged alerting the occupants of my presence. No one noticed. I moved toward the aisles of snacks and wished I had a bit more money. Breakfast would be nice and I really didn't want the blueberry crapola bars.

A few trucker-looking fellows gave me the once over before making tracks outside. A middle-aged guy in a business suit and a young mother bouncing a disgruntled toddler on her hip did, too. The food was too tempting. My mouth watered at the thought of my favorite. No! I need to get out of here. Stepping back outside, I didn't know how to do this. Did I ask random, non-serial-killer-looking truckers where they were headed? Did I stick my thumb out like in the movies?

I was so deep in thought I didn't notice it when a guy stopped beside me until I nearly walked into him while pacing back and forth. "You lost?" He sounded even more southern than I did with my hillbilly twang. Standing six feet tall, with a paunchy belly, red hair and a mischievous grin, he was middle aged and his eyes were kind.

"Sort of."

"I'm heading south if you need a ride."

"How far south?"

"Conway, South Carolina."

"Is that near Myrtle Beach?"

He chuckled. "Yep."

"Sweet! I'd really appreciate it if I could ride down with you."

He stepped off the curb and waved me on, "Come on. We've gotta log some miles." While he checked his load and tires and gauges and all things trucker guys do before they hit the road, I settled into the cab of the tractor. The outside was dark blue and the interior a simple gray. It sort of smelled like stale French fries, which made me giggle. Booger, which was the trucker guy's handle, had a pair of orange fuzzy dice hanging from his rear-view and a hula-dancer suction-cupped to his dashboard.

The driver's side door flew open and Booger climbed up and cranked the engine. I felt like I was sitting on the darn thing. It rumbled and shook so hard my butt was starting to feel numb. But it was a free ride and Booger seemed nice, and not like a Manson-type of guy. He wrote down numbers in a little book thing and checked his gauges, before donning a pair of wrap-around shades I was sure he'd had from the 1980s. The lenses reflected the rainbow and he smiled big, his cheek full of chewing tobacco. "Ready, Freddy?"

"Ready when you are, good buddy!" I teased.

"Ten-four, over and out! Let's get 'er done!" He maneuvered the massive vehicle out of the parking space and soon, we were rolling down Interstate 64 heading toward my future.

Made in the USA
Middletown, DE
17 May 2015